TIME BOMB

R.M. OLSON

ISBN-13: 978-1-7771778-4-3

To my writer friends, who consistently talked me off the cliff as I wrote this

TIME BOMB

A virus planted on a computer or system that is programmed to come into effect at some specified later time.

1

Jez tossed a handful of gambling chips onto the open cockpit floor of the *Ungovernable* and eased herself down into a slightly stiff slouch. "Alright, Olya, listen up. You know how to play fool's tokens, right?"

The eight-year-old gave her a skeptical look. "You know my mamochka, Aunty Jez. What do you think?"

From the copilot's seat, Lev gave a long-suffering sigh. Jez looked up at him and winked.

Despite the fact that he still looked like a damn scholar, something about his dark, tousled hair and mild, intelligent eyes made her heart stutter just a little. It had been happening far too often over the last couple days.

Which was completely stupid.

She shook her head and turned back to Olya. "Fair point. OK, first—"

The ship jolted, and Jez grabbed for the corner of her pilot's seat with her good arm as gambling tokens skittered across the floor.

She swore through her teeth.

"What—" began Lev, but she'd felt that kind of jolt before on a ship. She jumped to her feet, swearing louder as her broken ribs protested, and flipped the holoscreen up. A red dot flashed from behind them, then another, then another, and as she watched, a streak of yellow shot out from the one in the centre towards their ship.

Damn. This far out in deep space they shouldn't have to deal with this crap.

She slid into the pilot's seat and flipped power to the rear shields on instinct as it hit, and a crackling spark of energy shot up the back of the ship as it jolted again.

"We're being shot at," she gritted. "Someone's firing on my damn ship. Olya, get back to your mama, I'll teach you to gamble later." Olya nodded, face pale, and slipped out the cockpit door.

Adrenalin crackled through Jez's body, but she couldn't stop grinning. Probably shouldn't be, but hell, it had been way too long since she'd gotten into a decent fight.

Three days, at least.

She shoved down on the controls, and the *Ungovernable* nose-dived as another shot skimmed their port side.

"Strap down, everyone," she called over the ship's com. "Things are about to get interesting."

Lev had already strapped in, his face slightly pale.

"Get Ysbel onto the guns," she snapped at him, and he nodded and hit the com.

Jez whipped the *Ungovernable* in a tight circle, the pressure of the restraints against her injuries bringing momentary stars to her vision, then yanked back on the controls as another shot whispered just under them, her beautiful, perfect ship responding to her lightest touch as if reading her thoughts.

That was the secret—if you got too far, they'd adjust their aim. Let them think they had you, every single time.

A red damage report scrolled across her screen from the last hit, and she swore under her breath.

Whatever these ships were using, it wasn't a short-haul ion-cannon.

"What the hell was that?" she snapped over the com. "Tae?"

"I don't know." Tae's voice over the com was strained. "Stand by, I need to get on the shields."

Another shot, and at the last moment she pulled into a roll, the shot sliding past her starboard side.

She had visuals on her attackers now, three bright points against the clean, cold black of deep space—sleek, fast short-hauls with the slim body and short wings of something that could go in-atmosphere as well as out. Something designed for speed and maneuverability, and from the looks of it, a hell of a lot of firepower.

They'd be fast.

But they had no idea what they were getting into.

"Ysbel, you on?" she called into the com.

In response, Ysbel's guns cracked out, a thin line of blue slicing through the black, and caught the wingtip of one of the sleek flyers, sending it spinning away from them, energy sparking across its shields.

"That shot should have vaporized them," Ysbel grunted over the com in her heavy outer-rim accent. "They're running shields I've never seen on a short-haul."

The two remaining ships spun in formation, and another yellow crackle of energy jolted past her, followed by two more—the damaged ship had, apparently, rejoined the fight. At the last second Jez pulled into a roll, biting down hard against the pain as her body pressed against the restraints. Two of the shots slid past her starboard side, but the last slammed into her shields. More red scrolled across her holoscreen.

Tae staggered into the cockpit, trademark scowl on his dark face, dressed, as usual, in his worn mechanic coveralls that almost made him look like the street-kid he'd been, up until a month ago. He shoved his hair out of his eyes and glared at her. "For heaven's sake, Jez, I said—"

"Bit busy now, trying to keep us all alive and everything," she shot back. She pointed her ship's nose starboard, then spun hard to port, whipping the *Ungovernable's* stern around so she was coming up on the belly-side of her attackers.

Another blue line from the *Ungovernable*'s gunports lit the black of space, narrowly missing the foremost ship.

Ysbel swore over the com. "I can't aim if you won't let me line up, you idiot pilot."

"Might not have to," she murmured. "Just give me a sec."

The ships had caught on to her maneuvers now, and split up, flying in close. They were going to hit her from three sides, which, if they were firing regular ion cannons, wouldn't be a problem with the kind of shields her angel was running. But whatever they were firing —

Three bolts of yellow crackled on her screen. She waited until the last second, then she jammed the thrusters, sending the *Ungovernable* leaping up and out of the way. The three ships scattered to avoid friendly fire, but one of them took a bolt to one wing.

She grinned.

"They're using modded Aro tech," Lev said in quiet triumph, glancing up from his screen. "That's why their shields are so good."

Tae looked up from where he was crouched by the control panel to one side of Jez, feverishly re-connecting wiring. He'd somehow managed to strap in, anchoring his harness to the cockpit floor.

"I'll hook something into our blockers to take out the shields. They're flying close enough it should work. Lev, I need specs."

"Give me a second." Lev scowled in concentration as he scrolled rapidly down his com screen. "Got it," he said at last. "Sending it through."

The lead ship swung around, staying under the *Ungovernable's* port side and out of range of the guns. Tae yanked out a wire and re-connected it.

"Now," he snapped, and Jez hit the blocker.

The ships sparkled for a moment, their surface glowing with a thousand glittering stars of dying electricity as the blocker took down the shields.

"Alright, Ysbel," she said over the com. "Shall we show the pla-guers how a real ship fights?"

"For once in my life, Jez, I think you and I completely agree on something."

The ships were still riding low under her belly, out of range of the guns. Once their shields had disappeared, they'd apparently decided that keeping out of the damn way was the better part of valour.

She grinned.

Probably should have thought about that before they decided to pick a fight.

She barely had to nudge the accelerator, and the *Ungovernable* launched herself forward like a desert-dog after a rabbit. Jez sighed in ecstasy and played her fingers over the perfect, beautiful controls, the ship reading her movements like it was alive.

"Get ready, we're going back through the middle," she murmured.

A bolt of yellow lit her holoscreen, and she twitched the ship out of the way, letting the shot hiss past the shields with millimetres to spare, then whipped the *Ungovernable* around on her axis and jammed the thrusters.

Two of the attackers peeled off in panic as the *Ungovernable* shot between them.

"Now!" she called. "Get their attention, Ysbel."

Her holoscreen lit up again, and twin blue jolts of energy shot out. The ships swerved wildly to avoid them, only to be met by two more bolts. One ship managed to dodge, but the second was clipped, what was left of its shields sparking like a reflection of the stars that cut the blackness behind it.

"Hey, you dirty plaguers," Jez called over the general line. "Might want to learn how to fly before you come after someone." She paused. "I told my friend on the guns to play nice. But the thing is, she doesn't like playing nice. And I'm going to stop trying to hold her back pretty soon here."

For a moment she thought the ships might make a break for it, but at last a sullen voice came over the com.

"Stand down. We don't mean you any harm."

She grinned. "That's nice. Me on the other hand, I mean you a hell of a lot of harm. Why'd you attack us?"

"We mistook you for another ship." The man on the other end of the com didn't sound convincing.

"Ysbel?" She didn't bother turning off the general com.

"Would you like me to vaporize them, or just take off pieces?" asked Ysbel. "I could hit their oxygen supplies. On ships that size they'll have about ten hours of emergency backup. The nearest wormhole is eleven hours away, but who knows? They might get lucky."

"We don't want a fight!" It was a new voice this time, slightly panicked. Jez smiled to herself. Ysbel did tend to have that effect on people. Even if they couldn't see her shaved head and muscles and the modded heat pistols she always wore.

"Yeah? Well maybe think about coming up with a better way to introduce yourselves next time, you bastards."

"We mistook you for someone else," said the same voice. There was a stubbornness to the undercurrent of panic this time.

"Yeah? Who?"

There was a long moment of silence.

"Hey Ysbel, that oxygen idea was actually pretty—"

"OK! Alright. We have a contract for a ship that looks like yours."

She raised an eyebrow and turned to Lev. He frowned. Beside her, Tae typed rapidly into the holoscreen on his com, brows lowered in concentration.

"Just give me a sec," he muttered. "Keep them talking."

She hit the general com line again. "Yeah? Who gave you the contract?"

There was another long pause, and then the line went abruptly dead.

"Got it!" said Tae, just as a yellow jolt lit the ship's holoscreen. Jez brushed the controls, the *Ungovernable* shivered gracefully, and the shot passed harmlessly over their heads.

The three ships turned as one and shot off towards the wormhole coordinates.

She flipped the com back to the internal line. "Give them something to remember us by, Ysbel," she said. "No point killing them before they learn how to actually fly their plaguing ships."

"And now you and I disagree again," said Ysbel. "Alright. They get home in one piece." She paused. "Mostly in one piece." She paused again. "At least, no really important pieces missing."

Three more crackling lines of blue streaked out towards the ships in rapid succession. Jez flipped back to the general line and listened with satisfaction to the swearing.

"What'd you do to them, Ysbel?"

"Well," said Ysbel, "I hit them in the rear of the ship, where I assume they store their waste gasses. If I'm correct, they will have a slow-burning fire that will likely explode once they hit atmosphere wherever they're going. I assume it will give them time to land before their ships blow up. Probably. If they're fast. But, I may have miscalculated." She paused. "I'm going to run some tests on the guns. I'll meet you down on the main deck in a few minutes."

Lev, face still slightly pale, let out a long breath and shook his head. "What in the name of everything sane was that about?"

Jez grinned and leaned back in her chair. "Bet Tae can tell us. You hacked them, didn't you, tech-head?"

"Yes," he said. "Can I stand up now, Jez? I swear I have more bruises from your flying than from breaking out of prison." He scowled at her, but she'd known him long enough to see the faint smile under it.

Once Tae had left, Jez unstrapped, stretched, and winced, swearing softly.

"Jez. You have four broken ribs, remember?" said Lev from the copilot's seat.

She glared at him. "They're my ribs, genius-boy. Pretty sure I'm the one who got them broken."

"You didn't remember," he murmured, and there was a look of faint amusement on his face. She glowered at him, and he chuckled, shaking his head. "Come on, let's see what Tae pulled up." He stood and turned towards her, and she found suddenly that she was looking directly into his dark eyes. Her heart quickened, and there was something warm and tingly and not entirely unpleasant in the pit of her stomach.

She swallowed hard.

Alright. This was not OK.

Well, at least, she wasn't entirely certain if it was OK, and she was way too close to him every single day, and the way her damn heart had started jumping every time she saw this soft-boy who really should have been a scholar made it far too difficult to think about it clearly.

He reached out, hesitated, then put a gentle hand on her unbroken arm. "How are you feeling, Jez?" he asked softly. "Really."

There was a concern on his face that made her breath catch.

She managed a grin, even through her heartbeat thrumming in her chest, and his hand tingling against her skin like a buzz of electricity.

"I'm fine. Besides, I learned how to swear through the boneset, so —"

He raised an eyebrow. "I'm pretty sure you never stopped swearing."

She shrugged. "Maybe not. But now it doesn't hurt."

"Jez. It's been exactly three days since you were beaten almost to death. You have four broken ribs, a broken arm, a broken jaw—"

She tried for a jaunty smile, although she felt less jaunty than breathless. "Yeah, well, I'm fine. Your doctor friend did good."

He shook his head slightly, still watching her with a faint, rueful smile on his face. "I'd tell you to be careful. But I know that's never going to happen."

"Nope." She grinned, somewhat shakily. "Anyways, we should get in there. Pretty sure whatever Tae found is going to be good."

2

Lev shook his head wryly as Jez sauntered out of the cockpit. Her tawny face was a gruesome rainbow of bruises, but she still somehow managed to look cocky.

He drew in a long breath and ran a hand over his face, trying to bring his heart rate back to normal.

What was it about that damn pilot that turned him into an awkward teenager again?

Still shaking his head, he followed her down the short, narrow hallway and ducked out onto the *Ungovernable's* main deck.

The semicircular deck had the same old-fashioned atmosphere as the rest of the ship, the antique wood paneling smooth from years of use, the metal of the floors and ceiling a dull, burnished shine. Tae was already seated at a one of the low tables, a holoscreen open in front of him. He glanced up as Lev entered, his face creased in concentration and his dark hair falling over his eyes. He still looked residually exhausted from their two weeks in prison, and Lev couldn't help a slight smile. Yes, Tae was probably the best techie and hacker in the entire system, but you wouldn't know it to look at him—with the dark circles under his eyes, he looked even younger than his twenty years.

Jez dropped into a chair across from Tae and pulled up one knee, wincing as she did so, and stretched the other leg out in front of her. She studiously avoided Lev's gaze.

And then her whole body stiffened, and the grin on her face turned a bright shade of dangerous.

Lev sighed and closed his eyes for a moment.

"Masha," he said.

"Hello Lev." The woman's voice was bland and calm and completely unremarkable. Lev blew out a breath and turned.

He still found it slightly disconcerting how entirely average Masha appeared. Her face was pleasant and competent-looking, her skin an unremarkable brown, her shoulder-length hair pulled into a neat rat's tail, buttoned shirt crisp and long pilot's coat showing signs of wear. She'd been the one, a month and a half earlier, who'd broken them out of prison, promised them credits and a pardon in exchange for one simple government job.

And from the moment he'd met her, and noticed the glint of calculation hidden behind those calm, competent eyes, he'd known it was never going to be that simple.

One heist on the most dangerous weapons dealer in the system, a double-cross on the government, and two thousand people broken out of a prison planet later, he'd been proven completely right.

And he still had no idea what Masha really wanted with them.

"Tae." Masha pulled up a chair next to Tae. "I assume you managed to hack into their database. Tell me what you found, please."

"Hey Masha," Jez drawled. "Haven't seen you for the last three days. Thought maybe we'd got lucky and you'd died."

Lev braced himself to grab for Jez's arm in case she decided to try to punch Masha in the face again. From the corner of his eye, he noticed Tae doing the same thing.

"Tae?" prompted Masha pleasantly, ignoring the pilot completely.

"I—" Tae glanced between Jez and Masha and blew out a breath. "Here. I haven't finished looking through it."

Lev cast a quick warning glance at Jez, then leaned over the back of Tae's chair, peering at the holoscreen. He scanned the information quickly, frowning. "So. It appears they weren't lying. Correct me if I'm wrong, Masha, but we were completely wiped from every database in the system when we pulled the Vitali job. How can they set a contract on someone who doesn't exist?"

"That," Masha murmured, "is what I've spent the last three days trying to figure out. I've been studying every record we took from the prison. The information they had on Jez was surprisingly accurate, and included things I doubt would have been on the database in the first place, considering her—rather unconventional history. And it was less than two weeks from the time we broke into prison to the time we broke out again."

Lev turned and raised an eyebrow at her. "So—"

"So, as we guessed, someone is looking for our pilot. And I believe she might be the impetus for whatever it was that happened back there."

"Well, can't say I blame them," said Jez lazily. "I am pretty damn hot."

Lev sighed. "Jez—"

He wasn't entirely certain if she didn't see the cold calculation behind Masha's calm expression, or, more likely, she just didn't care. Either way, between Jez's unstoppable force and Masha's immovable object, he wasn't certain any of them would survive the impact.

"So," he said at last. "The plan?"

"The plan, Lev, is the same. I have no intention of changing it when we don't know what we're up against. We'll pick up supplies tomorrow, as scheduled, and then we'll head back to deep space to shake any potential pursuit. Whoever it was who betrayed us in prison, they're out now, and could make contact with anyone in the system. And if, as it appears, there's a contract on Jez—I believe it continues to be in all of our best interest to get somewhere other ships will have trouble reaching us. Considering our ship is the only one I am aware of in the system with hyperdrive tech, that shouldn't be difficult."

"Those ships that attacked us today," he said quietly. "We're six hours' flight from the nearest wormhole, off any major shipping line. They should never have been able to find us out here, no matter how high the contract was."

Tae nodded. "They looked like smuggler ships, but I've never seen that kind of tech on a smuggler ship." There was concern in his voice. Masha shot him a sharp glance.

"Nor have I. But I have seen that tech before."

"Where?"

"As—part of my work," she murmured. "Before I joined forces with the four of you."

Lev studied her for a moment.

He'd gone through every record in every database to which he had access. And considering he'd been locked up for accessing highly-classified files, and considering he had a photographic memory, that was quite a number of records.

Masha was exactly who she'd told them she was—perfectly-clean record, attended university in Prasvishoni and gone straight from there to a low-level government job, gradually working her way up into higher positions through a combination of competence and people's inherent desire to make this friendly woman's life just a little easier.

And yet …

He shook his head.

It didn't matter at present. Whatever Masha's ultimate goal, she was probably right as to the best course of action for the time being.

Still—he couldn't shake the faint unease that lurked under the instinctive draw of Masha's calm charisma.

"Aunty Masha is a dirty plaguer!"

The door to the main deck slammed open, and a solidly-built six-year-old, with straw-coloured hair and a rebellious expression on his chubby face, burst through.

There was a badly-disguised snort of laughter from Jez. Lev sighed resignedly.

Apparently three days was the outside limit children could be around Jez without learning her particular brand of swearing.

"Jez?" The voice from the hallway was sharp and layered with menace.

Jez straightened, grinning. "Hey Tanya! Your kid's a quick learner."

Tanya stalked into the room, her expression promising murder and possible dismemberment. She looked somehow much more intimidating than her slender frame and wistful features should allow.

Still, she had married demolitions expert and mass-murderer Ysbel, so …

"Hello Uncle Lev."

He looked down at the small hand slipped into his, and smiled despite himself.

"Hello Olya."

"Did we get shot at this morning? Was mama shooting them back?" Olya's eight-year-old face held its usual expression of determination mixed with slight skepticism.

He knelt so that he was at her eye level. “Yes on both counts.”

She tipped her head to one side, considering him, then nodded. “Good. My mama’s a pretty good shot. And she’s very good at blowing things up.”

“I would say that’s an understatement, Olya,” he said gravely.

“I will be one day, too. She said she’d teach me. Mamochka already taught me lots of things. And you promised you’d finish teaching me about black holes.”

He gave a small smile. “I did. But as I recall, you were supposed to be helping me clean the deck last time we had this conversation. I seem to recall doing the whole thing by myself while you watched and asked me questions.”

She grinned at him. “I was going to help. But then you got distracted, and you looked like you were enjoying yourself. Mamochka always says, don’t interrupt a person who’s enjoying themself, because life is short and enjoyment doesn’t last.”

Lev raised an eyebrow at her, smiling despite himself, but there was a faint, sick guilt in the pit of his stomach that never seemed to go away these days

Three days. That was how long it had been since they’d broken Olya and Misko and Tanya out of prison.

And five and a half years since he’d sent them there.

He hadn’t realized it at the time, of course, employed by the government, too caught up in his own misery to know or care who he was hurting. It had been an interesting intellectual exercise, that was all. Extract someone they’d told him was a rogue agent.

And so, he’d planned the extraction that snatched Ysbel from her home and sent Tanya and Olya and Misko to a harsh, remote prison planet at the far end of the system. And Ysbel still had no idea.

None of them did.

"Olya?" he said quietly. "How are you doing?"

She frowned at him. "What do you mean?"

He gestured around, trying to smile. "This is a little different than what you're used to. Are you settling in OK? Are your mama and mamochka doing alright?"

She tilted her head to one side, thinking.

"Yes," she said at last. "I'm OK. It's nice to not be locked up all the time. And it's nice that we don't have to worry about someone hitting us or hitting Mamochka if we don't listen."

There was something hard and cold in the pit of his stomach. "Did the guards used to hit you?" he asked gently. She nodded.

"Yes. One time one of them gave me a black eye. I was pretty little, and I didn't know you weren't allowed to cry when you got hurt, and I fell and hurt my knee. So he hit me. Mamochka tried to stop him, but she couldn't."

He nodded, trying not to let the sick feeling show on his face, because Olya was much more perceptive than she had any right to be. Still, growing up in a place where crying over a skinned knee could earn you a black eye, he supposed that was only to be expected.

At first, after he met Ysbel and realized what he'd done so many years ago, he'd thought that finding Ysbel's family would somehow redeem him. And then he thought that maybe, if he managed to pull off the rescue attempt, that would clear his conscience.

But the thing was, of course, that nothing could redeem him. Nothing could change what he'd done. And at the very least, he owed Ysbel the truth. Because if she told him thank you one more time, if she gave him that look of a shared joke one more time, if she looked down at her wife and children and shot him a look of silent gratitude one more time, he thought he might actually throw up.

"Well," he said at last. "No one here will hurt you if you cry."

Olya frowned at him again, then shook her head decisively. "No. I never cry. Nor does Misko."

Eight years old. Eight and six, and they never cried, and the thing was, he believed it.

He swallowed down something in his throat.

He'd tell Ysbel. Soon. She'd probably kill him, of course. But it couldn't possibly be worse than being the reluctant recipient of her gratitude, of Olya's hero-worship, of Tanya's cautious friendship, as the guilt ate him from the inside out. He'd spent the last month and a half trying to convince himself that she didn't need to ever know. But—well, at the end of the day, he owed her the truth.

He owed her that much, at least.

Ysbel took her hands off the guns regretfully and glanced around the small gunner's tower. It had been a long time since she'd been on ship's guns. Still, it was nice to know the skill didn't go away.

She closed her eyes and took a deep breath, running her hand over her shaved head, and tapped her com.

"Tanya?"

"I'm fine, Ysbel. The children are fine too, before you ask." There was the hint of a smile in her voice, and Ysbel sagged with relief.

She'd had them back for three days now, her wife, their daughter, their son, and still every time she called Tanya, she thought her heart might stop, and every time Tanya answered, the relief that coursed through her was almost enough to make her faint.

She shook her head wryly and made her way out of the cramped tower and down the ladder to the main deck.

Tanya was waiting at the door, with that wistful smile of hers.

Ysbel smiled back, took her wife in her arms, and gave her a lingering kiss.

"Are you sure you're alright?" she whispered. Tanya pulled back, eyes twinkling slightly.

"Ysbel. I'm not quite as fragile as all that, if you recall."

"The children?"

"Already inside."

Tanya put her arm around Ysbel's waist and drew her into the room.

The others were there already. Misko had crossed over to where Tae was sitting and climbed onto his lap, and Tae was looking down at him fondly, and for once not scowling. That in and of itself was something of a surprise, especially since she was almost certain he hadn't strapped in before Jez began her maneuvers. Olya had attached herself to Lev, as usual. And Jez sat in the centre of the room glaring daggers at the woman in the corner, who was dressed in a long pilot's coat and wearing a pleasant smile with an edge to it that could shear steel.

Even three days from having been beaten within an inch of her life, the lanky pilot looked dangerous. But Masha didn't seem worried in the slightest.

"Has Jez tried to kill Masha yet?" Ysbel whispered. Tanya shook her head slightly.

"Not yet."

"And has Masha tried to shoot Jez?"

"I think that might be coming."

"Ah. So I didn't miss much, then."

Tanya gave her a slight smile, and then turned back to the centre of the room.

"So," Ysbel said. "Do we know who was trying to kill us?"

Jez turned and grinned at her. "Nope. Still trying to narrow it down. Kind of a big list, at this point."

Lev was shaking his head slightly. "They seem to have had a contract on us. I still don't know how. And with a ship like the *Ungovernable*—finding us would be difficult."

"And even if they knew where we were somehow, why would they fire on us?" Masha murmured. "Usually contracts require the subjects be brought back for verification."

"Well," Jez drawled, leaning back in her chair, "guess you haven't lived much if you have to wonder why people are firing on you. Me, I always wonder why they don't."

Masha studied her. "Perhaps you're right, Jez," she said, but there was a layer of meaning behind her words that Ysbel couldn't read. "I suppose you are the person with the most expertise in that field, after all." She straightened. "I suggest that we put an alert on the ship's sensors in case we run into anyone else. And in the meantime, I'm sure there are things all of us should be doing."

"Yep. Some of us don't have the option of just sitting in our cabins for three days while everyone else runs the ship," said Jez. Masha raised an eyebrow, but didn't respond.

"Well," said Lev, clearly trying to defuse the situation, "let's get to work then. Jez, you want to run the diagnostics, see if anything was damaged?"

Jez grinned and got gingerly to her feet. Ysbel bit the inside of her lip, watching her. She could still remember the sick despair of three days previous, watching Tanya and her children being led away to certain death. The cocky, restless pilot had been almost killed saving them.

Ysbel owed her a debt she could never repay.

Jez tripped, stumbled, and swore colourfully. She glanced around the cabin, grinned at Olya, and said, "That's how you swear, kid. You should practice. Never know when it'll come in handy." She winked over her shoulder at Ysbel and Tanya, then sauntered out of the room.

Ysbel shook her head. She owed the idiot a debt she could never repay, and also she wanted to strangle her at least three quarters of the time.

Tanya glared at the pilot's retreating back. Ysbel drew her back gently. "It's alright, my love. You get used to it." She paused. "Or, you don't get used to it, but you learn how to picture in your head things blowing up. That makes it a little easier."

Tanya sighed, gave a rueful laugh, and turned to the children. "Alright Misko, Olya. Come on. You two are on mess-hall duty today, and breakfast needs cleaning up."

"You dirty plaguer," Misko muttered. Tanya's face darkened.

Tae sighed as well and stood. "I'll help. May as well, since apparently no matter where I go or what I do, whenever I get comfortable, Jez will decide to take us through an asteroid belt or pick a fight with three ships with Aro tech. Come on, Misko, let's get in there before your mamochka decides to wash your mouth out with soap."

"I will still wash your mouth out with soap," said Tanya.

Misko gave a fair approximation of Tae's signature glower. "I like soap. It tastes good."

Ysbel chuckled to herself as the two children pulled Lev and Tae out the door after them. Lev, possibly the most intelligent human being she'd ever met—even if he could be a complete idiot—and Tae, who was almost certainly the best hacker and techie in the system, bar none. And they were off to do the children's dishes. Well, it was good for them. Possibly not for the children, but certainly for them.

"Those children are going to be spoiled rotten in two weeks' time," said Tanya, moving closer to Ysbel and nuzzling her head into her shoulder. Ysbel smiled and put her arms around her wife, pulling her close.

She tried to ignore the panic that still welled in her chest every time she touched her, the sick anger that still swirled through her brain every time she saw that familiar face, lined now with a faint hardness that hadn't been there five years ago.

She had her family. They were back with her, and she wasn't going to lose them ever again.

And yet …

And yet. Five years she'd lost. Five years of waking up alone, five years of prison, five years of wishing she were dead, of living only for revenge because that was all that was left to her. Five years of Tanya raising two children by herself in the middle of hell. Olya, the stubborn, determined, three-year-old was gone forever. And Misko, the tiny, solemn, chubby toddler. She had Misko the six-year-old hellion, but she'd lost her baby.

She clasped Tanya tighter, and squeezed her eyes shut against the tears that shouldn't be there.

She should be happy. She owed it to them to be happy. And she was, she was desperately, exhaustingly, dizzyingly happy, but underneath the happiness there was a hole, a place that could never be filled up.

"Ysbel?" Tanya murmured questioningly, stirring against her shoulder. Ysbel swallowed hard and blinked quickly.

"What is it, my love?"

"Are you alright?"

"I'm fine," she whispered, pressing Tanya's head gently back into her shoulder and kissing her hair.

Something inside her hurt at the lie. But it was a stupid truth; that even now, even clutching Tanya to her chest, even with her love for this woman who was her whole heart burning through her, there was a sense of loss so deep and so aching that it took her breath away.

One day, she'd find the person who'd planned this. And then she would kill them.

It would be easy. She'd killed plenty of people before.

It wouldn't soothe the ache. She knew enough to know that. But maybe it would make it easier to sleep at night, rather than lying awake, her arms around the woman she loved, staring at the ceiling with silent tears running down her cheek.

"My love?" Tanya whispered. "I believe the children will be busy for a while. And if I recall correctly, we had some business we left unfinished this morning, in the bedroom." She lifted her head and gave Ysbel that smile that still made her weak in the knees. She managed a smile in return, and as Tanya leaned in for a lingering kiss, she kissed her back, clutching her as if Tanya was the only thing keeping her from drowning.

3

Jez's muscles hummed with tension as she lowered the *Ungovernable* gently to the planet surface.

It wasn't the landing that balled a tight knot in her stomach—that was simple as breathing.

It was the fact that the copilot's seat, usually occupied by Lev, contained the woman in the long pilot's coat who seemed to think she was Jez's damn boss.

Masha's expression was bland and pleasant, her eyes straight ahead. She didn't even deign to glance over at Jez as the ship settled onto its landing gear.

Jez stood abruptly, for the first time in her life actually looking forward to leaving her beautiful cockpit, since it meant leaving plaguing Masha behind as well.

"Jez," said Masha, without looking at her, and there was a hint of ice in her voice. "I expect no trouble on this stop."

"Yeah? Well, guess you'd better not cause any trouble then, you bastard." Jez smirked, and flipped Masha a rude gesture as she sauntered out the cockpit door.

Damn that woman to hell.

When she reached the main deck, the others were waiting. Lev gave her a small smile when he saw her. "You and me today, I guess," he said. "Ysbel and Tanya are staying back on the ship with the children, and Masha's going with Tae."

She narrowed her eyes at him. "I don't need a babysitter, genius-boy."

He raised an eyebrow. "Jez. We're going into a zestava where none of us knows anyone. We just got shot at yesterday by ships none of us recognized, someone is after you, and, if you recall, you have—"

"I know, I know, four broken ribs and a broken arm and a broken damn jaw," she grumbled. "Fine."

He looked like he was biting back a small smile of amusement. She rolled her eyes and hit the control for the landing ramp. It lowered with a faint *hiss*.

"Be careful out there, pilot-girl," called Ysbel. "I don't want to have to blow this place up to rescue you."

Jez shot the woman a jaunty grin. "If I remember right, I'm usually the one rescuing you."

"Yes, well, it might be nice if nobody had to be rescued, for once."

"Sounds kinda boring to me."

Lev shot her a look. She grinned at him, and made her careful way down the loading ramp.

She couldn't hide her wince as she stepped off the ramp and onto the soft ground of the small outer-rim planet. Still, it had only been four days, and much as she hated it, it always took more than four days to get over being beaten.

The wind was chilly, cutting across what looked like a wide grassland. In the distance, mountains rose, blue against the darker blue of the sky. It was early morning here, apparently, and the cool of it cut through her jacket and the thin material of her trousers, and her boots had already sunk a few centimetres deep in mud.

She shivered slightly, and pulled her jacket a little closer around her.

"Reminds me a little of outside of Prasvishoni," said Lev beside her.

She glanced over at him. He was looking out over the grasslands towards the small town, and there was an expression on his face, half wry, half wistful.

"You know," he said, "there's a small university on this planet. Not in this town, farther east. One of the women I met in prison taught there."

"Yeah." She looked down. "I'm … sorry."

He turned to her, and this time his smile was genuine. "You know, my whole life I wanted to teach at a university. But in the last few weeks—" he shrugged. "I'd never understood how much I'd enjoy flying."

She met his eyes, and for a second her heart did its customary jump. She swallowed hard, and managed a grin back at him.

"Guess that means you can learn something after all."

He raised an eyebrow at her. "For the record, I did almost throw up yesterday when you were dodging those shots."

She gave a snort of laughter. He tried to look stern, but the glint of humour in his eye ruined it.

"Come on, genius-boy. Let's go, before it starts to rain and Masha blames me for breaking the plaguing clouds."

They made their way down the rutted dirt path towards the town gates. The intricate carved wood of the gates must have been recently painted, because the colours practically glowed against the dark blue-grey of the sky. There was a guard at the gate, but she stepped back and gestured them inside as they approached.

"You're lucky. Gates opened five standard minutes ago," she said.

"Thank you," said Lev. "We're looking for ship parts. Which side of town?"

The guard gestured with her chin, and Lev nodded his thanks.

They wandered through the narrow, almost-deserted packed-dirt streets. The air smelled like rain, and the boardwalks were liberally caked with mud. The houses and apartments were tumbledown constructions of prefab, but even in this backwater they'd managed to paint the carved wooden shutters on the buildings brilliant jewel tones.

It was easy to tell when they reached the merchants' sector. The buildings were smaller, closer together, and if possible, even more tumbledown, some of the doorways nothing more than a rough space-blanket pinned between the blocks of prefab forming the doorway, but all with a small sampling of their wares laid out in a neat heap on tables along the boardwalk.

And ... there. At the end of one of the streets.

She wandered over, drawn almost by gravity.

The speed capacitors.

She ducked through the blanket-doorway and into the small, cramped, dimly-lit shop, and Lev followed.

The *Ungovernable* was her perfect, beautiful angel. But there wasn't a ship in the world that couldn't use a couple extra speed capacitors.

She could get a couple, too, as long as that damn Masha hadn't been too stingy with the credits on her buying chip. Of course, last time Masha'd given her credits, she'd staked the whole chip on a game of fool's tokens ... she smiled fondly to herself at the memory of the bastard's face when Jez had told her.

Some memories were worth more than all the credits in the world.

She ran her hands along the jumble of capacitors, the metal

surfaces smooth and gleaming under her fingers.

"Jez," Lev whispered. She jumped, winced, and swore.

"Sorry," he said. "I'm going to see if I can find some specs on those ships we ran into, and maybe some newscom broadcasts I can upload. Never a bad thing to know what's going on. Will you be OK here?"

She looked at him in mild incomprehension. He sighed and rolled his eyes.

"Fine. You sit here and make sweet love to the ship parts, and I'll meet you back here in a standard hour, OK?"

She grinned. "Sure, genius-boy. You know where to find me."

He started to turn, stopped, and shot her a suspicious glare. "No kabaks. I don't want to have to haul drunk Jez anywhere. I've done it before, and it's not an experience I want to repeat."

She smirked. "Guess you'd better come back before I get bored then."

He sighed. "Jez—"

"Fine, genius. I won't get drunk." She paused. "Too drunk, anyways." She paused again. "Unless—"

"Jez—" he was speaking through his teeth. She laughed.

"Relax. It's way too early in the morning for sump. If I'd wanted to be drunk now, I would have started hours ago."

He shot her a look of complete exasperation. She grinned to herself and turned back to the speed capacitors.

She wandered up and down the aisles for a while, ignoring the people who came and left as the shop grew busier, letting her hands slide over the ship's parts and smiling dreamily to herself at the thought of what she could do with her angel-ship if she had unlimited credits and a little bit of time. She was handling an inline capacitor, running her fingers over its smooth surface with a sort of rapture, when she realized the light reflecting off the dull, polished-metal surface was coming from much higher on the horizon than she'd expected. She tapped the com on her wrist.

It had been almost three standard hours.

She frowned, glanced around the now-crowded shop, and hit Lev's private line.

"Hey, genius. Where are you? Thought you were coming back two standard hours ago."

There was no response.

"I'm heading for a kabak, if you want to come," she said. That should get him to answer, if nothing else did.

Still, nothing. She tapped the general line.

"Hey Tae, you seen Lev?"

"No." Tae's reply came instantly. "I'm with Masha. We've just about done getting supplies. I thought he was with you."

"He was, but then he ran off to go look for something."

"What was he looking for?"

She rolled her eyes. "How am I supposed to know? I was looking at speed capacitors, OK? I wasn't actually listening."

Tae gave a long-suffering sigh. "Ysbel? Did Lev end up back at the ship?"

There was a moment's pause. "No," came Ysbel's voice. "I have not seen him, and nor has Tanya." There was another pause.

"Dirty plaguer!" came a small boy's voice from what sounded like she ship's com. There was the sound of a scuffle in the background.

"Tell our pilot that I am going to have a word with her when she gets back to the ship." Ysbel was speaking through her teeth.

Jez grinned and hit her com. "Hey Ysbel, know I'm hot and all, but you probably shouldn't flirt with me in front of your wife."

"Piss off."

"So to be clear, no one knows where Lev is," said Tae in a flat voice.

Jez glanced around quickly. The small shop was filled with men and women in dirty peasant smocks or worn flight clothes browsing through the small stock of parts, but none of them had the relaxed but still slightly formal posture or the disheveled black hair of the absent Lev. She narrowed her eyes and slapped the com.

"Don't worry, tech-head. I'll find him. I'm good at finding things."

"Yes. Things like gambling games and places they sell sump," grunted Ysbel.

"Those too," she said, grinning, then slapped off her com.

She glanced around the shop one last time. Despite herself, a small tendril of worry snaked through her gut.

What had he said? Something about newscoms, she was pretty sure.

She'd spent nine years as a smuggler. She knew her way around a backwater zestava.

When she ducked out through the low shop door, a light rain was falling. She pulled up the hood of her jacket and hunched her shoulders against the wet, squinting through the greyish haze.

Where would he have gone? And why the hell wasn't he answering his com?

She wandered down the boardwalks, the wet, muddy wood glistening in the dim light filtering through the rainclouds, and scowled at the world in general.

She was supposed to be the irresponsible one.

He'd probably just found something on an information chip and got distracted.

She was getting close to the edge of town, and the buildings here were shabbier, the colourful shutters on the windows crooked, paint blistered with age and neglect. There was a distinct air of lawlessness to this part of town, and she relaxed slightly. This was more like her kind of place. Across the street from her, muffled voices came from inside a dimly-lit kabak. Then there was the distinct sound of a fist hitting flesh. She grinned to herself, then stopped suddenly.

The sound hadn't come from the kabak. It had come from the small, tumbledown building beside it.

And she was almost certain she'd recognized one of the voices, words crisp and cultured and not even a little bit at home in a place like this.

She sucked in a quick breath.

Not good.

Heart pounding, she pulled out her modded heat pistol and crossed the muddy street, holding the weapon inconspicuously behind her leg. The muffled sound of her boots on the wet wooden boardwalk were loud in her ears, even over the faint morning sounds of the kabak next door. She put her back against the dirty, splintery siding of the building, and crept cautiously towards the closed doorway.

From here, she could hear the voices more clearly.

"I told you. I have no idea who you're talking about." Lev's voice was strained, but his tone was as calm as ever, if slightly irritated. Someone else spoke, but she couldn't make out the words. Then the voice raised slightly. It was unfamiliar, but she recognized the meaning in his tone instantly.

"—better damn well hope this will refresh your memory."

She kicked the door hard, swinging up her heat pistol as it slammed open, and glanced quickly around the bare room.

Three unfamiliar figures, all dressed in the nondescript flight clothes she recognized instantly as smuggler gear. All three had weapons. And in the back of the room—Lev, tied to a chair. He was frowning, and blood trickled from the corner of his lip, and a woman stood beside him, heat pistol raised as if to hit him a second time.

Suddenly, Jez was very, very angry.

"Back the hell off, you bastards," she ground out through her teeth, holding her pistol level. "That's my damn copilot."

All three of them turned to face her. The man who appeared to be the leader gave her a long, speculative look.

They were standing too close to Lev for a shot with this thing—beam wasn't narrow enough.

"You Jez Solokov?" the leader grunted. She gave him a dangerous grin.

"Don't see how that's your business. But that scholar-boy you have tied up over there, he is my damn business. So unless you feel like a heat-blast to the face, you might want to let him go." She shrugged. "'Course, someone as ugly as you, heat blast to the face might not make that much of a difference."

"It's her," the man said to his companions. "Must be. They said she had a mouth on her." He turned back to Jez with an unpleasant smile. "Looks to me like you lost the last fight you were in."

"Guess I need practice," she said. "Don't usually fight with people as plaguing stupid as you, but hell, this time I'll make an exception."

Lev shot her an exasperated look. She winked at him, then pointed the modded heat gun at the floor in front of the three smugglers and squeezed the trigger. The boards erupted in an explosion of air-blistering heat and light, and then sizzled into ash, small flames licking at the edges of the hole she'd just blasted in the formerly-wooden floor. She grinned.

Ysbel was a damn marvel with guns.

"Now, you dirty plaguers," she said in a friendly tone. "You feel more like talking?"

"Jez, they have a—" Lev began in a strangled tone. The woman standing next to his chair cuffed him hard alongside the head, yanking out a small cylindrical tube with her other hand and pointing it towards Jez. Jez's brain recognized it at the same time as she pulled the trigger a second time.

It clicked uselessly

Damn.

"EMP blocker," Lev finished unnecessarily. She drew back her arm and flung the useless heat-pistol as hard as she could directly into the face of the leader, cursing breathlessly as her broken ribs protested. He stumbled back, cursing and clutching his face, and she braced herself and lunged forward, grabbing the woman guarding Lev by the front of the shirt. She jerked the woman towards her, grunting at the pain, kicked her legs from under her, and shoved her backwards. The woman's head hit the wall with a satisfying crack, and Jez ducked on instinct as a heat-blast sizzled through the air above her.

"Jez! What are you—" Lev hissed.

"Busy now," she snapped. The leader was coming at her, heat-pistol drawn.

This was going to bloody hurt.

She yanked a knife out of her boot, shoved it at Lev, then gritted her teeth and spun, kicking out with her booted foot. She hit the man's hand and he grunted in pain, the pistol spinning away across the floor, and for half a moment she thought she might black out. The man on the other side of the room stooped and grabbed for it, but before he could shoot, Jez yanked the leader around in front of her, between her and Lev and the heat guns, spots dancing before her eyes.

"May as well stop," said Lev. He'd managed to jam the knife blade between the magnetic cuffs. They'd popped open, and now he was holding the EMP blocker he'd snatched from the disoriented woman on the floor. Jez raised an eyebrow. For a soft-boy, he moved fast when he had to. The man thrust the heat-guns back into his belt, but as he lunged at them, Jez shoved the man she was holding forward. He stumbled, and both men went down in a heap. She grabbed Lev by the arm and shoved him ahead of her out the door.

"Run!" she hissed, and they took off down the narrow streets.

Every step jolted through her ribcage, and her head spun with the pain, but on the other hand, getting caught by whoever was chasing them would probably hurt a hell of a lot worse.

"What the hell were you doing?" Lev panted, irritation clear in his tone as they ducked around a corner into a dirty alley. She could already hear shouts behind them. Whoever it was after them, they must really want Lev.

"Saving your damn life. What did it look like?" She was still grinning.

The broke back out onto a larger street, and he shot her an wry glance. "I was in the middle of convincing them I'd never heard of you."

She managed a shrug. "Didn't look like it was working out for you."

People turned to stare as they pounded past. Jez dodged around a man with two children in tow, and almost ran headlong into a startled woman pulling a load of boxes attached to an anti-grav.

"Sorry," Jez grunted, sidestepping just in time.

"This may surprise you, Jez, but I did manage to survive for twenty-six years without you there to rescue me." Lev still sounded irritated, if slightly breathless.

"What, in a university?" she shot back.

"More complicated than it sounds," he panted. "Watch yourself. They're going to be shooting us in a moment."

"Use the EMP blocker." She ducked down another alley, and he followed.

"It's broken. Broke when she fell."

She turned to glare at him. He shrugged.

"They didn't know it was broken when I grabbed it." He paused. "Up there. Go right. I saw a map of this place. There's a back way out of town."

Behind them, there were shouts and the sound of boots, approaching fast. She dodged down the narrow street, Lev hard on her heels. Behind them, a heat-blast left a charred scar on the building on the corner, and another scorched their heels.

"Back here," Lev ground out, pulling her into a narrow alley and coming to a stumbling halt. She collapsed against the wall, swearing and panting, the smell of wet dirt and garbage filling her nostrils, and he twisted the heavy cuff down his wrist, posture tense.

"What are you—" she began. He held up a hand, breathing hard. Their pursuer rounded the corner after them, heat-gun drawn, and Lev stepped forward and swung his wrist out, the heavy cuff snapping sharply against the butt of the gun. The man's hand dipped, but he didn't lose his grip on the gun.

Damn, damn, damn. She wasn't close enough to do anything, and the world seemed to slow, and the man raised the gun and fired point-blank into Lev's face.

The gun clicked uselessly.

Jez's heart re-started, and she lunged forward and drove her fist into the man's sternum. He stumbled backwards, and she grabbed him by the greasy hair with her good hand and introduced his face to her kneecap. He dropped, momentarily stunned, and she snatched the spare pistol from his belt, spinning around just in time to plant the muzzle of it into the stomach of the smuggler leader as he rounded the corner. He stopped so quickly that he almost tripped over his own feet.

"Go on, ugly," she panted, blinking back the tears of pain. "Get back."

He did as he was told.

The man in the street stirred, blood streaming down his face, and she gestured him up to join his companion. He stumbled to his feet and obeyed.

"Thought you said the EMP blocker didn't work," she whispered to Lev. He raised an eyebrow.

"It doesn't. But I happen to know that particular model of heat pistol is quite sensitive to percussive force."

She rolled her eyes at him, but she was grinning.

"Alright you," she said to the two smugglers. "What—"

"Jez," said Lev from behind her. His voice held the sort of calm that meant something very, very bad was about to happen.

In front of her, the man who she'd assumed was the smuggler captain smiled.

She cast a quick glance over her shoulder.

The deserted street to either side of them was no longer deserted. Instead, it was now filled with at least two dozen grim-faced men and women that she was pretty damn sure weren't innocent bystanders.

She shoved Lev out of the way as a heat-blast crackled through the air beside her ear, and again they ran for their lives.

The streets were getting smaller and dirtier as they approached the end of town, and the light rain was quickly turning into a downpour.

"This way," Lev gasped, yanking her down another alley. "There's an old back gate. I don't know if it still opens."

She jumped a puddle and landed in another, the wet soaking through the worn places in her boots, her teeth clenched. "Trust me. It'll open," she said, patting the butt of her heat pistol.

A laser blast ricocheted off the wall of an abandoned building in front of her, and she leapt to one side as it hit the ground at her feet, sending up steam and a scent of burnt mud. Lev's jaw was set in a sort of resigned horror.

She slapped her com. "Time to go, kids! I found Lev, and we're coming in hot."

"What—" Tae began.

"Meet us at the ship. Ysbel, might want to have a welcoming party."

She glanced over her shoulder.

It wasn't easy to see through the rain, but it looked like more smugglers, or whoever the hell they were, seemed to have joined in on the pursuit. She tapped her com again.

"A big welcoming party."

A shutter in one of the ramshackle houses twitched, but it looked like everyone on this side of town was smart enough to stay out of the street right about now. Everyone except her and Lev, and the whole damn army of smugglers who were chasing them.

A stray heat blast singed the hem of her coat, and she swore loudly.

"You're enjoying this, aren't you?" Lev asked with breathless exasperation. She shrugged one shoulder.

"You get used to it."

"I'm fairly certain that I'm not going to get used to it," he said through his teeth.

She grinned at him. "Hang around me long enough and you might."

At the end of the dirty, narrow street, lined with broken-down buildings and boarded up windows, the town walls rose up, wooden and too high to jump. She gritted her teeth.

"Hope you weren't kidding about that door."

Lev narrowed his eyes, frowning slightly. "No, it should be there."

"Well, if it isn't, we're going to find out the hard way in about ten seconds."

"Ah." His face cleared. "There. It's boarded up. Can you—"

"On it, genius," she said, yanking the heat pistol out. Wasn't easy to hold steady when you were splashing down a muddy street, and also when your entire damn ribcage felt like it was being cut open with a heat-knife, but still, it was a pretty big target. She drew in a shallow breath, let it out slowly, and squeezed off a blast. It didn't have Ysbel's mods, but it wasn't a bad gun, and at this range it burned a respectable hole in the thin boards. She fired again, and even wet as it was, the flimsy wood ignited and sputtered fitfully.

"Stand back," she panted.

"Jez. You have four broken ribs," he said. "I am capable of some physical exertion on occasion."

She sighed and fired one last time, and, with a look of extreme distaste, Lev rammed his shoulder into the weakened wood. It splintered, and the door swung reluctantly open.

"Go, I've got the gun." She shoved him through the entrance as the first of their pursuers rounded the corner. The smuggler's heat pistol was already raised, and as she dived through after Lev, the man slowed, aimed, and fired.

The bolt hit her squarely in the side, and she tumbled the rest of the way through the door, swearing through her teeth and biting back tears of pain. Lev's face was bloodless as he dragged her clear of the entrance.

"Jez!" he was shouting. "Jez, are you alright? Jez, answer me."

Her head was spinning, and it hurt like hell, but it didn't hurt nearly as much as she'd expected. She put a gingerly hand to her side as Lev pulled her out of the way and touched where the blast had seared through her jacket.

Then she gritted her teeth and swore more loudly.

"Jez, can you hear me? Answer me." Lev's expression was grim, and slightly terrifying.

"I'm fine," she grunted. He grabbed the pistol from her hand, stalked to the entrance, and snapped off three shots. Judging from the cursing from the other side of the wall, his aim had improved immeasurably since she'd first met him.

She staggered to her feet, still swearing. He turned back, grabbing her good arm to steady her.

"Jez. Where did it hit?"

"Hit something in my pocket. I'm fine. Come on, we don't plaguing have time for this."

"You—"

"Come on!"

He slipped an arm around her, and they set off at an awkward run. She stumbled slightly on the uneven ground and the long grass, and pain jolted through her ribs and the round burn mark on her side.

Lev tapped his wrist com against his thigh. "Jez is hit," he said, voice grim. "Masha, get a kit ready."

"Jez?" Tae sounded almost frantic.

"I'm fine!"

"You don't damn well look fine," Lev snapped.

They turned the corner, and despite everything, Jez couldn't hold back a sigh of pleasure at the sight of her beautiful, perfect ship, its metal sides burnished to a dull polish, every old-fashioned rivet on it gleaming, it's sleek, clean lines making it look like it was straining against gravity, yearning to get back into the sky.

"You can swoon over your ship later, Jez, come on," Lev growled.

Ysbel stood on the loading ramp, wearing her usual flat expression.

"Duck," she commanded as they approached.

Jez had spent enough time around Ysbel not to question, and apparently Lev had as well. They dropped, and Jez almost blacked out. Ysbel drew back her arm, and something small and cylindrical sailed over their heads and landed in the mud several metres behind them.

"Now, run," the woman said, and they scrambled to their feet and sprinted for the ship.

They were half-way in when the ground behind them erupted in an explosion of grass and mud and dirt and deafening noise. Ysbel smiled in a satisfied way and stepped after them up the ramp. Tae was already closing it behind them.

"Jez," said Lev through gritted teeth, "You need to—"

"Help me into the cockpit," she grunted.

"Masha can—"

She turned to glare at him. "If you ever think you see Masha flying my ship, either I'm dead, or you're drunk."

He shook his head in exasperation, but helped her down the corridor and through the cockpit door. She dropped thankfully into the pilot's seat.

"Strap in!" she called over the com. Then she hit the thrusters, the ship leapt forward, burning through the atmosphere.

And despite the pain throbbing through her body and the spots dancing before her eyes, as the surface of the planet receded behind them and the beautiful blackness of space opened up in front of them, for one perfect moment everything was right with the world.

Then Masha's voice came over the com.

"Jez. Please do a small jump to get us into deep space. Then please come to the main deck, both of you. And I hope you have a very, very good explanation for what happened back there."

4

Gingerly, Tae released his harness strap and got to his feet, glancing around the cozy living quarters for something to grab onto if necessary. Ysbel, who was sitting across from him on one of the soft couches, gave him a small smile.

"Strapped down in time this time."

He scowled at her. "If Jez didn't treat every time she sat in the cockpit like we were trying to get away from an entire squadron of enemy ships, it might be a little easier."

Ysbel chuckled and tapped her com. "Tanya?"

There was that strain on her face, and he could tell when Tanya answered by the relief that flooded her expression.

He shook his head slightly.

It had only been a few days. She'd be fine. But there was something haunted in the woman's face, something he'd hoped would disappear when they finally found Tanya and the children.

But, he supposed, wounds that deep didn't heal overnight.

Speaking of wounds—Jez really hadn't been looking good when she'd stumbled up the ramp, leaning against Lev for support.

"Come on," he said. "We'd better get in there before Masha and

Jez kill each other."

Ysbel gave him a reluctant smile and followed him to the main deck.

When he stepped through the door, Lev was lowering a swearing Jez against the wall. His face was grim, and hers—well, it was difficult to tell under the colourful mass of bruises, but there was anguish in her expression. Tae crossed the deck quickly and crouched beside them, worry twisting his chest.

Trust Jez to get herself in trouble. He wasn't actually certain whether she could spend ten minutes anywhere in the system without getting herself in trouble.

"Is she OK?" he asked. Lev shook his head grimly.

"I don't know. She said the blast glanced off something in her pocket, but—"

Jez touched her side and swore fluently.

"Jez, what happened?" Tae asked, his teeth gritted with worry. She looked at him with an agonized expression.

"I think the blast hit my damn speed capacitors," she whispered.

Ysbel rolled her eyes, kneeling beside them. "Open your jacket and pull up your shirt, you idiot, or I'll have to cut it off you."

Jez did as she was told, for once. Tae swallowed, feeling slightly sick. The bruises she'd taken from her beating a few days ago had turned a dark purple and stood out in stark relief against the flexible white bone-set that the prison doctor had applied four days earlier, and there was a new, round, bright red burn-mark where the overheated capacitor had seared into her skin. Ysbel shook her head and held out a hand, and Tae jumped to his feet, grabbing the nearest heat-blast kit. She ripped it open and stuck it over the burn, sealing it carefully.

"Is that all that happened to you then, you crazy lunatic?"

Jez nodded without speaking. Her face had gone bloodless.

"Jez—" began Lev, in that steady tone which usually meant he was much more upset than he was trying to let on. Ysbel shook her head.

"I doubt whatever it was that you two were doing was good for broken ribs."

"Yeah," Jez whispered, with an attempt at a grin, "but you should have seen their faces." She reached into her pocket and, with an effort, pulled out the damaged capacitor. She looked at it for a moment, shaking her head sadly. Then her eyes went unfocused, and her head lolled back against the wall. Tae's heart stuttered in panic.

"Ysbel," Lev snapped, but Ysbel shook her head, pushing herself to her feet.

"I'll go get the scanner, but I think it's just the strain." She paused and looked at Lev's face. "Don't worry. I don't think you could kill this lunatic with an ion gun. And believe me, there are days I've thought about trying."

Tae blew out a faint sigh of relief and tipped his own head back. He wasn't certain how Jez managed to earn the number of beatings she got—well, he supposed that wasn't entirely true—but he could still feel the panic of four days ago, seeing the restless, irritating pilot who had somehow become something like a really, really annoying older sister, bloody and unconscious in the prison courtyard.

Ysbel returned a moment later with the medi scanner, took a quick scan, and nodded.

"She's fine. I'll give her something for the pain when she wakes up."

"Yes, that would probably be a good idea," said a cold voice from above them. "And then, I hope, she'll explain exactly what happened back there."

Tae sighed and opened his eyes.

This really, really wasn't going to end well.

Lev turned, shaking his head ruefully. "Masha. I know how this looks. But this wasn't—"

Jez's eyes snapped open. "My capacitor! Tae, can we fix it?"

Tae turned and glared at her. "Jez, you just got shot. You're lucky you weren't killed. And you're really lucky that the capacitor was non-reactive, or it would have burned a hole through the middle of you."

"Can we fix it?"

"Jez—"

She scowled at him, and pushed herself gingerly up against the wall. "Look, I spent three hours in that plaguing shop, and all I could buy were two capacitors, because someone—" she shot a venomous look at Masha, "loaded basically no credits onto my chip. And then someone damn well shot them!"

"Jez," he said in what he hoped was a patient tone, "we're on the *Ungovernable*. We have a hyperdrive, we have tech that no other ship in the system has, and I'm pretty sure even without hyperdrive no one and nothing could keep up to us. Why in the system were you buying speed capacitors?"

"I bet I could make it go faster," she grumbled.

"Jez." Masha's voice had the icy tone it always seemed to take on when she was talking to the pilot. "Lev was just about to explain why the two of you were running back to the ship with what looked like half the zestava after you."

Tae winced. Jez grinned, but there was something sharp behind her expression. "Well Masha," she drawled, "Thing is, when someone tries to kill genius here, I get mad. Guess I don't like it when people hurt my copilot."

Lev gave her a rueful look. "I was fine."

She snorted. "You were cuffed to a damn chair."

"And you, Jez, were barely on your feet, and if you recall, you have—"

"Yeah, yeah, four broken ribs and whatever," she said, waving her hand airily.

"For someone who just fainted, you seem remarkably unconcerned about it."

She grinned. "What do you mean, fainted? I was resting my eyes."

Despite everything, Tae had to bite back a laugh at the expression on Lev's face.

"Is that what happened?" Masha asked Lev. Her voice was still cold, but there was a speculative look on her face. Lev looked up at her, shaking his head wearily.

"Yes, Masha. I was buying a couple information chips and someone pulled a heat-gun on me and hit my com with an EMP blocker before I had time to put a call out. I suppose I should have been expecting it, but—" he gave a slight shrug. "In honesty, I assumed this was one of the few places in the system where no one wanted to kill us at the moment."

"That," said Masha icily, "is apparently the one thing we can never assume, at least, not with our present company." She turned her cold glare back on Jez, who gave her a cocky grin.

"Masha," said Lev patiently. "This wasn't Jez's fault. She was back in the parts shop when all this happened."

"And what did they want?" Masha asked, with no noticeable thawing in her tone. Lev hesitated.

"They—wanted to know if I knew Jez," he said at last.

Jez shrugged. "Not my fault people are looking for me. I mean, Ysbel here can't seem to keep her hands off me, and she's married."

She smirked at the others. Lev put his face in his hands, Ysbel sighed heavily, and Tae shook his head.

Masha eyed the pilot speculatively. "We unfortunately can't change whatever it is you did before you came here—"

"You know damn well what I did before I came here, you bastard," said Jez, still grinning. "If you didn't want a smuggler in your crew, you shouldn't have recruited a damn smuggler into your crew."

"I have no problem with having a smuggler in my crew," said Masha, in that pleasant voice. "However, having someone in my crew who is irresponsible and reckless enough that she puts every other member of my crew at risk—that's where I begin to draw a line."

"Listen, you dirty—"

Masha held up a hand. "For once, Jez, I believe that your actions today didn't directly cause this. But you could have called for the rest of us to come help, and I believe we could have extracted Lev with much less notice."

"Someone was going to hit him in the face with their damn pistol butt when I came in," Jez said through gritted teeth, and Tae raised an eyebrow. Jez wasn't usually that upset when someone was going to get hit in the face.

Perhaps Lev's crush wasn't entirely one-sided.

"I understand that. However, now there's an entire zestava who knows who we are. I can't imagine there are many ships like the *Ungovernable* in the system. It won't take people long to start putting things together. If it was just Vitali after us, that would be bad enough. But now that we've broken two thousand people out of prison? The four of you are very talented, true, but the fact remains that there are only four of you." She paused and looked around at them, and Tae could see the slight strain-lines behind her mild expression.

He frowned.

It took a lot to worry Masha. But she was clearly worried.

"There was someone in the prison looking for you, Jez. They managed to tag your prison file, which should have been impossible. I've spent the last four days going back through every piece of information we have to figure out who it was and what they wanted."

She sighed, and took a seat in one of the padded chairs. "I was hoping to have this discussion this afternoon, when we'd finished picking up supplies. But I suppose now is as good a time as any." She pulled a small chip out of her pocket and tossed it to Tae. He caught it, frowning.

"Open it," she said. He slipped it into his com and brought up his holoscreen, glancing quickly through the lines of code.

Something cold stirred in his chest. He glanced up at Masha, and she nodded slightly.

"What is it?" asked Lev.

"Smuggler tech," he said quietly. "Someone managed to install some sort of smuggler tech on this ship. They've been tracking us."

"Yes," said Masha quietly in the silence. "Since we left the prison planet, I believe. I doubt the ships that attacked us yesterday were random. And someone must have guessed we'd land on this zestava for supplies. They have a tag on each of us, not just Jez. If they knew Jez was alive, it wouldn't have been difficult to figure out who the rest of the crew might have been. But, as Tae noted, there was a date on Jez's file, what appeared to be an internal note that wasn't completely scrubbed. There were dates next to each of your names as well. I was not able to ascertain what the dates might refer to, and there's a range on them of over thirty years. I've sent them to your coms. Let me know if you think of anything important. I don't know if it will be helpful, but I'd always prefer to go into a situation with as much information as possible."

Tae looked up, stomach tight with worry. "That's not all," he said grimly. "Here Lev, let me send this to your com. You should take a look at it."

Maybe he was wrong. Maybe Lev would take a look and tell him he was wrong.

He glanced over at Jez, leaned up against the wall. Her bruised face was tight with pain, even though she was clearly trying to hide it, but there was something sharp and reckless in her expression.

Masha had mentioned the tag on Jez's prison file to him, and he'd spent the last four days trying to figure out how whoever it was had tagged her. It wasn't impossible—he could have done it himself in thirty seconds. But you wouldn't be able to tag someone like that unless you knew they were there, and there was no reason anyone should have known Jez was there.

But … that alleyway, what felt like at least a lifetime ago, back on Parasvishoni. He was pretty certain he knew now who the people who'd jumped Jez were. He hadn't even bothered to ask at the time —for someone like Jez, there were probably half a hundred people who would have wanted to jump her in an alley. But looking at the long list of code on the chip Masha had given him had brought a name back to his mind.

Lev looked up. His face was grave.

"Lena," he said.

Tae closed his eyes for a moment.

He'd really, really been hoping he was wrong.

Why was he never wrong when he wanted to be?

He took a deep breath, and nodded. "I checked the specs. As far as I know, her smuggling crew is the only one who fits. I'm no smuggler, but when you're on the streets, you hear things. Her crew's callsigns are pretty unique."

Lev raised an eyebrow wryly. "I'm something of an expert on Lena's crew, for reasons much too long to get into. I'm certain it's her."

Tae glanced back at Jez. Her eyes were narrowed, and there was the beginnings of a grin on her face that probably meant really bad news.

"Well," she said in a thoughtful voice, leaning back against the wall. "Lena. Been a long time since I saw her."

"Jez," said Lev, his voice serious, "why is she after you?"

Jez sat up slightly, shrugged, winced, and swore. "Let's see. I mouthed off to her a few times. Alright, a lot of times. And then I pulled a job for her that she'd tried to turn into a setup, and I got out. And then I stole her ship. It was a really nice ship. And I also stole some of the cargo she took." She grinned, a look of faint nostalgia on her face. "And, I put wall spikes through the thrusters on every single one of the rest of her ships." She paused. "And, she might not have been too happy that the last time she sent Antoni to kill me, you and Tae got the jump on him with a heat pistol and Ysbel threatened to blow him up. Probably a bit of a sore spot, if I'm being honest."

Tae stared at her with a mixture of horror and disbelief. Lev's face echoed his.

"Jez," said Lev carefully. "You're exaggerating, right? You didn't actually do all that to Lena?"

She grinned at him jauntily. "Yep, sure did. Probably a few other things that I forgot, too."

"You—how did she not kill you? This is Lena we're talking about!"

Jez shrugged. "Hard to kill someone when you can't catch them."

Tae and Lev exchanged glances. Lev seemed to have been struck speechless for once, and Tae couldn't blame him.

Lena had a reputation. Her crew had a reputation. And the reputation was, you get on Lena's bad side, you might as well start planning your funeral. He knew Jez had flown for Lena once, but he'd assumed they'd mutually agreed to part, mostly because he couldn't imagine Jez following anyone's orders for more than about three days, and he also couldn't imagine someone like Lena putting up with Jez's mouth for more than about three days.

He glanced back at the pilot, and shook his head ruefully.

He'd spent the last several weeks with Jez. He should have known it would never have been that simple.

Still …

This wasn't good news.

Behind him, Ysbel was trying to hide a chuckle. Lev glared at her.

"You think this is funny?"

Ysbel shrugged, clearly trying to keep a straight face. "No. Not really. But I think Lena probably had no idea what she was getting into when she decided to go up against our pilot."

"I think that's true of everyone who meets Jez," Tae muttered, and this time Ysbel did crack up. Jez gave the room a smug look.

"Can't say I'm not good at what I do."

"Jez, this is not something to be proud of!" said Lev in a strangled tone. "I have no idea how Lena tracked you down, but this is not a good thing!"

She shrugged again. "Took her four years to catch up to me last time. I figure with this sweet, sweet angel I'm flying, it'll take her longer this time."

At last Masha stood. There was something in her posture that made Tae look up quickly, and then there was something in her expression that made his stomach drop.

Masha walked slowly over to where Jez sat against the wall. She studied her for a moment, something calculating in her expression, then she crouched down in front of the pilot.

"Jez. Lena is a problem we can't afford right now. That means the only way we stay alive is by staying off the radar. And I've come to the reluctant conclusion that that is something that you are currently incapable of. And so, Jez, you are confined to the ship for the foreseeable future. You will pilot the ship as I direct, and you will do absolutely nothing to attract attention."

For a moment, no one spoke. Tae held his breath, tensed to jump forward and grab Jez's fist when she inevitably went for Masha.

But Jez just leaned her head back against the wall, eyes half-closed, a small smile on her face.

He frowned, and something chilled inside him.

Whatever came out of Jez's mouth next, there'd be no taking it back.

"Well, Masha," said Jez at last, not opening her eyes. "I figured this was coming, one way or another. I could swear at you, you dirty bastard, but you already know what I'm going to say. So. We'll do a nice long hyperdrive jump, find a safe planet. And you and whoever wants to stay with you can get off. I'll keep the *Ungovernable*, you can have the credits. You're the one who stole them, and there's plenty there for you to get a decent ship." She paused, and there was total silence across the deck.

Tae couldn't breathe.

Jez shifted, sitting up slightly. "See, you don't actually give a damn.

We're just a sharp set of tools for you to use. You wanted someone to fly your ship and take your damn orders—well, I've never been too good at taking orders. So you take whoever wants to come with you. I'll drop Ysbel and Tanya and the kids off on their planet if they want. And then—" she gave a sharp grin. "I'm going to raise absolute hell, all through the system, for as long as I can until someone shoots me down. And every time they try, I'm going to give you the finger, Masha. Because of all the bastards I've worked with, and I've worked with a few, you're the biggest damn piece of work I've ever met."

For a long moment, no one spoke. Tae felt like someone had punched him in the stomach, and he was still trying to catch his breath.

He couldn't look at Jez.

He couldn't blame her, really. Maybe if he was in her place, he'd have done the same thing. But …

But for just a few weeks, he'd thought he could trust them. He'd thought they might actually go back. That they might actually be able to help the street kids—his friends—he'd left behind. That it might be as important to them as it was to him.

He should have plaguing well known better. He'd thought he'd learned his lesson when he got thrown in jail, back on Prasvishoni, when he'd turned himself in because not turning himself in would mean the police burning out the street-kid gangs until they found him, who cared how many they left dead.

It was just like it always was. Like it always had been. You start with a dream, but then you find out that it costs a hell of a lot more than anyone is willing to pay. And then you're back to fighting for your next meal and trying to keep away from the police, or whoever it is that wants to kill you. Just keeping alive, that's all it ever was.

He shook his head, with a small, bitter smile. The anger was a sick knot in his stomach.

Then again, he'd always been stupid.

Masha was watching Jez. She didn't look as surprised as he'd expected. But of course she wasn't surprised. It was always going to end like this, because Jez was never going to follow orders, and Masha was never going to stop giving them. She probably knew it from the moment she met Jez, and she probably already had a contingency plan in place.

"I see," Masha said, after a moment. Her voice had returned to its usual pleasant, businesslike tone. "I suppose that's that. You will not be keeping the *Ungovernable*, Jez, but you will get exactly what you contracted with me for—credits, and a ship of your own. You can pick the one you want, I'm certain we have enough credits to pay for it." She stood and glanced around. "As for the rest of you, if you stay with me, I will have plenty to keep you busy. Including you, Ysbel, if you choose. Although if any of you would like to 'raise absolute hell until someone shoots you down,'" she turned a cutting glance at Jez, "you are, of course, more than welcome to go with our pilot." She paused. "I will tell you, though—there is more behind what we are doing than just staying one step ahead of our bad debts." She looked down at Jez with a thoughtful expression. "Jez. I suggest we plan on docking tomorrow morning."

Jez nodded, without speaking. Tae watched her. Even through the despair and anger thickening in his chest, he could see the stricken look behind her carefree expression.

She'd been the one to pull the trigger. But Masha had handed her the gun.

He glanced around the room quickly. Ysbel still wore her usual stoic expression, but there was something in her eyes—pain? Hope?

He couldn't tell.

Lev looked slightly sick.

Tae stood restlessly.

He had no idea what he was going to do. And it didn't matter. Jez, Masha, Lev, Ysbel—they might have grand dreams, but in the end, they were just like him—a bunch of starving outcasts, trying to grasp at the fringes of something, scrabbling to get by. No time for causes, or dreams, or friendship, or loyalty, or anything else.

He turned quickly and left the room. He was choking back a lump in his throat, and no one on the damn ship needed to see that.

5

"So, my heart," said Tanya quietly, once they were back in their cabin. "We're going home."

Ysbel nodded. She still didn't trust herself to speak.

This was what she'd wanted, of course. This was everything she'd ever wanted—Tanya, Olya, Misko. They could go back home. And one day, she'd stop feeling sick when she looked at her wife and remembered everything that had happened to her. One day she'd look at Olya and Misko and feel only happiness, not happiness mixed with a stabbing pain. One day …

"Are you alright, Ysi?"

"Yes. I'm fine." The words almost choked her on the way out. Tanya drew back and studied her.

"What's the matter?"

"Nothing," she said, forcing her voice to remain level. "Nothing is wrong. This is what I wanted. What we both wanted."

Tanya was still studying her, that familiar face more lined than Ysbel remembered it, each line tracking a joy or pain or grief that Ysbel would never know.

"You are going to miss them, aren't you?" Tanya asked quietly.

Ysbel tried to smile.

"I've been trying to get rid of that pilot since I met her."

Tanya smiled in return, that wistful smile of hers. "I'm sorry."

"Don't be sorry. Please," said Ysbel. "This is what I wanted, and I would give up everything in this world for you and the children."

"I know," Tanya whispered. "I wish you didn't have to."

"It's better this way," said Ysbel. "We need to be on our own again, I think. We need to be a family again."

Tanya nodded, her head against Ysbel's shoulder, and Ysbel blinked back tears.

Damn everything. Damn Masha's stubbornness, and Jez's attitude, and the whole system.

"Ysbel?" Lev's voice came through her earpiece, and she jumped. Tanya pulled back again, looking at her questioningly.

"My com," she said apologetically, and tapped her wrist. "What do you need?"

"Ysbel." Lev paused. There was something strange in his voice. "I … there's something I've been meaning to tell you for a while now. I thought I'd better do it now, while I have the chance."

She frowned. "Alright."

He paused again. "Would you mind coming somewhere where we can talk?"

"Of course," she said. "I will meet you on the main deck. It should be empty now."

"Yes," he said quietly. "I believe it is."

Tanya was still watching her. She tapped off her com. "It's Lev. He wants to talk to me."

"About what?" asked Tanya. Ysbel shrugged.

"I have no idea. I never know what that boy is thinking." She paused. "But he's a good man. If it hadn't been for him—" she had to stop speaking for a moment. Tanya smiled fondly.

"I know," she said. "I won't ever forget him either."

"I don't think it will take long. Is everything mostly packed?"

Tanya shot her a wry look. "Yes, considering that the only things any of us own at the moment are what we're wearing, we are packed."

"We do have plenty of weapons, though."

Tanya gave a soft laugh. "Yes. We do. I don't think I would recognize you if you weren't surrounded by explosives, my heart."

Ysbel kissed her wife on the forehead and slipped out the door. Once outside, she paused for a moment, leaning against the wall.

This was maybe the stupidest thing she'd ever experienced.

She was going to get everything she wanted. When she'd first come here, she'd have been happy to blow this entire crew to pieces just for a taste of revenge against whoever had done this to her family.

It was strange how things changed.

Now she had her family back, but losing the crew made her feel like another part of her was being torn away. She could hold onto one, but not the other.

Still—she shook her head and tried to smile. A few weeks. That's all she'd had with this ridiculous, genius, crazy crew. A few weeks wouldn't take long to heal.

She was almost certain.

She straightened and sighed, heading for the main deck.

Lev was waiting for her, sitting on one of the padded chairs. The deck was empty apart from him, the warm yellow artificial lights casting soft shadows from the tables and benches. He gave her a brief, wry smile as she came in, and gestured to the chair across from him. His face was calm, like it usually was, but his foot moved restlessly against the leg of the chair. She frowned. She'd never known him to fidget.

She pulled out her chair and raised an eyebrow at him.

"Well?" she said after a moment.

He sighed. "Ysbel," he said. His voice was quiet. "I—there's something I've known for some time. I had always intended to tell you, but I never seemed to find the right time." He gave a rueful smile. "Or maybe I'm just a coward. That's also a possibility."

Her frown deepened. "Well? Go ahead and tell me then."

There was something about his voice, his posture, that made something inside of her twist with a faint dread. Whatever it was he was about to tell her, she wasn't sure she wanted to know.

He took a deep breath. "Ysbel. As you know, I worked for the government for several years before I … left their employ."

"Were arrested, you mean," she grunted. He nodded.

"Yes. And while I was working there …" he paused again, closing his eyes for a moment. "Ysbel," he said quietly, "While I was working there, my superiors came to me with a problem. They said there was a rogue agent who needed to be extracted from some outer-rim agricultural planet, and they needed someone to come up with an extraction plan."

She stared at him for a moment. Her heart was pounding, and her hands were almost trembling, something sick and cold lodged in her stomach.

He couldn't be saying what she thought he was saying. She must be misinterpreting him.

"You—" she began hoarsely.

He opened his eyes and met her gaze. "Yes, Ysbel," he said quietly. "That was me. I was the one who planned your extraction five years ago."

"I—" Her voice didn't seem to be working.

She had to have misheard.

Lev. The man who had strong-armed Masha into going down to the prison planet to rescue Tanya. The man who had sat on his cot in prison and asked her to tell him about her wife, and then let her talk until she couldn't talk any longer through the tears. Endlessly polite, always courteous, with his calm, thoughtful expression and his measured tone.

But … she'd seen his face, when Jez was hurt and they were breaking out of prison, that cold, calculating thoughtfulness that wasn't thinking of anything but how to produce the maximum amount of pain with the minimum amount of effort. She'd seen something in him then that she hadn't known was there.

And suddenly, she was very certain that he could have done it. He could easily have done it, and he might not have thought about it twice.

"Whatever it is you're thinking, Ysbel, believe me, I've thought it already." His tone was a little wry, and there was a tension underneath it that probably came from fear. "And whatever it is you want to do to me, I deserve it. I know. I could tell you I didn't know it was you, I could tell you I didn't realize they were going in to kidnap an innocent woman rather than a rogue operative, but the truth is, I didn't even try to find out. It was a job, and I did it." He paused a moment. "And I've finally realized that nothing that I say or do, from here on out, will ever change that, although believe me, I've tried."

"I—I believed you were my friend," she whispered.

"I believed I was too," he said quietly. "I'm—I'm sorry, Ysbel. I'm sorry."

The one who'd found her family, the one who saved them.

The one who'd sent them there in the first place.

She couldn't breathe. She couldn't think, because the blood pounding in her head made it impossible.

She'd trusted him. And he'd known, this whole time.

"Why didn't you tell me?" she asked hoarsely.

He lifted his palms, that wry half-smile still on his face. "Because as I said, I'm a coward, Ysbel, as well as a murderer. I have no excuses."

She half stood. She felt lightheaded somehow, dizzy, as if the world had turned upside down.

The pistol she always kept in her belt was already in her hand somehow, pointed at his forehead, and her hand was steady, even though the rest of her felt as if she might shake to pieces.

"I'm going to kill you." She hardly recognized her own voice. "You destroyed my family. You hurt my children, you hurt my wife, you burnt my home to the ground. You destroyed me, Lev, and I will kill you for it."

He should have stood up, probably, should have run. Some part of her wanted him to run, because some part of her still looked at the scholarly, slightly disheveled young man, with his tousled hair and his thoughtful, piercing eyes, and saw a friend. A person she'd trusted with her life, and who had in return been able to trust her with his.

But he didn't. He sat there in his chair watching her, and he didn't move. There was regret behind his gaze, and she couldn't tell if it was for himself, or for her.

"Hey. Ysbel. I wouldn't do that if I were you."

She looked up. She still felt half-way dizzy, and the blood pounding in her brain made it hard to focus on anything, but she saw the lanky pilot leaning up against the doorway to the room.

In the back of her mind, she noticed Lev turn as well, an expression half of irritation, half of guilty relief washing over his features.

"Jez—" he began. Jez gave him a quick smirk.

"Not your business, genius-boy. I'm talking to Ysbel." She turned back to Ysbel, and there was something sharp beneath her grin. "Listen to me, Ysbel. That's my damn copilot. And if you want to kill him, you're damn well going to have to kill me first."

"That would not even be a problem, you idiot," Ysbel hissed. "You stay out of this."

"Nah," said Jez, still grinning. "Not going to stay out of this."

"Look at you." Ysbel's voice was shaking with anger. "You can hardly stay on your feet, you damn fool. You really want to get in my way?"

Jez smiled lazily. "Well, here's how I see it. So maybe I'm not up for much right now. If you remember, by the way, I got these saving your damn skin and breaking your wife and kids out of prison. But you're probably right. You could probably kill me." She straightened, wincing slightly at the movement, and her eyes were hard as steel. "But here's the thing, Ysbel. You touch him—you touch one damn hair of him—and I'll make you wish you were dead. I promise you that."

Ysbel glared at her for a long moment. Her heart was pounding so hard she thought it might break through her ribcage.

Lev had destroyed her. He'd destroyed her, and he'd hurt Tanya, and he'd made her children grow up in a place that was the closest thing to hell she could imagine.

And he sat here in front of her, defenceless. He wasn't even going to try to stop her.

And across from her, the lunatic pilot girl who'd risked her life, taken a beating that probably should have killed her and almost had, to save Ysbel. More than that, to save Tanya and Olya and Misko and every person on this ship.

She was shaking, and she wasn't sure that she'd be able to fire the pistol she had pointed at Lev's head. But then, her hands had always steadied when she was holding a weapon.

"I'll do it, Ysbel," Jez said softly. "Zhurov couldn't kill me four days ago, and believe me, he tried. You really want to do this?"

She could almost feel the tension in the air, crackling out from the pilot, the fear that surrounded Lev like a fog.

At last she shoved the pistol back into its holster and dropped her hand.

"For you, Jez," she said quietly. "Because you saved my family, I will not kill this boy. Not this time. But I'd better not see his face again, because believe me, if I do, dying is the best he can hope for."

Jez didn't drop her gaze from Ysbel's face, and she was still wearing that faint, dangerous grin, but at last she nodded.

"Fine. I'll make sure he stays out of your way, and you will leave him the hell alone."

"Jez," said Lev, faint resignation in his tone. "I am capable of speaking for myself."

"Not sure you are," said Jez, without taking her eyes from Ysbel. Lev sighed and stood.

"Listen. Jez, there's nothing I can do to convince you to stay out of this, is there?"

She shook her head. "Nope."

"Alright." He turned back to Ysbel, and she turned to face him. She could still feel Jez's eyes on her, sharp as razor blades.

"Ysbel. I'm sorry. Believe me, this was not what I planned. But—" he paused. "The next planet we stop at, I'll leave. You don't deserve to have to deal with this. That's all I can do, but that, at least, I will do."

She stared at him, her eyes narrowed.

She was so angry she could hardly breathe.

"I hope very much that you do that," she said, her voice soft with anger. "Because I owe Jez a debt, and I'd hate to have to find another way to repay it."

She caught a movement from the corner of her eye, and she spun. Tae stood in the doorway. His face was stricken, and he gaped at the scene in front of him.

"Lev? Ysbel? What's—" he began.

Jez leaned back against the wall casually. "It's fine, Tae," she said, sparks still cracking from her tone. "Ysbel here decided to kill Lev. But I talked her out of it."

"I—what?" Tae glanced between Ysbel and Lev, then back to Jez.

Lev shook his head, shooting a mildly irritated glance at Jez. "It's not—"

"What's happening?"

Masha's voice was crisp and sharp. Jez turned slightly, her grin becoming a little more dangerous.

"None of your damn business anymore, Masha. Back the hell off."

"Jez—" Tae began through his teeth.

"As long as I am on this ship, Jez Solokov—" Masha said over him.

"Ysbel, my heart? I'm going to—" Tanya stepped through the door, glanced around her, and raised an eyebrow. "Perhaps I came at a bad time."

"Nah," said Jez expansively. "Join the party. We were all just having a discussion."

"Discussion?" asked Tanya, glancing meaningfully around the room. "Is that what you call it when at least half the room wants to murder the other half?"

Jez's grin widened. "Yep. Because if you want to see what happens when it stops being a discussion—"

"Jez, cut it out," Tae snapped, taking a step towards her. Ysbel was faintly impressed. Even she would have thought twice about approaching Jez when she was in this mood.

And then the deck jolted and shuddered, and she grabbed for the table edge to keep her balance. Tanya fell against the wall, Lev grabbed a chair, and Masha, Tae, and Jez landed on the floor, Jez swearing loudly enough for all three of them.

"What—" began Lev, his face slightly pale.

Ysbel knew that feeling, though, knew it through her bones.

Ship's guns.

The ship jolted again, and Jez scrambled awkwardly to her feet, cursing fluently and creatively. She and Ysbel locked eyes.

"They're shooting my damn ship," she said.

Tanya, and Olya, and Misko.

"I'll get on the guns," said Ysbel, and she turned and sprinted from the room.

6

Jez swore as she staggered down the short corridor to the cockpit, arms outstretched to catch herself as she half ran, half stumbled.

Lev, the damn idiot, was behind her, she could hear his footsteps, and Masha too from the sound of it.

She reached the cockpit as another bolt hit them, and she just managed to catch the back of the pilot's chair to keep herself from being thrown into the wall. She cursed again and pulled herself into her seat, strapping down.

"Hold onto something," she called over her shoulder. "This is about to get interesting."

She pulled up the holoscreen and touched the controls with the tips of her fingers.

Damn. Maybe interesting wasn't a strong enough word.

There were six or seven ships around them, and from the look of them, they were orders of magnitude worse than what they'd faced the day before. They were close enough that she had visuals on one of them through the front cockpit window, sleek and deadly against the black of space.

Lev staggered to his feet and managed to pull himself into the copilot's seat.

"Give me specs on those ships," she snapped. She yanked down on the controls and hit the starboard stabilizers, and the *Ungovernable* flipped up on its side, barely missing another blast from the ship in front of them. Another blast jolted across her holoscreen from behind, and she shoved the *Ungovernable*'s nose down as it cracked over their heads, sparking across the edge of the shields.

"You on the guns, Ysbel?" she called into the com.

"I'm here, but the guns aren't working."

She glanced back at the screen, looking quickly over the red damage report.

"Must have been hit in the stern. Knocked the guns offline. They shouldn't have had anything powerful enough to do that," she said grimly. "Stay up there, just in case they come back on."

"They won't come back on," said Tae in her earpiece. "Not if we got hit where I think we did. I'm going to have to get up there and fix them."

"Then plaguing get up there!"

"They're hydo-class ships," said Lev from beside her. "They shouldn't have guns that powerful, but it looks like someone modded them. How are our shields?"

She glanced down at the screen again. "Not good. I didn't have them on full power when we got hit, and we lost a capacitor." She yanked the ship's nose up again. Her beautiful ship, usually so responsive it could have been reading her mind, was sluggish under her hands, and she swore to herself, gritting her teeth. "I'm sorry, baby," she whispered. "Just get us through this, and I'll fix you up, I promise."

"You'll need to get us out of here." Masha's voice was businesslike. "We're not equipped to fight back at the moment."

"Tae?" she snapped.

"Sorry." Tae's voice over the earpiece was strained. "It'll take me a few minutes. The wiring's been fried, and I have to pull it out and re-wire."

She chewed her lip for a moment and glanced out the front window. Another ship had slipped into view to join the first, blocking out the stars behind it. "We'll have to make a jump."

"Hyperdrive?" asked Lev.

She nodded. "Don't like going in blind, but we're not outrunning them, not like this, and I don't want my angel hurt any more than she has to be."

"Give me twenty seconds, I'll get you a course."

"Lev, I suggest quadrant three," said Masha.

Lev nodded, expression tense as he typed something into the com.

"Got it," he said, looking up. "Go."

She glanced at the coordinates and hit the com. "Hold on to something." Then she pulled back on the hyperdrive and shoved the throttle forward.

And just as space began to stretch and distort around them, something slammed into the side of the ship, jerking her hands from the controls. The strange hypnotic colours and patterns of the space between hyperjumps appeared, but they were distorted somehow, and the *Ungovernable* was trying to shake itself out of her hands. Lev clung to his seat as the ship jolted and rolled, and she could feel through her fingers the *Ungovernable* screaming, breaking apart.

"We've got to come out," Masha said through her teeth, and Jez almost swore at her, but she didn't have the time because her ship was breaking up, and she and Masha and everyone on this ship was about to be crushed into nothing. She wrestled with the controls, fighting against the force that was hammering against the ship, pounding it into pieces, but it didn't respond, and she couldn't hear the ship talking to her anymore, and in an instant of clarity she realized that if she somehow survived and the *Ungovnerable* didn't, she wouldn't care because if she couldn't get back into this cockpit, life wouldn't really be worth living anyways.

She glanced at the holoscreen quickly, then winced.

"I'm sorry, baby," she whispered. She gritted her teeth, grabbed the throttle, and jammed it all the way forward. The ship shuddered and jerked and the scream of tortured metal scraped against her ears, and right before it became too much to bear, she jerked hyperdrive backward. The *Ungovernable* shuddered again, harder, and for a moment she knew that this was the end, and they'd be torn to pieces and scattered across deep space and still every single piece of her would miss this perfect, perfect ship—

And then the ship jerked one last time, and the distorted view of hyperspace slipped away, and they were surrounded once more by the black nothing of deep space.

She closed her eyes and drew in a shallow breath, and then another.

Then, not wanting to do it, not wanting to know what her gut had already told her, she touched the controls.

There was no response.

But she'd known there wouldn't be, because the faint hum that sang through her bones like a melody, that was the heartbeat of the running ship, was gone.

The *Ungovernable* was dead in the sky.

7

Tae struggled to his feet and leaned against the wall of the gunner's tower. He was breathing heavily, and when he touched the throbbing spot on his forehead, his fingers came away red.

He turned and locked eyes with Ysbel. Her face was pale, expression grim.

Neither of them needed to speak.

"We'd better get down there," said Ysbel at last. He nodded, and followed her out the door and down the ladder.

His head ached, and his arm, where it had been slammed up against the gunner's seat, throbbed. But it was nothing next to the sickness in the pit of his stomach.

When they reached the cockpit, Jez was still in the pilot's seat. She looked stunned, her face bloodless, her expression desperate. Her eyes found him the moment he stepped into the cockpit, and from the look on her face, he knew it was bad.

He'd known it was bad the moment he'd felt the gentle, almost imperceptible hum of the ship shudder and disappear.

He shoved his way past the others and crouched beside the paneling. Jez unclipped her harness, hands fumbling with the straps. She leaned heavily on the arm of her chair as she got to her feet, her movements slow and uncertain, and knelt beside him as the others stepped back to give them room, and carefully, he removed the paneling.

Even before he had it all the way off, he caught the thick charred scent of burnt wiring and scorched controls.

Jez looked like she might faint.

He pulled the paneling free, and they both leaned over to look inside.

It was gone. It looked like the entire control section had burnt, the wires and components melted together in an ugly tangle.

Jez met his eyes. Her face was haunted. "The shot must have hit us right as we entered hyperspace, knocked us off course," she said, her voice barely more than a whisper.

He nodded.

She didn't speak, just put a hand on the ship's paneling, and there were tears in her eyes.

"Well," said Masha from behind them, "there's no point in all of us staying here. Lev, please come with me to check the damage to the body of the ship. Ysbel, would you and Tanya look over the shields? The sooner we have an accurate damage report, the sooner we'll be able to plan our next steps."

Jez didn't react. Tae wasn't certain she'd even heard, or if she had, if she'd understood.

Lev got to his feet. He looked down at Jez and hesitated. Tae gave him a slight shake of his head.

There was nothing Lev, or he, or anyone else could do for Jez right now. She probably didn't even know they were in the room.

Lev gave him a wry half-smile of understanding, and stepped out after Masha.

Jez reached into the paneling, touching the smoking internal controls with the tips of her fingers. It was probably hot enough to burn her, but she didn't pull back. He sighed and stood, walking over to the holoscreen. That, at least, was working, which was more than a miracle.

He glanced down at Jez again.

He'd studied the hyperdrive tech, and what she'd done, pulling them out of an off-balance hyperjump, should have been impossible. The ship should have been torn to pieces, and pieces of him and every other person on this ship should have been strewn across about three different galaxies.

Although, with Jez behind the controls of a ship, 'impossible' became much more flexible of a concept.

He pulled up the readout and studied it more carefully. Something like dread sat heavy in his stomach.

The entire screen was a red damage report. He wasn't frankly certain if there was anything that wasn't damaged.

Controls—offline

Weapons—damaged, unresponsive

Shields—down

Body—damaged, but somehow still intact. He blew out a breath. Of course, if it hadn't been intact, they'd already know, because they'd all be either dead or in the process of getting there.

Oxygen supplies—

He felt suddenly cold.

"Hey, Jez," he said quietly. "The oxygen converter is offline."

She looked up, staring at him as if she hardly recognized him, and it took a moment before he saw understanding on her face.

"Oxygen?" she murmured, as if it was a concept she hadn't heard of.

"Yes, Jez," he snapped, suddenly angry. "Oxygen. The stuff we damn well breathe. How many days' reserve do we have?"

"Two, I think," she murmured.

"Alright, then we have two days before we all suffocate."

"Oh." She turned back to the burnt wiring.

He slammed his hand down on the dash. "Jez!"

She jumped. "What?" she said at last, in a low voice.

"Can you just pay attention, for the Lady's sake? We have problems right now. You can't just—"

"Yeah," she said, and there was a weariness in her voice he hadn't heard there before. "I know. We have all sorts of problems. The oxygen is offline, I saw that before you came in. We have damage to all the main ship systems. We didn't finish stocking up on supplies at the last zestava. Someone's after us, and our weapons are damaged and our shields are non-functional. I know. But the thing is—" She turned back to the control panel, shoulders slumped. "The thing is, this ship—I—" she paused helplessly for a moment, then dropped her head against the arm of the pilot's seat. "What do you want me to do, Tae? I can't fly. I can't get us out of this. My ship's dead, and if my ship's dead, I might as well be too. There's nothing I can do."

He bit back his anger. "Come on," he said at last. "I think we've learned everything we can here. Probably should get everyone else's report."

They were the first out on the main deck, but Ysbel appeared not too long after, Tanya behind her. She shook her head when she saw them.

"Perhaps before the jump you could have pulled the weapons online by fixing the wiring," she said. "Not now. I'll have to repair them, and I don't think we have any of the components we need to do it. I'll look through what I have, but—" She gave a helpless shrug.

Tae nodded. It was no more than he'd expected.

"Shields too," she said. "Those aren't my area of expertise, but I did look at the physical components on my way back. Three of the capacitors are broken, snapped in half, and two others are burnt. I'm not certain if they're fixable." She broke off as Lev entered the room, her face going cold, and turned away quickly.

Tae gritted his teeth in frustration. Whatever had happened before he stepped through the doors to the main deck earlier, Lev and Ysbel had picked a stupid, stupid time to get into a fight.

Masha stepped in after Lev, and her face was grim.

"It's not good news," Lev said quietly. "Looks like several of the back compartments burned out. I assume you already know about the oxygen situation."

Tae nodded.

"Tae," said Masha, "would you please summarize for us?"

He nodded again and took a deep breath. "As it stands right now, the ship is dead. The oxygen converter is fried, and we have maybe two days' worth of oxygen stores before we run out. Even we get everything fixed up, without the hyperdrive it's twelve hours to the nearest wormhole than another ten or twelve to get planet-side. I haven't had time to go through the wiring and the controls in depth, but I've seen enough to know that it's not just re-wiring. We're going to need to replace half of what's in there, and I don't know how many of the components we have. Internal and close-range coms are online, but we're not going to be calling out long range for help. Even if there was anyone we could actually call who wouldn't try to kill us. Weapons are down, shields are down, and life support systems are running on redline. If the thrusters didn't overheat, maybe we can pull them back online. That's our first option. If not, we'll just hope we can get the oxygen converter repaired to give us time to fix the thrusters. And that we have the right parts."

"And if we don't?" asked Lev.

He shook his head and didn't answer.

"And we can't forget what put us here in the first place," said Masha in a quiet voice. "Even if we get out of this, Lena isn't going to let up. We'll be maneuvering ourselves straight back into a space battle, and with our ship like this? It's a battle we aren't going to survive. We have credits from the heist. If I know what we're up against, it's possible we can negotiate our way out of this. But if I don't—" she broke off, and gave a meaningful glance around the room. "I need to know what those dates on your tags indicate. I need to know everything I can about this situation. Because if I don't, fixing this ship will only take us back to be killed more quickly."

Tae glanced around at the rest of the room.

Jez slumped in one of the chairs, staring out at nothing, but he'd noticed the stiffening of her posture every time Masha spoke. Lev looked tired, and was steadfastly avoiding Ysbel's eyes. Ysbel stood next to Tanya, but there was a look on her face that would have terrified him if he'd had the energy to be terrified.

He swore quietly to himself.

Maybe Masha was right. Maybe they had a chance of getting out of this alive.

But if they did, it was pretty damn slim.

8

Hour 1, Jez

Jez was pretty sure people around her were talking. She wasn't paying attention, and to be quite honest, she didn't care.

Who the hell had time to care about stupid crap like oxygen when her ship, her sweet, beautiful, perfect angel, had died?

Once she'd seen that—once she'd looked under the paneling and seen the scorched remains of the gorgeous thing that had talked to her, sung to her, responded to her every movement and her every thought—everything else had been a sort of haze.

Tae was upset, she could tell that. Still, Tae was the kind of person who would get upset about irrelevant crap like that.

She still hadn't managed to wrap her mind around the enormity of what had happened.

Sure they'd all be dead in two days, probably, but that seemed distant and unimportant compared to the sight of those scorched, melted controls under the paneling.

"Jez!"

She blinked and looked up into Tae's scowling face.

"What?" she muttered sullenly.

"I've been talking to you for the last five minutes."

"Oh." She didn't have the energy to say more.

Tae narrowed his eyes. "Jez," he said deliberately, "I will slap you in the face if that's what I have to do to snap you out of it."

For a moment, she contemplated letting him try. Damn tech-head had never been as quick as she was.

Still—she probed the aching swollen spot on the side of her mouth with her tongue.

Still, being slapped in the face while she had a broken jaw was probably something she'd want to avoid. She assumed. At this point, she didn't really care, but she assumed that once he'd slapped her, she might.

She sighed and turned to glare at him.

Everyone else had been here too at some point, she was pretty sure. She'd heard Masha's voice and tried to block it out, which, in fairness, she did pretty much every time Masha talked. And Ysbel, and Lev—she was pretty certain she remembered something about Ysbel and Lev before her whole world had exploded in smoke and flames and charred wiring.

Something about …

Damn.

She looked up at Tae, actually seeing him for the first time since they'd pulled out of hyperspace.

"Tae. You should probably know. Ysbel's pretty mad at Lev."

He glared at her. "What? Is this important right now?"

She somehow managed a grin, although it felt weak and shaky. "Probably, since if she tries to kill him, I'll try to kill her and she'll probably end up killing me instead, and I don't think Masha can fly this thing well enough to get us somewhere safe if we're trying to limp her in."

Tae's scowl deepened. "Noted," he said icily. "Would you mind telling me why everyone on this ship wants to kill each other suddenly?"

She grinned again. "Well, Ysbel wants to kill Lev because he's a damn idiot, and also he told her he was the person who planned her extraction five years ago,"

"Wha—" Tae began, face going slack with shock.

"And I want to kill Ysbel, because she's trying to kill my copilot. And I also want to kill Masha because she's a plaguing bastard, and Masha wants to kill me because let's be honest, who wouldn't?" She paused a moment. "I don't think anyone wants to kill you at the moment."

He glared at her in disbelief. Finally he shook his head and muttered something about the feeling not being mutual, because at this point he'd happily kill all of them. She grinned wider.

"Looks like you might not have to. We're pretty well on our way all by ourselves."

"Shut up, Jez," he grumbled. "I'm going to go take a look at the thrusters. Are you coming, or are you just going to sit here and use up our oxygen?"

She glared at him and pushed herself painfully to her feet.

She hadn't realized until just now, but being thrown around the cockpit hadn't done anything good for her bruises. Or her broken ribs, or, for that matter, her arm, which throbbed painfully every time she tried to move it. She looked at Tae more closely, and frowned.

"You got something on your head."

He glared at her in exasperation. "I know that! It's called blood. I was plaguing well thrown head first against the gunner controls, you plaguing idiot."

“Oh.”

“Come on.” He turned in disgust and started down the hallway that led to the engine room. She followed, shaking her head.

When they reached the engine room, she ducked in after him, wincing at the movement.

The massive, cylindrical thruster engines on either side of the room took up most of the space, and as she stepped inside, the sharp, chemical stink of overheated metal took her breath away. The thruster engines themselves groaned dangerously, smoke trickling out from the cracks in the panels.

“Tae,” she began, suddenly wide awake. From the look on his face, he’d seen the same thing she had.

“Get the access ports open,” she snapped. “We’ve got to get them cooling down.”

He jumped for one of the access ports, and she jumped for the other, ignoring the jolt in her ribs at the movement. She yanked it open, and smoke poured out, choking her.

Too hot. Way too hot.

“Wrench,” she said through gritted teeth, and Tae tossed one towards her. She jammed it onto the nearest bolt, but the bolt was glowing a dull red and the metal twisted as she tried to turn it. It would only be a matter of seconds before the wrench was far too hot to touch anyways.

“Use the mallet.” Tae’s voice was tense. She snatched one and, gritting her teeth, hit the red-hot bolt, shearing it off.

The creaking intensified.

“Get on the other one,” she said over her shoulder. “Get the bolts off, I don’t care what else you have to take off to do it.”

He nodded, grim-faced.

She sheered off three more bolts. The panel vibrated under her hand, smoke curling from the edges.

Five more to go.

Sweat trickled down her face, the heat from the metal scalding her skin.

Two more bolts.

The whole thruster engine was groaning, and there was the *hiss* and *ting* of overheated metal from inside.

She struck the last bolt with the mallet and leapt backwards as the heavy panel sprang open, the compressed smoke billowed out, stinging her eyes and throat.

"Tae!" she coughed, waving ineffectually at the air in front of her eyes. "Did you—"

"Almost." His voice was strained. She blinked uselessly. She couldn't see a damn thing in here.

"Tae—" Then she saw his dark form through the smoke and sprinted over to him. He was doubled over coughing, his breath coming short. She brought up her mallet and slammed it into one of the two remaining bolts. It jarred loose, and the pain in her side almost made her pass out, and then Tae managed to land a blow on the last bolt. They both stumbled backwards as the panel sprang free, and she grabbed his arm and dragged him from the room. The smoke was choking, and she was lightheaded from lack of oxygen. He pulled her down, and despite the screaming agony of her ribs, she dropped.

The air here, at least, was fresh enough to breathe, and for a few minutes they sat coughing and choking the soot from their lungs, and she almost whimpered at the pain of it.

By the time they'd recovered, the engine room had cleared enough that she could see through the billows of smoke.

Tae looked at her, the black streaks on his face making his expression appear even grimmer than usual. He pushed himself to his feet, and she followed painfully, swallowing back the sickness in her stomach.

The panels on the two bulky thruster engines lay open like a body prepared for autopsy. Their insides, usually a display of smooth, clean silver lines, were blackened now, delicate internal fins twisted and warped from heat and strain. Most of that was probably from her last push, when she'd managed to shove them forward hard enough that she could jolt them out of hyperspace.

She'd known what she was doing. Probably hadn't had a choice, honestly, because from the look of it, they'd been burning up.

Still …

She felt like she'd killed someone.

"So much for the thrusters not overheating," Tae muttered. "No wonder they're offline. Look at that carbon buildup. There's not a millimetre of clean surface on any of these fins. Let's hope that Lev and Ysbel get the converter up."

She swallowed hard, selected a wire brush and the narrowest chisel-tip she could find, and started to chip away at the blackened carbon choking the fins. Get those cleaned up first, and then she could see how bad the rest of the damage was.

Tae grabbed a wrench, and started yanking on the half-melted bolts holding together the still-intact side panel on the thruster engine opposite her, much more violently than he actually needed to.

As she brushed gently at the buildup, the narrow, delicate lines of the fins began to emerge from under the carbon. They were blistered with the heat, and the force of her maneuver had ripped some of them apart like paper. She touched one gently, and it disintegrated under her finger.

For a moment she thought she might throw up. She might start crying, and once she started, she might never stop. She couldn't lose this ship. It would kill her to lose this ship. She couldn't—

"Jez! Snap out of it," said Tae through his teeth. She looked over, startled. He'd already turned back to his work, grabbing a mallet and banging at the hopelessly-melted bolts in an attempt to break them free.

She took a deep breath, then another, watching him.

"Hey. Tech-head," she said finally. "What's wrong?"

He turned on her in disbelief. "What's wrong? What the hell do you think is wrong, you damn idiot?"

She stared.

He turned back to his work, smashing the mallet into one of the ruined bolts.

"Tae?"

He didn't look at her, and for a moment she wasn't certain he'd answer.

"It doesn't even matter to you, does it?" he said at last, his voice low and bitter. She frowned.

"I—"

He turned back, and she was shocked at the bitterness in his expression. "Not the ship. What happened before that, you and Masha. I thought we were supposed to be a crew. But hell, it's much more important that all of you get to air your damn grievances with each other, isn't it?"

She blinked, feeling suddenly sick.

She'd been so angry, on the main deck with Masha, she'd hardly had time to think about what it meant. About what she'd done. And then there had been the situation with Lev and Ysbel, and then the attack.

But … he was right. Even if they fixed the ship, something had been broken that she had no idea how to put back together.

"You'll all be fine without me," she said finally, trying to insert a jauntiness into her tone she didn't feel. "It'll be fine. You can all go with Masha and do whatever it is you were going to do in the first place. I'm not going to stop you." She had to swallow hard against the words, though.

For the first time in her life, she'd found people she cared about, and who actually cared about her in return. Who didn't leave her, even when they probably should, who took her side and laughed at her stupid jokes and rolled their eyes in exasperation, but never actually stopped caring about her, even when she was a complete idiot.

And what did she do? She decided to leave them, instead.

Tae was studying her, shaking his head slightly. "You really believe that, don't you?" he asked at last. The bitter edge in his voice was cut with tiredness now. "You really think you can do that, you can break this crew wide open and smash your way out, and nothing will change."

He shook his head and turned away wearily. "Doesn't matter. It was bound to happen eventually. The thing is, Jez, I don't even blame you. I don't think you're even capable of working with someone for more than a few weeks, because you don't deal with your problems, you just run away from them, and any time people work together for more than a few weeks there's bound to be problems. You're just not interested in solving them."

He bent down and picked up the mallet from where he'd dropped it, and started banging half-heartedly at the bolts again.

Jez turned back to her own work. There was something cold inside her, something that spread from her stomach out through her arms and into her fingers, making her grip on the wire brush clumsy.

Masha had been right, after all. She was bound to wreck things. She couldn't help but wreck things. That was why she'd never really wanted a team, before she'd been thrown head-first into this one.

She glanced sideways at Tae. He wasn't looking at her, instead glaring at his work.

He'd been angry plenty of times, at her, at Lev, at Masha—he'd been exasperated, and frustrated, and furious. But now—it wasn't the anger that had shocked her. It was the hurt behind it. Like he'd trusted her, and she'd screwed up and let him down. Like they all had.

She brushed gingerly at the carbon coating the fins, even though she knew it was useless. The metal beneath was damaged so badly that when she got the carbon off it, it would crumble at her touch.

Everything was broken. And it was probably her fault, but she honestly didn't know what else she could have done. Masha hated her, and Masha wanted her gone, and one of these days she'd have had to leave anyways. May as well have been on her own terms.

You're just not interested in solving them.

What the hell did he know?

She sighed and dropped the wire brush back into the tool kit, and grabbed the other mallet.

At least with a mallet, she could make a damn difference.

9

Hour 7, Jez

When she'd dropped the mallet for the third time, and for the third time been reduced to choked, breathless swearing, Tae picked it up and refused to give it back.

"For heaven's sake, Jez, go lie down in the med bay for an hour. If you pass out here, I'm not hauling you back to your cabin."

"I wasn't going to ask you to," she muttered, but a sudden wave of lightheadedness washed over her, and she had to grab for the wall to keep from falling over.

"Please, Jez," he said with a sigh. "Lev's going to actually kill me if I let you keep going."

"Don't see how it's any of his damn business," she grumbled.

Still, he was right. She was probably going to fall over in a minute, and she really didn't feel like picking herself up off the floor again today. She settled for glaring at Tae, then she made her unsteady way out the door and into the small, tidy med bay.

When she reached it, she paused in front of the cot.

She basically hadn't laid down in a bed since they'd come onto the ship. She lived in the cockpit—she usually slept in the leaned-back pilot's seat, an alarm set to alert her if anything happened, the feel of the ship soothing her to sleep and her hands on the controls even in her dreams.

The uncanny stillness felt strange and unsettling now, and she wasn't sure she could have borne stepping back into the silent cockpit.

She sighed and sank carefully down on the narrow cot. It was softer than she'd imagined it would be.

She couldn't stop seeing the look on Tae's face, hurt and betrayal and a sort of exhausted hopelessness.

Damn him.

She dropped her face into her hands, scrubbing gingerly at her eyes, because the bruises from prison were still far too sore.

479 Standard, three-month, seven-day. That was the date on the tag Lena had put on her.

It had been a long, long time. Three years was a long time, and a hell of a lot had happened since then. Never really kept track of dates much. But—well, something had happened around that time. She'd managed to almost shove it out of her mind, but … she never quite succeeded. And even the memory of it made her stomach twist, and a faint taste of vomit climb the back of her throat.

She'd been flying on her own for a solid year by then. Lena'd said she'd never make it on her own, but Lena didn't know spit. Of course, it hadn't hurt that, thanks to Lena, she'd had probably the fastest smuggler-ship in the damn system.

And it really didn't hurt that there wasn't anyone else in the system who could fly like she did.

She'd just come in from a long run. The clammy, cool Prasvishoni morning air clung to her nostrils, cut with the burnt ozone smell of her jacket and the usual faint scent of dirt and mildew and forgotten trash from the alleys that lined the narrow streets. She shoved her hands in her pockets as she sauntered back through the filthy streets from the loading docks where she'd dropped her ship after the run, the dim morning sun barely filtering in through the city's force-field. She had plenty of credits loaded onto her chip, and she had two days off before her next three runs. Find a kabak, maybe? Or she could look up her last girlfriend or one of her other old flames, probably find someone with nothing to do and plenty of time to do it in.

It wasn't until she reached her seedy apartment—a second-story one-room in a dingy prefab building, white walls almost grey with mildew—that the unease twinged in her brain. It wasn't anything she noticed. It was what she didn't notice—the normally-quiet alley was more quiet than usual, dead, completely deserted. There should have been at least some street kids huddling around the entrance. But there was nothing.

Still—it was early morning. Maybe it had been a cold night, and they'd found somewhere warmer.

Frowning, she held her com-key up to the outside door and pushed it open.

The noise it made opening was usually enough to set off a round of sleepy curses from the surrounding apartments, especially if she was coming in early. But it was silent on its hinges, and the unease in the back of her brain spiked. For a split second, she was tempted to run. Maybe she should have. But she set her jaw and stepped carefully through the door, letting it swing silently shut behind her.

Her apartment was up a narrow, dirty staircase, and she climbed it with careful steps. Her heart was pounding, and her mouth felt dry.

As far as she knew, Lena was the only one after her, and Lena couldn't have caught up to her yet. She'd been careful. OK, maybe careful was the wrong word. But she'd damn well made sure that the plaguer wouldn't have been able to track her here.

She pushed open the door from the narrow landing and into the hallway, and the alarm in her head sounded louder when it swung open easily. She'd given up a long time ago asking the landlord to fix the plaguing thing, and she usually had to set her shoulder against it to get the ancient hinges to move.

She should run. Whatever had happened, it was bad, she could feel it in her gut.

But she couldn't, not yet. Not until she knew what the hell was going on.

She walked silently down the grungy hallway. Her door was second to the end, and she paused in front of it and glanced around.

The door next to hers had a faint mark by the handle, like someone had forced it. Had it been like that last time she came? Probably not, but then she'd been gone for three days. Could have happened anytime.

Her door was clean, and she took a deep breath.

Must have been the neighbours whoever it was came for. No surprise there. Didn't know what they did, but you didn't rent a place in this dump unless you really didn't want the government knowing where you were.

She held her com-key to the door lock, and when the click sounded, she pushed the door gently open.

Her eyes swept over the tiny, dingy room, and it took her a split second to realize what she was seeing.

When she did, she felt suddenly, unaccountably sick.

It wasn't the violence of it. It was the sheer, methodical destruction.

Everything she owned had been torn to pieces—the sagging cot, the sitting cushions, her suitcase of spare clothes. The cleanser had been dumped over on its side, the rusty metal of the heating compartment pulled apart like a swamp-crab shell. Every dish in her cupboard was smashed, piece by piece, on the floor. Her clothing was torn deliberately to pieces, and someone had taken a razor-blade to her spare pilot's coat, ripping it down every seam. And the stack of grey cargo-boxes she'd stolen from Lena were gone, every last one of them.

She wasn't afraid of Lena, or anyone else. Now that she had her own ship, did her own runs, she hadn't been afraid of anything in a very long time.

But suddenly, she was terrified.

She stepped back abruptly, letting the door swing shut in front of her, and it was just the tiniest sound as the door touched the doorframe, something she wouldn't have even noticed if every nerve in her body wasn't on edge.

A small click, like something mechanical had been triggered.

Whatever it was, it sent her sprinting full-tilt down the hallway towards the stairs.

As she ran, one of the neighbours's doors swung gently open, as if at the breeze of her passing. She caught a glimpse of what was inside, and with a sudden sick feeling, she knew exactly why no one had made a sound as she came in. An older woman lay on the dirty carpet, a red stain bleeding outwards in a widening circle around her throat.

No, not the stairs, she'd never make the stairs. At the end of the landing was a narrow window of cheap glass, and she yanked a spare wrench out of her pocket as she ran and hurled it end-over-end at the glass. It hit with a crunch, and a spiderweb of cracks appeared in the wavy surface. She set her shoulder and hit it at full speed, and the glass exploded under her weight, and she burst through the narrow opening, legs flailing and shoulders tucked, as behind her the entire apartment building erupted in a fountain of flame.

She landed in the courtyard below in a shower of glass shards and burning prefab, rolled, and scrambled to her feet. Then she ran, hands and face cut and bloodied, down streets and alleyways until she was far enough away that she could stop and catch her breath.

She hadn't looked back. Not once.

Because the thing was, not even Lena had the kind of pull to rig something like that.

There had to have been at least fifty apartments in that building, fifty or a hundred or two hundred people crammed into those tiny, dingy spaces.

If any of them had been alive when she reached the building, none of them were now.

And she didn't even know who'd done it.

10

Hour 1, Ysbel

Ysbel closed her eyes for a moment, pausing on the small ladder down to the life-support room, trying to hold onto her frayed temper.

Lev had climbed down before her, tension obvious in his posture.

Fourty-eight hours. That's how long they had before they all died. She could work with this bastard for that long, surely. She could keep from killing him for that long.

Probably.

When she reached the ground, she bent down beside the control panel of the massive oxygen converter, which took up most of the cramped space, ignoring Lev completely. Her hands, thankfully, were steady as she lifted it gently free, even though her breath was coming too fast and there was a sick, shaky feeling in the pit of her stomach.

She'd been dreaming about killing him for five and a half years now, without knowing it was him. It had been the only thing keeping her alive.

He pushed the door open and slipped inside, moving quietly around to look over her shoulder.

"What's it look like, Ysbel?" he asked, and the familiar, calm voice jolted her. Somehow, she'd expected it to be different than it had been, now that he'd revealed who he was.

She didn't speak, just gestured to the panel. He hesitated, then crouched down beside her, frowning.

"Everything offline," he murmured. "That's probably to be expected. I assume the conversion panel burned out."

"I've seen this before," Ysbel said reluctantly. "If there's a power surge that's too high for the regulators, the panel will overheat and burn through the wire filaments. Then no more oxygen conversion."

He nodded, forehead still creased in a frown of concentration. "So unless we have replacement filaments, there's no fixing it."

"Yes. But we knew that before we started. What I'm concerned about is this." She pointed to a small, flashing red light at the corner of the panel. "The filaments are usually close to the external walls of the compressed oxygen storage tank. Which usually isn't a problem, because they never get above fifty degrees, even at high usage."

"But if they're burning out," he said slowly, "then at that temperature—" He stood. "You're right. We'd best check. If it's venting into the waste gas tank, it'll run out in a couple hours, and we'll all be dead."

He turned to the wall where the repair tools hung and studied them for a moment. Ysbel rolled her eyes, reached past him, and pulled two wrenches off the wall, shoving one into his hand.

"For someone who's so smart, you are remarkably useless," she grumbled. He gave a rueful smile.

"I'm open to the possibility that you're correct."

For a moment, she had to bite back a smile of her own. Instead, she glowered at him, and he dropped his eyes.

She felt along the back of the cylindrical main compartment until she found the access hatch, and started pulling the bolts free.

Even from here, it didn't look promising. The bolts screeched against metal, warped from the heat and the strain. She frowned as she worked, handing the bolts back to Lev as he waited behind her.

At last the control panel was unbolted, and she took a deep breath and lifted it carefully off. Immediately, the room was filled with the charred smell of scorched metal and burned components. Lev coughed.

"I assume that means your guess was correct," he said.

"Yes, I—" she broke off. "Do you hear that?"

Lev's face went tense, and he pushed in to stand next to her.

Something was hissing through the vent, pushing the smell of scorched air through the compartment, and behind it, fainter yet, there was a thin sound of escaping gas.

"You were right," he said in a tense voice. "The storage compartment is bleeding out. We need to—"

"Get back," she shouted, and she shoved him backwards as the panel on the compartment creaked and burst open at the seams. He stumbled backwards into the small doorway, she almost fell on top of him. He caught his balance on the door frame, then pushed past her and set his shoulder to the broken compartment, shoving it back.

"If we can get it closed—" he began through his teeth. She set her shoulder next to his, and somehow, centimetre by centimetre, they managed to shove it back into place.

Gas was still hissing from the cracks, their precious oxygen bleeding out.

"The pressure's pushing it open," he said through his teeth. "Listen. If the filaments burned, where would the crack in the tank be? On the top seam?"

She shook her head. "No. The heat from the filaments superheats the round seam around the centre of the tank, so when they burst it usually already has a hairline crack."

He nodded, eyes moving slightly as if scanning some information in his head.

"Alright, listen," he said at last. "I'm going to step away. Can you hold this?"

"For the moment, yes," she grunted.

"I'll be right back." Carefully, he removed his weight from the panel she was holding. The pressure on her shoulder increased, but it wasn't anything she couldn't hold, at least for a few moments. He ducked around her and into the main compartment, and returned a moment later with a long tube of internal sealant. She frowned.

"Alright," he said. "Listen. When I tell you, let go of the panel and jump back, alright?"

She frowned at him. "You can't—"

"Listen to me! Neither of us can hold that closed forever. I'm going to spray sealant into the system at the same time you let the panel open," he said, slightly breathless. "The pressure should suck it into the cracks and seal them."

"I've never heard of something like that," she grunted.

"I haven't either." His voice was tight. "But I think it should work."

Reluctantly, she nodded. He slipped in behind her and reached his hand through the access port, his fingers running delicately across the seams. Then he wedged himself into the small space between her and the ship wall and shoved the tip of the tube into the crack where the air was escaping. He braced himself against the back wall and put his hand on the plunger.

"Alright, Ysbel," he said. His voice was calm, but she could hear the strain under it. "On my count, please. Three. Two. One. Now."

He shoved down on the plunger as she leapt back. For a moment, there was a sucking, splattering sound, and then, finally, silence. She glanced up cautiously. Lev leaned back against the wall, face drawn, sweat standing out on his forehead. They listened for a tense moment, but the hissing noise had stopped.

"I think we did it," he said softly, a smile of relief spreading over his face, and for a moment she grinned back at him.

Then she turned away abruptly.

Damn that idiot boy. Damn him to hell.

She turned back to the oxygen converter, checking all the places where more cracks might have appeared in the explosion. Lev stood back, giving her specs when she asked for them, never speaking unless she spoke to him first.

She'd never seen him so subdued.

It could be that he was afraid of her. But then, she'd never known him to be afraid of much of anything.

Of course he wasn't. Because he'd never take a risk unless he'd thought it through from every angle and considered every possible outcome. Which meant, when he'd called her onto the main deck to talk with her, before everything exploded, either he was certain she wasn't going to kill him—or he knew she was, and he didn't care.

The thought choked off her breath for a moment.

There were a hundred ways he could have told her. He could have left the ship and slipped a note into her com, he could have waited until she was back on her home planet with her family and gambled that she wouldn't leave it again to come after him. He'd probably have been right.

But he hadn't done that. He'd either believed that she cared enough for him that their friendship would keep him alive, or he'd known it wouldn't, and told her anyways, and been prepared to die for it.

She wasn't entirely certain which of the two options was worse.

When they finished, she tapped her com and said brusquely, "We're done down here."

"Let's meet in the mess hall, then," said Masha. She sounded weary, and when Ysbel looked at her com, she realized why.

"It's 0300 standard time," said Lev from behind her. "We were down here longer than I thought."

She turned her glare on him. "I have a com, you idiot."

"I'm sorry."

She could kill him, right now. Jez wasn't here.

Instead, she gestured him ahead of her up the ladder. He stepped around her without meeting her gaze and started up towards the corridor that led to the mess hall.

11

Hour 8, Ysbel

She glanced back at the oxygen converter as they left. It was an older model, a type she hadn't seen in years.

That date on her tag.

She tried to push back her unease.

She couldn't be certain, of course. She'd been very young, far too young to remember dates.

But it was possible. The timing would have been close, anyways.

She closed her eyes for a moment.

It was the suffocating, thick air she remembered the most, the way the heavy fabric had caught against her mouth when she tried to breathe. She'd tried to pull it off once, but her mother had caught her hand.

"Not now, Ysi," she said, and there was something in the tone of her voice that had made Ysbel obey.

It was early, so early that it was closer to night than morning, and the streets of Prasvishoni were chill and deserted. She was wrapped in a heavy jacket, one of her father's scarves pulled up over her face and head, but the chilly morning air wound itself through her clothing, making her shiver. Or maybe it wasn't the chill at all.

Her mother, too, was covered in a bulky coat, face obscured by a scarf, and her father, walking slightly ahead of them, was a shapeless dark mass in the dim of the flickering streetlights.

She glanced around her as they walked. Through the small slit where the scarf had been bundled over her face, she could make out the walls of the buildings, looming dark over the narrow alleys they made their way along. There was something tight in her throat, and she squeezed her hands into fists in the pockets of her coat.

"Where are we going, Mamochka?" she whispered. Her mother looked down at her and shook her head slightly, her posture tense.

She'd heard her parents talking, long into the night, for over a week now. She'd laid awake and listened, but she couldn't make out the words, and what words she could hear didn't make sense.

But the tone in their voices had been unmistakable.

They were afraid.

Her legs ached and her feet were sore with walking, but her father had refused to take the skybikes.

And then, ahead of them, as the grey of early, early dawn began to lighten the sky, she saw the loading docks.

She could see her father's posture tense as they stepped out of the alley. He turned slightly, and whispered, "Keep your head down, Ysi. Don't look up, whatever happens, alright?"

She nodded, something tightening around her chest and choking off her breath. Her mother pulled at her hand, and she followed them out of the alley.

Even at this hour, the loading docks were busy. Ysbel had never liked people all that much, but she'd never been afraid of them. Now it seemed that every shadowy form they passed was watching them, weighing them, out to hurt her, to hurt her father and mother.

She kept her eyes on the dirty concrete and tried to swallow down her fear.

At last she stood shivering on the loading dock of a ship she'd never seen before in her life. Her mother had gone ahead to talk with the ship's captain, but her father must have seen the tension in her posture, because knelt beside her, and pulled down his scarf just enough that she could make out his face in the harsh shadows of the ship's outer deck.

"Ysi," he'd said in his quiet, gruff voice. "Don't worry. We'll be going somewhere that's much better than this. No more of this cold, forever."

"I like the cold," she said, her voice sounding small and frightened in the impersonal bustle of the loading docks.

"I know," he said, face creasing in understanding. "But you'll find something you like better. I'm sure of it."

She turned to him, his familiar worn coat and high brown boots, and his soft beard that was starting to grey.

"I'm scared, Papachka," she whispered. "Why are we leaving? I don't want to leave."

He'd sighed, and his face was cut with worry. "It's a long story, Ysbel. But believe me, it's for the best." He paused. "Ysi. Look over there. You see, on that crane? The converter?"

She turned, glancing at the huge black cylinder suspended by a mag-beam just above the dock.

"Yes," she said, without interest.

"Pay attention to it. When we get to our new home, your mother told me she would start teaching you explosives. And I will let you help me with my weapons design, if you want. You think you can do that?"

She turned back to him, eyes wide. "Yes."

"Well then. You want to watch the oxygen converter. Learn as much about it as you can. Because have I ever shown you my heat-pistol designs?"

"Yes."

"The heat-sink runs on a similar principle. And if you ask your mamochka about the explosives she uses, you'll understand them better if you understand the chemical conversion that happens in the filaments. Alright, my Ysi?"

"Yes." She was staring wide-eyed at the oxygen converter now.

"That's an old one. But I want you to keep your eyes on it, alright?"

"Yes Papachka."

He straightened, and she noticed, absently, the dark figure shoving their way through the crowd, brushing up against the converter for a moment before hurrying away, but she wasn't paying attention to anything but the converter itself. She watched it as the crane lifted it from the dock and swung it towards the hole in the upper deck of their ship, squinting and concentrating with all her ten-year-old might.

If she hadn't, she might not have even noticed.

"Papa," she said urgently, tugging on his trousers. He was speaking to the captain now, who'd followed her mamochka back.

"Papa!"

He looked down in faint irritation. "Ysi—"

"Mamochka, look!"

Her mother turned at the tone in her voice, and it only took her a moment to see what Ysbel had seen. She snatched Ysbel up and shoved her husband and the captain to the ground as the slight bulge Ysbel had noted, right in the place where her papa had pointed out where the filaments would be, expanded, turning from black to a dull red. And then a dull explosion shook the ship's dock, and pieces of red-hot shrapnel rained down on the ship's hull and the docking-bay around them. There was shouting and screaming from outside the ship, and a high, shrill shriek of pain.

And for a moment, Ysbel caught the look that passed between her mother and father—terror.

And that was the instant she'd realized that this was for real, and forever. That she and her mamochka and papachka were never coming back to Prasvishoni.

12

Hour 8, Lev

Lev stepped into the mess hall, his shoulders slumping with relief, even though he fought to hide it.

The walk up the corridor, with Ysbel behind him, it had taken every bit of willpower in his body to keep from spinning around to see if she was about to kill him.

Masha was there, of course, and Tanya, her face exhausted. The children had joined her, and they had the pale, drawn look of too much stress and too little sleep on faces too young to hide it.

Olya brightened slightly at his entrance, but he couldn't bear to look at her, so he avoided her gaze.

Tae stepped into the room a moment later, followed by Jez. She looked almost as bad as the kids, her face still bearing traces of the stunned disbelief of earlier, the circles under her eyes apparent even under the gruesome colours of her bruises, and his chest constricted a little at the sight, like it always did.

Her eyes went to Ysbel behind him, and her expression grew slightly dangerous.

"Masha," she said softly, "did you send Lev with Ysbel?"

"Yes, Jez," Masha said, her voice sharp and clearly discouraging questions.

Jez ignored it, as usual. "I always knew you were an idiot, Masha, but I didn't realize—"

"Jez," he said tiredly. "Leave it. It's fine."

She glared at him. "Not your damn business, genius-boy. I'm having a conversation with Masha right now."

"Yes, and we all remember how well your last conversation with Masha went," said Tae through his teeth. Lev glanced at him, startled. Tae's face was tight with strain.

"Listen, tech-head," Jez snapped.

"Jez—" Lev began again.

"You're all a bunch of dirty plaguers!" Misko shouted over the noise, then started crying loudly.

"Now look what you've done," Ysbel growled, and finally Tanya held up her hands.

"Please. Everyone. It's been a long day. Why don't we get some food. The children need to eat, anyways."

They glared at each other for a moment longer, and then reluctantly, everyone turned back to the table. Tanya handed out rations packs, and they ate in icy silence. Lev hadn't realized how hungry he was until he bit into the food, and then his stomach pinched in protest.

He gave a wry smile. To be honest, he hadn't felt much like eating ever since he'd decided to talk to Ysbel.

He glanced over at Jez again. She was glaring at everyone, and when she caught his eye, she narrowed her eyes further. Still, behind her glare, he could see a sort of empty hopelessness.

He shook his head. He probably would never understand exactly how she felt about this ship, but he'd seen the look on her face when she was flying it—an almost transcendent joy. It was the only place she ever seemed at peace.

Now she looked like someone she loved had been murdered, and she was staring at their corpse.

Once everyone was eating, Masha stood.

"What's everyone's status?" she asked quietly. "Ysbel?"

Ysbel shook her head. "We still have forty or so hours' worth of oxygen, but no way of getting more until the thrusters are back online."

"Thrusters are in bad shape, but we might be able to limp back to a planet," said Tae. His face was blackened with soot. "It won't be quick, but if we get them running, it should pull the emergency oxygen generator online. Keep us alive, at least."

"How long to fix it?"

He shrugged. "Five or ten hours?"

There was a moment's silence.

"With that in mind," said Masha, "I'd advise that everyone get a few hours of sleep."

"We can't afford to plaguing sleep," snapped Tae. "We have maybe forty hours of oxygen left. I'd love to spend it sleeping, but somehow I don't think that will fix this."

"I understand that, Tae," said Masha. "However, nor can we afford a mistake because we're too tired to think straight. I'll wake you in three hours' time. That should at least be enough that we're not falling over from exhaustion."

She paused a moment and looked around the table. "Have any of you made any progress on the dates on your tracking chips? I need every scrap of information I can gather if we want to survive our trip back to shallow space"

"Assuming we make it that far," Tae grumbled.

Lev frowned in slight unease.

The date had been niggling at the back of his mind since he'd seen it pop up on his com. It was back from his days in university, and he wasn't likely to ever forget it, but he also had no idea what importance it would have to a smuggler like Lena.

Across the table from him, Ysbel shifted slightly. "I don't remember the exact date. But that would have been around the time I left Prasvishoni with my father and mother. I don't know what sort of meaning it would have to anyone else."

Tanya smiled and laid her head on Ysbel's shoulder. "Besides me," she murmured, and for the first time in a long time, he saw Ysbel smile.

"Tae?" asked Masha. Tae was frowning.

"I—that was a week or so before I got thrown in jail. That's all."

Masha nodded thoughtfully and turned to Lev. "And you?"

"I—would have to think about it," he said carefully, tapping his com off.

He wasn't entirely certain what significance the date had for anyone but him, but he'd rather have time to consider it before he put it in front of anyone else here.

Masha studied him for a moment, but at last she nodded.

"Very well. We'll sleep and get back to work in a few hours. Tae, you can tell us what you need, since it appears getting the thrusters back online is our first priority."

Tae nodded.

For a moment no one moved, seeming too weary for the effort. A wave of exhaustion hit Lev, and for the first time he realized exactly how long it had been since he'd last slept.

First the zestava, then Jez's fight with Masha, and then his conversation with Ysbel, then the explosion—it felt like it had been at least three days.

He shook his head and pushed himself to his feet. Jez looked up, glaring at him, and Ysbel pointedly ignored him. Tae was scowling at everyone.

He supposed he couldn't blame them, really.

"I'll see you in three hours, Masha," he said, with a faint, rueful smile. Then he turned and made his way down the hallway to his cabin.

He fell into his cot, but for some reason he couldn't sleep. Every time he tried to close his eyes, he saw Ysbel's face when he told her what he'd done, Jez's face when he'd stepped into the cockpit after she'd somehow managed to save them, and killed her ship.

Finally, he sighed wearily and stood.

It was a bad idea, but then that seemed to be his specialty these days.

He opened the door to his cabin and made his way down the hallway. At the door to Jez's cabin, he hesitated.

This was stupid.

Still, they were all likely to die in forty hours or so, so if there was a time for doing stupid things—

He tapped lightly at her door. For a moment there was no answer, and he thought maybe he'd guessed wrong and that she was asleep. Finally, though, she said, "Who is it?"

He pushed the door gently open and stepped through.

She was sitting propped up in the corner of the small room, one knee up, the other leg stretched out in front of her, her head tipped back against the wall. She raised her head with an effort as he came in, and then shoved herself up into a sitting position, swearing softly.

He hesitated again, then walked over and sat down on the cot beside where she was sitting.

"Hey, Jez," he said at last. "How are you doing?"

"How do you think I'm doing?" she said, letting her head drop back against the wall. Her tone was more weary than angry.

"I'm—sorry. About the ship."

"Yeah," she said.

He paused a moment. "Jez? You're angry at me."

She lifted her head and glared at him, and he was shocked to see tears in her eyes.

"Yes I'm angry at you, genius-boy. What the hell were you thinking? Look, I don't have time for this, OK? I don't have time to be worried about you. I don't have time to be wondering if you're going to be still alive next time I see you. I have plenty of other things to worry about. My damn ship is broken. I don't know if we're going to be able to fix her again, and if we do, I don't know if she'll be the same ship she was. Lena wants to kill me, and now all of us are going to die because Lena wants to kill me, and someone tried to beat you up back in the zestava, and I don't damn well have time for this!"

He stared at her. "I—"

"Just shut up, OK? Just shut up. Why the hell did you go tell Ysbel that?"

"I—Jez, because she deserved to know. I—"

"Well, you know what, you damn soft-boy? Next time you decide to go get yourself killed, why don't you find someone else to care?"

He let out a breath of exasperation. "Jez. I didn't intend for you to hear that. I wasn't expecting you to—"

"Yeah?" she turned on him. "You just expected her to kill you, was that it? And you thought that would be just fine?"

"Jez, listen to me." He was speaking through his teeth now. "I thought it through, alright? If she had chosen to kill me, it would have been her right. I—"

"Just shut up, you damn idiot," Jez snapped. "Just shut the hell up, OK?"

"Jez—"

"I'm fine. I'm trying to get some sleep."

He looked at her for a moment. She was steadfastly refusing to look at him, and she wiped her eyes angrily on the sleeve of her jacket.

"Jez, look, are you sure you're—"

"Leave me alone," she muttered.

He sighed and shook his head. "Alright, Jez, I'll leave you alone. I'm sorry for bothering you."

She didn't answer, and he stood slowly.

Something inside him twisted to see her like this. Something about Jez crying was wrong. She should be grinning, or laughing, or making some smart-mouth remark, and when she was crying he felt like something solid and constant in his world had turned upside down.

"Look, Jez," he said quietly. "I'm sorry, alright? I'm sorry for everything. We'll fix the ship. I'll do whatever I can to fix the ship. I've spent the last few weeks reading everything I can find on her, and we'll put her back together. I promise."

"Yeah," she said bitterly, without looking up. "And then you'll leave, right?"

He paused. "I'm beginning to think that's going to be the best option for everyone."

She didn't answer, and finally he turned and stepped out the door, closing it softly behind him.

He wanted to swear, but he couldn't even bring himself to do that.

Masha was probably right. He probably just needed some sleep, before he could screw anything else up.

13

Hour 11, Tae

"Tae." The voice came through his earpiece, and he jerked awake, staring around him at the darkened room and trying to remember where he was and what he was doing there.

"Tae, I'm sorry. It's time to wake up."

It was Masha's voice.

Masha. The ship.

Damn.

The heavy weight in his stomach, that had been there since Jez had told them she was leaving, breaking up the crew, settled back into place.

They had thirty-some hours before they all suffocated, unless they could get the thrusters back online.

He wasn't sure if the three hours of sleep Masha had promised had helped clear his head, or only served to muddle it more. He wasn't sure he wanted a clear head at this point, because he wasn't sure he wanted to have the energy to think about everything that had happened, and everything that was going to happen even if they somehow got the ship running again.

He sighed and staggered upright.

You'd think, after all this time, that he'd be used to running on no sleep. He kept thinking that if he just finished this one job, he'd finally be able to catch up on all the sleep he'd missed. But at this point, all the sleep he'd missed was starting to look too long for one lifetime. He fumbled for his com, and tapped Masha's line.

"I'm up."

"Good." She paused. "We're meeting on the main deck."

"Be there in a minute," he mumbled. He hadn't taken the time to change out of his clothes, so he leaned his head against the door-frame until he was pretty certain that he could stand up without falling over, and then he made his way down to the main deck.

The others had already gathered, blinking and shivering, and everyone was huddled in their own corner. Jez managed a tired grin as he came in.

"Thought we'd give you a couple extra minutes while the rest of us got up."

"How long has it been?" he asked, his voice thick and hoarse with sleep.

"Three standard hours and twenty minutes," said Masha. Of all of them, she was the only one who looked relatively normal, but then he'd seen Masha look relatively normal after she'd been hit by a blast from a heat gun, so that wasn't actually saying much.

"I'll go down to the supply room and grab the thruster parts," he said, still trying to clear the fog from his head.

"I can grab the thruster parts," said Jez, trying to get to her feet. He glared at her.

"You can stay where you are. I don't want you nearly passing out on me again, because I need some actual help putting the thrusters together."

"She nearly—" Lev started, throwing a concerned look in Jez's direction. She glared and muttered something that was probably rude.

"Looks like none of you are morning people, then," murmured Tanya, so low that probably only he and Ysbel could hear. He turned to stare at her. When he caught her eye, she gave him a small smile, like they'd just shared a joke.

He shook his head and turned away. There was plenty to get done, heavens knew, unless they wanted to suffocate to death as they argued on the main deck.

Ysbel stood. "I'll come," she said. "I can help you carry things, at least."

He nodded, lips pressed tightly together, and turned down the short corridor to the ladder-stairs that led down to the middle deck. By the time he'd reached the hatch to the storage level, he felt slightly more awake. He shook his head.

He wasn't entirely sure what all the way awake felt like anymore, at this point.

He caught a whiff of smoke on the air as he climbed down the narrow ladder under the hatch, and frowned. Probably just from the burnout the previous day. He'd checked the damage report, and it looked like there'd been a small fire on the bottom deck at some point.

His boots echoed on the metal floor as he made his way cautiously across the wide storage bay, its walls scorched and blackened. It was mostly empty, thank heavens—they'd loaded the ship's parts and most of their supplies into the smaller storage room, where they were easier to lock down, and if they were lucky, nothing had been banged around too badly.

He put a hand on the door handle. It was warm—probably

retained heat from the fire.

At his feet, a tendril of something that looked like smoke wisped out under the door, then sucked back inside. He blinked and shook his head, trying to push back the dull headache of too little sleep.

Behind him, Ysbel had reached the bottom of the ladder, and he could hear her boots on the floor behind him.

He twisted the door handle and it wasn't until his hand was pulling the door open that something in his brain screamed an alarm. Ysbel's shout came from behind him, and her footsteps broke into a run, and time seemed to slow. He half-turned to shout at her to stay back, something, but before he could do more than turn his head, the door exploded outward in a ball of flames. The corner of it slammed into his forehead and threw him to the ground, and a wave of fire leapt out over his head. The heat hit him like a wall, and he couldn't see or think or breathe. His whole body was burning, and for one brief, lucid moment, he knew he was going to die. And then something grabbed him by his jacket and dragged him backwards. He tried to struggle on instinct, but his body wouldn't respond the way it should, and a moment later he was clear of the flames and someone shoved him painfully against the hard deck. He tried to open his mouth to protest, but instead he choked on smoke. Fire licked hungrily around the walls of the storage bay,

"Go!" someone hissed in his ear, and then he was being pushed up the ladder, and somehow his blistered hands grabbed the rungs and he pulled himself up, Ysbel behind him. When they got to the deck floor above them, Ysbel slammed the hatch shut and shouted something into her com, and Tae rolled gingerly onto his side. His hands were blistered, his clothing blackened and scorched.

Ysbel dropped to the ground beside him, her face grim. "Are you alright?" she asked urgently.

"I—" his voice was a croak.

"It was a backdraft. When you opened the door it exploded."

He should have known. He would have, if he wasn't so plaguing exhausted. "The fire retardant—"

"Is down there. But we're not going to get to it. Any other ideas?"

"Did everyone get out?" Lev's voice was calm as usual, but there was sharp tension running beneath it.

"Yes. But we can't get to the fire retardant, and heat like that will melt the deck soon enough. Not to mention what a fire will do to our oxygen supplies."

He could feel the heat through the floor now, the deck warm to the touch.

"It's right under the engine room—" Tae began, voice hoarse from smoke.

"I know. And the life support system."

Jez was grinning, that grin that meant she was about to do something crazy.

"Jez—" Lev began. She shrugged.

"Been in plenty of ship fires before. It's under the oxygen converter, right? So vent the waste CO2 tank."

"That's a wonderful idea, Jez," said Lev through his teeth. "Except that someone would have to get the venting tube through a hatch that's currently on fire, and will blow up in their face the moment it's opened."

"I'll—" Jez began.

"No, you won't," Lev said at the same time. "You have four broken—"

She glared at him. "I know, genius."

"I'll do it," said Tanya.

They all turned to stare at her.

"Tanya—" began Ysbel.

"Ysi. Of all the times you'd have to worry about me, this is not one of them."

To Tae's shock, Ysbel nodded resignedly. "You are right, of course."

He stared, but to be honest, he didn't have the time to wonder about it at the moment.

"The rest of you, get somewhere safe," she said, her tone matter-of-fact. "The med bay should work."

He hesitated.

"Quickly!"

"Come on," said Ysbel, half-dragging him to his feet. "You need the med bay anyways."

He stumbled to the short hallway that led to the med bay, and over his shoulder, he caught a glimpse of Tanya kneeling at the access port to the tank of waste gas.

Then they were out of sight, and he heard a sudden roar of flame, and Ysbel's face paled for a moment. And then a long hiss of gas, and the noise of the flames quieted.

A few moments later, Tanya appeared in the doorway. Her face was blackened, but she looked unharmed.

"It's out," she said. "I'd give it a few minutes to cool down, though."

Tae sank down on the floor in relief and leaned back against the cot, closing his eyes. Now that he had time to notice, the burns on his hands and arms ached and throbbed.

When he opened his eyes, Masha knelt beside him, med kit open on the ground in front of her.

"I'm fine," he croaked.

She ignored him, and pulled out a burn kit. "Let me see your hands."

He sighed and held them out, and she applied the patches to the blistered skin, along his arms and to the raw skin on the side of his face and neck.

Ysbel came over and crouched at his other side, concern on her face. A moment later, Jez pushed her way through.

"Masha," she said at last, as if the name tasted slightly rotten, "How's tech-head?"

Masha glanced up. "First degree burns, mostly."

"The door knocked him backwards, so he missed the worst of the heat," said Ysbel, and when he glanced up, he realized there were raw, burned streaks up her arm. She'd reached over Masha and was applying the burn patches to her own skin with a stoic matter-of-factness. "How's your head?"

He touched the throbbing bump gingerly, then sat up abruptly. "I've got to get those parts."

"I don't know how many of them will be left," said Ysbel quietly.

"I've got to check. We lose those parts—" He didn't finish the sentence.

"They aren't going anywhere," said Ysbel. "You'll have to wait until it cools down in there anyways."

Tae nodded finally, sagging back against the cot. Every muscle in his body was tense, but Ysbel was right. No matter how urgent it was, there was nothing they could do right now.

He closed his eyes for a moment, fighting down the sick nausea that was a combination of pain and the smoke in his lungs and too little sleep.

To think, once upon a time, he'd thought this bloody crew could do anything.

They couldn't even bloody well keep themselves alive.

Maybe Jez had the right idea after all.

"Let me go down," said Ysbel, finally, when enough time had passed. He shook his head, struggling to sit up.

"I know what I'm looking for. And I'll have a better idea if any of the parts are still usable."

He pushed himself to his feet, steadied himself on the wall until he was able to stand, and then stumbled back towards the hatch, his whole body aching. He paused long enough to pull out an oxygen mask and hook in a tube from the oxygen storage, then he clipped it over his face and, after a moment of hesitation, pulled back the hatch.

14

Hour 11, Tae

He felt slightly sick as he started down the ladder past the blackened skeletons of the structural beams of the beautiful old ship.

It was just a good thing Jez hadn't come down with him. She probably would have burst into tears.

The bay stank of burnt metal, the deck still steaming slightly under his boots. When he reached the supplies room, he hesitated, dread settling into his stomach. The twisted husk of the door was hanging open, the metal of it warped and half-melted. He shoved it out of the way and peered inside.

The inside of the room was a graveyard of blackened ash and scorched metal. He stood looking at it for a moment, then sighed and bent down, sifting through the ash-covered mess in a sort of hopeless optimism.

He closed his eyes for a moment, letting his fingers run over the melted, warped metal of what was left of their spare parts, searching for something that felt even slightly salvageable.

Not like he didn't have experience salvaging stuff he knew was crap and trying to make it work anyways, back on the streets of

Prasvishoni.

482 Standard, seven-month, third-day. The date on his com.

He'd told them it was a week or so before he'd been thrown in jail. It was true.

It was also the reason he'd been thrown in jail. The day he'd made what turned out to be the biggest damn miscalculation of his life.

He'd been angry, of course, and it had been his own plaguing fault. He should have suspected from the beginning. No one hired street kids. Still, he'd known he had a reputation as a tech-head, and so when Vadym Dulik had brought his people to come find him, and offered him what seemed, at the time, an obscene amount of money for his help with some tech—

He'd probably still have refused, honestly, if he hadn't woken up that morning to find Mila delirious with fever. She was only six, the youngest kid in their rag-tag gang, and there was no money for medicine when you were a street kid. The others weren't his family, not technically, but he was the oldest, and they looked up to him to keep them safe, and Mila's brother, who was only thirteen, had looked at him with those pleading eyes, as if he thought somehow Tae could save his sister—so he'd said yes, in exchange for some fever medication and a few stacks of ration-packs.

And then, two weeks later, he found what Vadym really wanted—the plans for all the tech he'd built from scraps over the past few years, that made it possible for his little gang to beg or steal enough to keep them alive. And he found it when he woke to the man's hired thugs standing over his bed. They threatened to beat him, and when he refused to tell them anything, they threatened to go back to where they'd found him, find Mila, and beat her instead. So he'd told them. He'd given them everything he had, and they'd taken it, and then they'd thrown him out.

They'd expected him to slink back to where he came from. That's what he probably should have done. But he'd been angry. And so instead of going back to the others, he'd staked out a place near a tech building, where he could easily mask his signature, set up in a makeshift shelter in the doorway of an abandoned building across the alley.

482 Standard, seven-month, third-day.

It has been the chill of a late Prasvishoni fall, and a thin dusting of snow was falling, yellow-white against the dirty streets. He'd told Caz and Peti he had some work to do, and he'd be back in a couple of days, and they'd believed him. He shivered under the thin blanket as he pulled up page after page of information on his hacked com.

To be honest, he couldn't remember a time he hadn't been a little too cold, from his first memory until now, but he was used to typing into the holoscreen with fingers that were stiff from the chill that had worked itself into them.

It wasn't hard. He'd figured it wouldn't be. Vadym had let him into his system so he could make sure Tae's talents were worth stealing, before he stole them. He hadn't considered that by allowing Tae into his system, he'd given Tae every tool he needed.

Tae smiled grimly to himself as he worked.

He'd realized, about ten minutes after Vadym had given him access, that the man was arrogant. So certain of his defences that he hadn't bothered to mod them. Assuming that if he paid enough money for a system, that was all it would take to keep him safe.

He hadn't counted on a street kid hacker. Probably hadn't thought twice about him, once he'd gotten his tech. Tae doubted he'd remember his name.

Well, he might not remember Tae's name. But he was about to get something he wouldn't forget any time soon.

The first bug he planted was a simple one—set to activate the next time someone went into the system, copy down every last piece of information on Vadym's protected devices. Nothing too frightening—except then it would vomit it back onto the government's public servers, for anyone who wanted to take a look.

They'd shut that down quickly enough, but it was just a distraction. Because underneath it, he was currently planting the most malicious time-bomb he'd been able to devise. If the copy-paste was the distraction, this one was the ground-cannon. And as soon as they shut down the first one—it would go off, ripping the code to every tech device that was wired into Vadym's system into a million shreds of data.

It was a delicate trap to set, but he was pretty sure he could make it undetectable. He just had to get in deep enough … He paused for a moment, frowning at the screen.

There was a system here he hadn't noticed during the two weeks he was working for Vadym. Which meant it was probably something Vadym was being very careful no one should see.

He tapped on the system, and, almost holding his breath, worked his way keystroke by keystroke past the protection.

It was something to do with the government. Not completely unexpected—he'd seen plenty of money coming in from various government entities when he went through Vadym's financials—but still. Something that secret—it seemed strange.

Of course it didn't really matter, because in a few hours' time, the whole system would be blown wide open.

He worked his way quickly through the hidden system, priming his bomb to go off. He didn't have time to read details on what it was for, or why it had been so well hidden, because now that he'd started, he was working against the clock.

Still—there was something about it, the way it had been set up.

He shook off the feeling of faint unease. That was the last thing he had to worry about right now. What he really needed to worry about was getting back out again before he got caught. Because a street boy taking down Vadym Dulik—that would be something the police would be very interested in indeed.

And then the alarms went off. At first he almost imagined it was his own nerves that had triggered it, but the blaring alarms wailing from the building across from him were real enough. Lights flashed red and white, and people were shouting, the wrist-coms of every person in a twenty-metre radius of the building flashing, locking down. He glanced quickly down at his screen of his own com, stomach tight. They must not have got through his spoof yet, but it would be a matter of seconds. Frantically, he worked his way backwards through the system, trying to cover his tracks as he went.

And then, finally, he was out. He sucked in a shallow breath, jumped to his feet, slapped off his com, and took off down the alley as fast as he could run. When he turned to glance behind him, police were swarming the building, weapons drawn.

But whatever it was, whatever had happened, they hadn't detected his time bomb. The next day, Vadym was ruined.

And a week later, so was he.

He'd have thought that, combined with five months in jail before Masha broke him out for her crazy suicide-mission heist, would have been enough to teach him not to be an idealist.

But here he was. Believing this stupid crew was going to risk their lives to help him, and then risking his own life to help them even when they'd proved they wouldn't.

He hadn't actually learned anything after all.

"Hey. Tech-head. You find anything?"

He jumped and spun around. Jez was standing next to him. He glanced around quickly, as if he could somehow protect her from the sight, but she'd clearly seen everything. Her face, what he could see of it through the oxygen mask at any rate, was haunted, and she looked a little like she was going to throw up. Her jaw was set, though, and there was a slightly sick determination in her eyes.

He held up a handful of burned components.

"That it?" she asked. He shrugged, and she knelt beside him, sifting through the ash.

When they emerged an hour later, between the two of them they could carry every part that they could possibly salvage.

That was one good thing from growing up on the street, at least. He was used to working with junk.

15

Hour 12, Lev

Lev watched in concern as Tae and Jez emerged from the hatch with their small collection of scorched and warped ships' components. He was no techie, but he could make a pretty decent guess that it wasn't good. The looks on their faces as they pulled off their face masks confirmed his assessment.

"What do we have?" Masha asked as they dropped the parts in a pathetically-small heap on the deck floor.

Tae shook his head, not even attempting a smile. "This is all we could salvage. Even most of this is junk, it's just less melted than the other components."

"Do we have what we need?" she asked.

Jez managed something that could have been a grin. "Well, guess that depends on what you think we need. To make the ship run again? Nope. To throw at each other when we get into a fight? Maybe."

Tae glared at her, and, to Lev's shock, she subsided, staring wearily at the floor.

His stomach twisted slightly.

It was worse than they were letting on.

"I don't know," said Tae at last. "I can use a few of these parts, but the spare thruster fins were all melted. We can possibly rig something so she can run with the broken fins, but it'll be slow, and it'll tear her to pieces. I doubt the thrusters would be reparable. And this is something Sasa Illiovich created, and I've never seen another piece of tech like it. If we run it like this, it's lost forever."

Lev glanced involuntarily at Jez. She was staring fixedly at the floor, and she looked like she might either throw up or pass out. But she wasn't saying anything.

"I understand that, Tae," said Masha quietly, and Lev noticed that her eyes went momentarily to Jez as well. "But if we don't get them online, we won't get the emergency oxygen generator online either, will we?"

Tae shook his head.

"And if that's the case, then I'm afraid Sasa's tech will do no one any good."

"I know," said Tae quietly. He glanced at Jez as well. She seemed to feel the combined weight of their stares, because she looked up wearily.

"Jez," Tae began, his voice a little more gentle than it had been.

"I know," she said dully. "Guess we better do it, then. She—" she swallowed hard. "She was a good ship, but … well, guess Masha's right. Not going to do any of us any good if we're dead out here."

She dropped her gaze to the floor again, and Lev bit his lip.

She hadn't even tried to insult Masha.

Tae watched her a moment longer, and there was a look on his face, bitterness and concern warring with each other. He turned away finally and said, "Alright then. I'll put in the internal components. I'll need someone on the outside, though."

"I'll go," said Lev quietly.

Tae nodded. "Probably best. You know the specs, right?"

"Yes. I've looked them over."

"Can you pull them up on your com? I'll show you what we need to do. It will be easier for you to find out there if you're already familiar with it."

Lev pulled up his com, and Tae crossed over to him, an almost-unrecognizable piece of tech in one hand.

"Here," he said pointing. "This is the part that's blown. You'll need to replace it with this, and then we'll pray to the Lady and the Consort and all the plaguing saints that it holds." He paused. "Have you been on a spacewalk before?"

Lev shook his head. "I've never had to. But I believe I understand the principle."

Behind him Ysbel snorted, and for half a moment he forgot that she wanted to kill him, and almost smiled.

"It's not hard," said Tae. "Same as being suited up in the ship. You'll bite down on the oxygen release to get it flowing. The tank holds enough for about two hours, but you should be in well before then. Your mag-boots will hold you to the ship, and you'll have mag-patches on your gloves, but you'll be tethered in case anything happens. If you need to talk, there's a com in the helmet that's patched in to the ship's coms. It's possible that the damage the ship took will interfere with the external com interface, but there's no way to know until you're out there. Either way, three tugs on the tether will tell us you need to come in."

Lev nodded. His hands, he realized, were sweating slightly, and his heart beat slightly faster than normal.

Still, as Masha had pointed out, the alternative to trying was certain death, which made the risks slightly less significant than they otherwise might be.

Ysbel left the room and met them in front of the airlock with a space suit. She didn't meet his eye, but dropped the equipment in a pile in front of him. He suited up quickly, pulled on his helmet and clipped the fastenings, stepped into the heavy mag-boots, and pulled the gloves over his hands, sealing them to the suit. Tae stepped closer and inspected the suit for leaks, then gestured Ysbel over, and the two of them lifted the oxygen tank onto his back. He staggered a bit at the unaccustomed weight. Tae handed him the thruster component, and he clipped it to his belt.

"You ready?" Tae's voice came through his earpiece. He nodded.

"Ready," he said, and his voice echoed slightly inside the helmet. Tae hit the airlock controls, and the first set of doors slid open. He stepped inside, and the doors sealed shut behind him.

He closed his eyes for a moment.

It was fine. There was nothing to be worried about. There was no reason that his hands should be slippery with sweat. He forced his breathing back to normal.

They had limited enough oxygen as it was. No need for him to gasp the rest of it in some sort of self-created panic.

Still—he'd never actually enjoyed space. In fact, at the university, he'd always operated on the general principle of the farther he was away from it, the better. He'd assumed there were plenty of things planet-side that could kill you, and there was really no point in seeking out an environment that was designed to freeze you to ice long before you'd have time to suffocate on your own fluids.

He managed a smile of wry amusement. Jez would never let him hear the end of it if she had any idea what he was thinking right now.

Jez.

His smile faded.

He wasn't entirely sure if, even if they made it back, Jez would survive this, at least, not the Jez he'd come to know over the past couple months. She looked broken. Like the ship. Like maybe they'd be able to put her together as well, somehow, but not the way she had been.

There was a faint hiss, and Tae's voice in his earpiece. "I'm opening the outer doors. Hold on to something."

He grabbed for the rungs of the ladder, and then there was a sudden weightlessness as the airlock's grav controls kicked off, and the doors swung open to the glittering black of deep space. He took a deep breath and climbed out of the airlock, his mag-boots and his gloves anchoring him to the ladder's rungs.

When he glanced back, he could see Tae's worried face though the viewing port. He rolled his eyes slightly.

Apparently, any time he was forced to do something that required any amount of physical dexterity, half the ship wondered if he would survive it.

It was a slow climb to the outside port for the thrusters, and it took a mind-numbingly long time to make his way across the exterior panels of the ship. As he walked, he noticed the scorch marks that cut across the polished gleam of the paneling, and he shook his head.

It was a good thing Jez wasn't seeing this. He wasn't certain she'd survive another blow at this point.

When he reached the external access port, he hit his com. "Tae. I'm here. I'm going to remove the hatch now."

There was no response. He tapped the side of his helmet and tried again. This time, a faint clicking and some static answered him.

The coms must be down.

At least he knew the specs. He should be able to get this back together with a minimal amount of errors.

He pulled the multitool off his belt and set to work popping off the access hatch.

He'd only been working for a few minutes when he noticed, in the back of his mind, a slight hesitation, a sort of restless irritation. He frowned and tapped his helmet, bringing up the internal com screen.

The oxygen indicator on the side of the helmet was flashing yellow.

The tank must have malfunctioned. He'd only been out for maybe twenty minutes, but the indicator showed the percentage of oxygen he was breathing was frighteningly insufficient.

He almost had the hatch off. And besides, they had limited oxygen tanks, and limited time. By the time he got back to the ship, they found a new tank, and he was able to come out again, that would waste a good forty standard minutes he couldn't afford to waste.

Best get this thing done as soon as possible.

He fumbled with the access hatch.

How long had his oxygen been low? He wasn't certain, but somehow his hands were clumsier than they should have been.

Damn.

He fumbled again with the hatch, and this time it popped off. He managed to grab it before it floated off, and he clipped it awkwardly to his belt.

His thoughts were less clear than they probably should have been, but there was something in the back of his mind that was suddenly very worried.

Probably should tell Tae he was running out of oxygen. At this point, he wasn't entirely sure he'd get back to the airlock.

"Tae—" he mumbled, but there was no response.

Of course. The coms weren't working. For some reason, the thought was slightly funny, and he found himself chuckling at it.

A lance of panic sliced through his thoughts, although he wasn't sure where it came from. Something about this wasn't right.

Oxygen. He was running low.

There was something in his hand, and when he looked down, he saw it was a thruster component.

That was the whole reason he was out here, right? Replace the component.

He was pretty sure.

He was lightheaded, and there was a certain unreality to everything. Breathing in seemed to take more effort than it usually did, and his lungs ached dully. He glanced down at the port, and the part that needed to be replaced was instantly apparent, blackened and half-way disintegrated. He tugged on it for a moment, and at last it popped free. Carefully, methodically, he clipped it to his belt, since he apparently couldn't trust his fumbling hands to hold onto it for any length of time. Then he pulled out the spare part and began trying to fit it into the empty space.

This was more difficult, as the slot was narrow and his hands were unsteady.

Jez could probably do it. If she was here, it wouldn't even be a problem.

He smiled to himself, despite his growing headache and the dull burning in his lungs, then turned back to his task, frowning.

Breathing was getting more difficult, and he wasn't entirely certain why.

Oxygen. He was low on oxygen. Again that spike of panic.

He needed to get back.

No, he needed to get this component in.

Something crackled in his earpiece, static and clicking. Did he sound like that when he called back? Probably.

Get the part in. He had to get the part in.

Finally, it slipped into place, and he breathed a shallow breath of relief and fumbled with clumsy hands for the door to the access port. It should just slip on, he was pretty sure, but he managed to almost drop it twice taking it off his belt.

His earpiece crackled again, and he jumped.

His head was spinning now, and he felt dizzy. If he let go, he wasn't sure if he'd fall down or up.

He laughed again. No gravity. He was on a space walk. He'd just float away.

The thought was unaccountably funny.

He shook his head, and turned back to the port.

Get the access hatch back on, that was the first thing. Then he could worry about the rest. There was something urgent he needed to do, but he didn't have time to think about it until he got this damn hatch back on.

At last it popped into place, and somehow, with the multitool, he tightened it, but his awkward efforts let the tool skitter across the surface. He pulled it back and peered carefully at the place.

Good. No scratches. Because if he scratched the ship, Jez would kill him. And somehow he couldn't bear to hurt her. He didn't want Jez to be hurt, at all. He'd prefer if she never got hurt ever again.

He'd let go of the multitool, and it was floating gently away from him. He grabbed for it, but it took him two attempts before he could close his fingers around it.

He was having a hard time keeping his eyes open now.

There was something he was supposed to do. What was it?

Replace the thruster component.

Not that, he'd done that already.

Get back to the ship. Get back to the airlock, because he was out of oxygen, and his body was shutting down. He was going to die.

It seemed like a problem that was somehow academic, distant and not really important at the moment. More compelling was the sight, all around him, of deep space, the faint, burning lights of the stars in the far, far distance, the black that cloaked everything like a velvet blanket, rich and cold and endless.

His earpiece crackled again, and for one brief moment, it shocked him back into lucidity.

He was out of oxygen, and he was dying, and no one in the ship knew because they thought he had plenty of time left. He couldn't call in on the com, and he'd be dead long before he could make the painstaking walk back to the airlock, if he was even coherent enough to do it.

He was going to die.

He saw, for a moment, Jez's tearstained face from the day before, when he'd found her in her cabin.

He couldn't damn well hurt Jez again.

With the last of his conscious thought, he grabbed the tether and pulled as hard as he could, once, twice, three times.

And then his grip seemed to falter, and he wasn't sure what he was holding onto and why, and his head ached and he was so dizzy he wasn't sure if he could take a step even if he wanted to.

There was a click, and something was happening with his boots, and he found he was no longer walking on the ship, he was floating beside it, and then everything went slightly hazy. The last thing he remembered was Jez's face in his mind, and the thought, for some unaccountable reason, made him smile.

* * *

"Lev! Lev, can you hear me?"

He blinked, through the pounding ache in his head, and tried to focus his eyes.

"He's alive. Lev! Lev, answer me. Can you hear me?"

He squinted and tried to peer around him, but the effort was too much, and he let his eyes fall closed again.

Cool fingers pressed against the side of his throat, and Masha's dispassionate voice said, "He should be fine in a few minutes. His pulse is good. He'll need some time to recover."

"I'll take him to his cabin."

The new voice was quiet and dangerous, and it took him a minute to recognize it.

Jez.

What was she doing there? The whole point of … of whatever it was he'd done was to keep her from getting hurt anymore. He was pretty sure.

She sounded somewhere beyond hurt. She sounded like she was about to take the ship apart with her bare hands.

"Come on, you idiot, up," she whispered, and he felt himself being lifted upright, and there was someone supporting him on either side.

"Let's get him somewhere quiet. It'll take him a bit to recover from this. To be honest, I wasn't sure we'd been in time." Tae's voice was unaccountably grim. Lev managed to raise his head.

The headache was pounding through his skull now, making the whole world fuzzy when he tried to open his eyes, but he managed to mumble, "Got the part in. Should be able to run it, I think."

"You damn idiot," said Jez from his other side, but her words choked, and he was left to puzzle what he'd done to upset her.

At last they lowered him onto something soft—probably a cot, by the feel of it—and after a whispered conversation, he saw through half-opened eyes Tae slip out the doorway. He glanced around reflexively, and relaxed when he saw Jez, sitting beside the bed.

Her face was drawn with worry, and there was a frantic, desperate look in her eyes. Almost like when she'd lost the ship.

What in the system could have happened? Because he was pretty sure there was nothing as important to Jez as her ship.

He had to do something, because in the state he was in, he didn't think he could handle seeing Jez sad.

"Jez," he whispered.

"What is it, you idiot?"

"Jez. I got the thruster piece in. I … didn't scratch your ship, I promise."

"You damn bastard," she hissed. "You think I care about that right now?"

He felt awful. He felt drunk, and like he was well on his way to the worst hangover of his life at the same time. But this was important.

"Jez." He managed to push himself up on one elbow. "What's the matter, Jez?"

She glared at him. "What the hell do you think is the matter, you plaguing idiot?"

"I … I'm sorry about the ship. I wish there was something—"

"This isn't about my damn ship, OK? You almost died. You were almost dead by the time we pulled you in here. I thought—" she paused, and he was horrified to see she was crying. "You damn, plaguing idiot. Why didn't you come back sooner?"

"I—I was—"

"I told you last night. I don't have time for this! I don't have time to be worrying about you all the time, and I don't have time to deal with this, and I don't have time to—to—" She broke down completely, dropping her head down on the cot beside him and sobbing. He managed to put his arm around her shoulder, but that only seemed to make things worse.

"And you're just a damn soft-boy, and this is the stupidest thing in the entire system," she sobbed. "And I don't damn well have time for it. And you almost died, and you throw up when I do any sort of flying at all, and—"

"I'm sorry," he mumbled, since some response seemed expected. She burst into fresh sobs, and he put his other arm around her as well, and held her.

It felt right, somehow, to have her in his arms, even through the torpor of his thoughts and the pounding, screaming headache. She dropped her head weakly against his chest, still sobbing loudly.

"Jez," he whispered. "Jez. Listen to me. I'm going to do whatever I have to do to make this better, OK? Listen to me, Jez. I—I need you to be alright. I don't know how to handle it when you're not alright. OK, Jez?"

She looked up, sniffling. "You sound drunk."

He managed a slight grimace. "I feel drunk."

"You should probably stop talking now."

"Maybe. But Jez, you—that whole time I was out there. You were the only thing I could think of."

Somehow it was very important that she hear this.

"Pretty sure when you wake up you're going to wish you'd stopped talking."

"Yeah. Maybe."

He was so tired. His eyes were falling closed on their own, and his head glowed with pain. "You have any painkillers?" he mumbled. "My head—"

"Yeah. I'll get some." She stood, and he grabbed her arm.

"No. Don't go. I don't want you to go."

She frowned at him, but she didn't leave.

"Just—just stay here, OK? I like it when you're here."

"Yeah." She sniffled again and settled back down beside his cot, and he gathered her back into his arms. She leaned her head back down on his chest, and he closed his eyes, and even with the pain hammering spikes through his temples, everything felt somehow right with the world as he faded out of consciousness.

16

Hour 17, Lev

The headache woke him. He lay in the dark, squeezing his eyes shut against the pounding in his brain that made it completely impossible to think. He reached out a hand to try to figure out where he was and what he was doing there, and on the floor beside the cot, felt two small tablets under his fingers. He picked them up and, with an effort that felt almost too great, tapped his com for a light. They'd been wrapped in a paper, and he fumbled on the floor until he was able to grab that as well, then he squinted at it in the faint blue light of his com.

Hey genius, the note read, *if you feel anything like you sounded when you passed out, you're probably going to need these. I'll be back in a bit to check on you—got to go keep those other idiots from wrecking my ship any more than she already is.*

It wasn't signed, and it didn't need to be.

He swallowed the tablets with a sigh of relief and lay back on the bed, waiting for the pain to diminish to the point he could think again.

What the hell had happened? Had he gotten drunk? He couldn't imagine what else would have given him a headache like this. Still, he was pretty sure he hadn't, because that sounded much more like something that Jez would do.

Jez.

Damn.

The memories began to filter reluctantly back through the throbbing pain.

The space walk, running out of oxygen.

He shuddered involuntarily. He'd almost died. He hadn't realized it at the time, too incoherent and half-drunk from oxygen deprivation, but he'd almost died.

And then somehow he'd ended up here. He had a faint memory of Jez laying her head on his chest, his arms around her—but as nice as the thought was, he was pretty sure he must have imagined it.

She had been here, though, he was almost certain of that, and she'd been crying, for some reason. And he'd said—what? He couldn't remember, and he had the uncomfortable feeling that if he did remember, he'd wish he hadn't. He was pretty sure he remembered Jez telling him he should probably stop talking.

Damn. He probably should have.

What had he said?

He shook his head, and even that slight movement sent waves of pain washing through his skull.

Unfortunately, there were things that were a lot more important to worry about than what he may or may not have inadvertently said to the lunatic pilot who he'd somehow gone completely off his head over.

He groaned and tried to sit up, and almost passed out.

Alright. He'd give it a few minutes.

He lay back on the bed, trying to think of something other than the throbbing pain, or whatever it was he might have said to Jez.

There was something else, niggling in the back of his mind.

A date.

It took him a moment to remember why it was there, and then he frowned.

Why would that particular date have been on the chip under his name? There was no reason it should have importance to a smuggler like Lena.

There was no reason why that date would have importance to anyone but him. Except, of course, for his professor. His mentor. It would have had reams of importance to her, if she was still alive. Which was, admittedly, doubtful.

He'd been working with Evka for almost three years at that point—she'd been the one who had insisted to the committee that he was ready for graduation, a year and a half before his fellow students, and the one who had strong-armed the committee into admitting him into the graduate program despite the fact he was only sixteen at the time. He'd had, of course, perfect scores in every subject, but then, the committee had a tendency to be slightly more regressive on matters of policy.

Evka, however, had threatened to resign if they didn't accept him, and added that she'd publish his scores to the entire academic system to let them know the kind of student they'd refused to accept into their program because of his age, and his admittedly-humble background. Wasn't the system built on the idea, she'd argued, that the lowest of the low can rise to staggering heights given the opportunity, and that birth and wealth and even age mattered less than raw talent and intelligence?

And she'd won, because of course she'd won, because she was one of the top research scientists in the entire university, which was, in turn the top research university in the system.

That had been a year and a half ago. But she'd been on edge for the past three months. He'd noticed it, in the way she turned her head when someone entered the classroom, in the tension in her posture, in the faint spark of fear, half-hidden in her eyes. And if anything, whatever was worrying her was building. These days he announced his presence at her office door with a clearing of his throat before he even knocked, because he'd seen her start when other people knocked, and he'd begun to worry about her heart, the way she clutched her chest and had to pause a moment to catch her breath after every shock.

She wouldn't tell him. He'd asked her straight out, once, but she wouldn't tell him. Still, he noticed her eyes following one of the other research students she was mentoring, and he could see the fear in her expression. And, because he had no desire for something to happen to the woman who currently seemed committed to bringing him into a professorship, he had decided to look a little more deeply into the student's background.

And also, although he hated to admit it, because the sight of his favourite professor, the woman who had treated him almost like a son, leaning against the wall clutching her chest, worry twisting her face, made him sick to his stomach, and very, very, angry.

That morning, he'd stopped at her door on the way to the class he was co-teaching—although really, he was doing all the teaching at the moment. He paused and cleared his throat loudly, then tapped lightly on the door.

There was no response.

He frowned. It was early, yes, but he'd never known her not to be in her office at this hour.

He tapped again, a little louder, and when there was no response from inside, he tried the handle.

It opened, easily, and he stepped inside.

Someone else might not have noticed—perhaps they would have thought it was too early, for once, and she hadn't come in yet. There was really nothing there that spoke overtly of violence. But there was just enough. That shred of torn paper on her desk—she still used paper, one of the few professors who did—the chips spilled carelessly on the floor and caught in the corners. Something someone as fastidious as Evka would never have missed. And there, on the edge of the wall by the door, a tiny spray of something red, as if someone wiping the surface clean had missed a spot.

It was very red.

He knelt beside it, and, heart pounding, touched his fingers to the wall.

Some of the red smeared onto his fingertips and across the wall, and he felt suddenly very, very cold. When he looked up, he noticed an equation on the wall com. It was something she and he had been working on, and it was still projecting dimly. But it was wrong, somehow, different than when he'd last seen it.

He frowned. That number there …

And then he saw it. A message in the numbers and letters.

Lev. If I'm gone, whatever you do, don't come after me. There's no point.

He'd stared at it for a long time. Then, deliberately, he'd wiped the red stains from his fingers, gone over to the desk and signed into the com.

He erased the entire equation. They'd spent the last eight months working on it, but it hardly seemed to matter. Then he replaced it with something that looked just as complicated, but was completely useless.

It would take someone else months to figure out that it didn't calculate what it was supposed to calculate, of course, and further months to realize that the reason was that the whole thing was a bunch of gibberish, but he didn't actually mind that outcome.

He still felt cold, colder than he'd felt in a very long time.

He stepped out of the office, after one more quick look around. He closed the door behind him, and wiped his fingers again, gingerly on the hem of his coat. She'd bought it for him, when the coat he had was falling apart at the seams, his wrists sticking far out of the cuffs. He'd found it one day in his student dorm without a note attached, but then he hadn't needed a note. He'd pretended not to know who'd given it to him, and she'd pretended not to know that he knew.

Then he walked slowly down the hallway and taught his class, took the homework from students who were generally several years older than he was. It had been something of a problem on the first day of class. It wasn't any more.

And then he'd walked back to his tiny student dorm, and sat down on his bed, and pulled up the holoscreen on his ancient com.

He knew the name of the student she'd been afraid of. And everything else, he could figure out.

He was very smart, after all.

Two days later, the news was all over campus that one of the students Evka had been mentoring had been arrested. No one was quite clear on exactly what he'd done, or why the police had found out about it, but for a day or two, that was all anyone talked about.

No one had talked about Evka's disappearance, so Lev had felt it would only be just.

The headache pills had finally kicked in, and he tried to sit up again, with marginally more success than last time. He blinked hard, leaning against the wall, and then pushed himself to his feet. The room spun slightly, but it was better than he'd thought it might be. Considering how long he'd been oxygen deprived, it was actually a miracle the only thing wrong with him at the moment was a headache.

He tapped his com. "Tae?" he asked.

"Lev? Are you up? How are you feeling?"

"I'm fine," he said. Fine, he'd learned, was a relative term. "Where are you?"

"Just finished the thrusters. I'm on the main deck."

"On my way."

He took a couple deep breaths, and then made his careful way down the hallway to the main deck. When he reached it, Tae was waiting for him. Lev tried to smile, but the effort made his head ache more, so he gave up and sank into one of the chairs.

Ysbel was there as well, but he knew better than to try to meet her gaze.

"Did you get the thrusters working?"

Tae nodded slightly. "As well as I can. Ysbel's just going down to check on the reactor, and then we're going to try to fire her up." He managed something that almost looked like a smile. "We're even ahead of schedule. We still have something like thirty hours of oxygen left." He paused. "I checked your oxygen tank. It was compromised, probably from the explosion. Why didn't you call when you started running low?"

"Com wasn't working."

"We could hear you. After you called in that first time, we kept trying to call, but you didn't answer."

"I didn't hear anything but static."

"Why didn't you just come back, then?"

He sighed, and leaned his head back. "I should have. I wasn't paying attention, and by the time I realized it was getting low, it must have already started to affect me." He half-laughed. "Honestly, all I could think of was getting the part in. It was not one of my more lucid moments, I'm afraid."

Tae nodded, but his face was creased in concern. "Yeah. Well, you almost died out there."

Lev shrugged, despite the cold in the pit of his stomach. "I didn't, though. Thanks to you. Thank you for getting me back in time."

Tae raised an eyebrow. "Don't thank me. Jez hauled you in. All I can say is, thank goodness Olya wasn't around, because I haven't heard that kind of language in a long time. Even from her."

Lev allowed himself a slight smile.

Then he paused a moment, and glanced behind him.

Ysbel sat there. She was watching him, and there was a strange look on her face. He was generally good at reading people, but he had no idea what she was thinking.

She'd been the one to bring the oxygen tank.

It had probably been compromised before she'd picked it up. Almost certainly. And almost certainly, she would have had no way of knowing.

Still …

It was odd, really. The oxygen in the tank had been just enough to let him get to where he needed to be, and he very likely would always have managed to get the thruster component in. It's just the getting back that would have killed him.

Could she have done it?

He cast another quick glance at the stocky, silent woman, with her emotionless face and dead eyes.

She'd killed thirty-five people at the shuttle launch station the government had brought her in to build. She'd planned for it, probably for months, to get the exact composition of people there that she wanted dead. And that whole time she'd worked alongside them, eaten alongside them, slept alongside them, and not one of them had ever suspected.

No. If there was ever someone who would be capable of something like that, it would be Ysbel. He wasn't sure if she had, or if it had just been an accident.

But he was very, very certain she was capable of it.

He shivered slightly as he turned back to Tae.

It wasn't that he didn't deserve it. He deserved it as much as that student, back in the university, had deserved it. And aside from his obvious self-interest, intellectually he felt no more regret for what was coming for him than he'd felt for what he'd done to the other student.

But there was something about working with a woman who had once been his friend, and never knowing when or what she'd decide to do to take her revenge.

Honestly, he almost wished she'd just used a heat-gun in the first place.

17

Hour 18, Ysbel

Ysbel stood, without looking at Lev.

"Tae. I'm going to check the reactor. It will only take me a moment."

"Call me when it's ready," said Tae. "I'll head into the cockpit with Jez, so I can watch the controls."

She nodded, and turned back down the corridor to the reactor.

She was biting the inside of her cheek so hard she could taste blood.

In about five minutes, she was going to find out if they were going to live or die, if Tae's insane fix had worked, if they were going to tear Jez's ship apart, but by doing so save their own lives.

That was what she should be worried about. Not about the slightly pale-faced scholar-boy slumped in a chair on the main deck.

He'd almost died.

The thought should have made her happy.

He'd have done what he needed to do, and then he would have died, and it would have been exactly as it should have been.

But there was something sick and cold in her stomach, and something burning at the corners of her eyes.

She'd seen plenty of people die. But when the airlock doors slid open and he'd been laying there, limp, when Jez, face frantic, had depressurized his helmet and yanked it off and Ysbel had seen the blue tinge to his lips, the unnaturally greyish tint to his skin, she'd thought she might actually be sick.

She tapped her com. "Tanya," she whispered.

"Ysi?" Tanya answered immediately.

"Are you alright?"

There was a short pause. "Of course I'm alright, Ysi. What's wrong?"

"Nothing. I was only worried about you."

"No need to be." Ysbel could hear the smile in her tone, and she closed her eyes for just a moment. "I'm with Masha. We've finished up in the systems room. I'll meet you in the cockpit."

"I'll see you there in a few minutes," said Ysbel. "The children are still sleeping?"

"Yes. Hopefully by the time they wake up, we'll be on our way."

"Yes. Hopefully," said Ysbel. She sighed, and tapped the com.

They'd be on their way home.

And she wouldn't, for now, think about what that would cost them—the *Ungovernable*, Jez's pride and joy, ripped to shreds. Masha gone, Lev gone. Their crew torn apart as surely as their ship.

She'd be home, with Tanya and Olya and Misko, and a gaping wound where the past five years' memories should have been, and maybe one day she'd learn to live with it. And until then, she'd pretend to be happy for their sakes, pretend to be whole, pretend that she'd never wanted anything but this after all.

She blinked. She'd reached the reactor deck without noticing it. She pulled the door open and stepped through.

Just a short fix here, nothing major. She pulled up her com and checked the readout Tae had sent her, and made some minor adjustments to each of the controls.

Even here, in the reactor power core, she could see the damage they'd taken from the hit. Every readout was haywire, and the sides of the heavy reactor shell were misshapen from the blast, the faint red glow from the power cell inside it visible even through the metal.

She finished the adjustments, checked the bolts, tightened the ones that had come loose, and turned to go, grabbing her tools and closing the door firmly behind her.

"Tae. I've finished the adjustments. You should be good to fire her up," she said over the com as she started down the hallway.

There was something nagging at the corner of her mind, an unease, and she wasn't certain what it was.

Probably something to do with Lev, or maybe just the lingering dread of looking at Jez's face once they got out of this, and she had time to think about what had happened to her beautiful ship.

No, it was something else.

The memory of the day on the deck of that ship, that for some reason lingered in her mind.

The terror of that moment, of the shards of shrapnel raining like fire around them, the fear on her parents' faces. "Ysi," her father had said, kneeling next to her in their tiny cabin, when they were finally safe and the ship had finally left atmosphere. "How did you know that oxygen converter was going to explode? I didn't even see it."

"I—" she wasn't certain how to explain. "It was the metal. It wasn't shaped the way it should have been."

"Ah," he'd said, understanding in his eyes. "You saw it bulging. You have good eyes, Ysi. I wouldn't have seen that. I didn't see that."

Why was she remembering this right now?

Something bulging. Not misshapen from the blast, but warping under too much strain—

Behind her, she heard the low hum, underlaid with a harsh grinding, as the damaged thrusters came online, a low whine that shouldn't have been there, like the protest of a wounded animal.

She swore and hit her com. "Tae! Shut it down!"

"What—"

"Shut it down!" She was sprinting for the cockpit, faster than she'd run in her life. "Shut it down now!"

She wasn't certain she'd be in time.

Jez closed her eyes and rested her hands on the familiar shapes of the controls.

They felt different. Lifeless.

There was a reason she hadn't been back in the cockpit since the accident, and it was because she hadn't been sure she'd be able to handle it.

She opened her eyes and turned quickly at a noise behind her. Tae stepped through the door, followed by a pale, but upright, Lev. Masha and Tanya stepped in after him.

She jumped to her feet, swore at the jolt on her ribs, and glared at Lev. "What are you doing up?"

He gave her a wan smile. "I'm doing OK. Feeling a lot better, thanks to the painkillers you left me. I believe the only major side-effect will be a headache." He grimaced. "Although, I will say, if you're going to have this sort of headache, it seems slightly unfair not to have at least had some wild evening to remember for it."

She could still feel her breath catch at the memory of his limp form, the panicked realization that this time he might actually be gone, and there might actually be nothing she could do to save him.

She glared at him as he slipped into the copilot's seat and pulled up the holoscreen.

"I'm sorry," he whispered. She ignored him and turned back to her own holoscreen.

She couldn't think about it right now, because she couldn't afford to have a panic attack in the cockpit, right before she brought up the power and destroyed her ship for what looked to be the last time.

"Tae. I've finished the adjustments. You should be good to fire her up," Ysbel's voice came over the com.

"Alright, Jez," said Tae. His face was grim. "Go ahead." He was crouched to her other side, the paneling removed from the compartment under the controls. He and she had painstakingly gone through the melted, ruined wires, salvaging what they could, replacing what they couldn't with whatever meagre supplies they'd been able to scrounge.

The whole time she'd felt like she was taking a knife to her chest and cutting out her own heart.

She was fixing the *Ungovernable* up so she could kill her.

She'd thought she'd die rather than do that.

She would die rather than do that. But … she glanced at Lev in the seat next to her, Tae, scowling as he crouched by the open panel.

She couldn't let them die rather than do that. In the end, that was the one thing she couldn't do.

She took a deep breath, closed her eyes, and fired up the engines, pulling the ship online. She gritted her teeth against the grinding whine of the motors, where there should have been no noise at all, only a barely-sensed hum, the faint breathing of the ship.

She was tearing it to pieces, and it was all she could do to hold her hand steady on the controls.

"Go ahead and bring the thrusters online," said Tae quietly. The strain in his voice was audible.

Slowly, she pulled the thrusters online, and there was a faint, grinding *thunk* and the ship shook slightly under her feet.

Sweat was forming on her forehead, and a drop of it trickled down the side of her face into her eye. She brushed it away with her elbow, not daring to move her hands from the controls.

"Tae! Shut it down!" Ysbel's voice came over the com, and she jumped.

"Shut it down! Shut it down now!"

She glanced at Tae, then shoved back on the controls, pushing the thrusters offline.

The ship, though, was still trembling, shaking beneath them.

Ysbel burst through the cockpit door.

"The reactor is overheating. It's going to melt down. Get everything offline, now!"

There was half a moment where they all stared at her. And then everyone seemed to move at once. Tae leapt to his feet, Lev jumped up, Masha and Tanya both started for the door.

"Lev, Masha, Tanya, come with me," said Ysbel. "We'll have to try to shut it down from down there. Jez, Tae—"

"I'll do what I can," Jez said through her teeth.

Damn.

A meltdown.

She'd always managed to avoid a meltdown up to this point. But this—wasn't looking good.

"Go!" Tae snapped. "Jez and I have the cockpit."

The others almost sprinted from the room, but Tae had already turned back to the wiring.

"Jez," he snapped. "I can't do anything from here."

"I know," she murmured. She closed her eyes, and let the ship talk to her through her fingers.

It wasn't talking. It was screaming, shrieking, dying.

"Come on," she whispered. "Come on, my sweet, sweet angel. One last time. You need to talk to me one last time."

"Jez—"

She didn't even look at him. Gently, she pulled the ship power down, just a hair. If she tried to pull it all the way offline now, it would cause a chain reaction and the whole thing would go up.

"Get the converters lined up," she whispered, and Tae bent over the control panel.

She nudged the thrusters back online, just enough to engage them. Under her, the ship was shaking harder, the floor trembling so that she could feel it through the walls and the panel. The grinding whine of the damaged thrusters was audible now.

She nudged the power down another notch. The whine increased, and she flipped on the side stabilizers.

"Ask Ysbel how they're doing," she murmured.

"Ysbel," Tae hissed, but she was only half-listening.

The ship was crying, she could feel it all the way through her bones. But it was talking to her too, telling her everything she needed to know.

Stabilizers forward. They were dead, of course, wouldn't do anything, but it would shunt some of the power away from the main reactor.

Thrusters online a little harder. They whimpered in protest, but she ramped them up, ignoring the tearing, shredding screech of tortured metal.

"Ysbel is holding down the override button, Lev and Masha have the manual bars, Tanya's got the access panel off," said Tae. "What do you need?"

"It's going to melt down in about sixty seconds," she said. Her voice sounded slightly dreamy in her ears. "If it does, they're going to die, but then, all of us will. On the count of ten, I'm going to pull everything online—shields, weapons, everything—and try to shunt every last bit of power I can out of the reactor. And then I'm going to shut it down. On my count, Ysbel needs to let go of the override, Tanya needs to hit the accelerator, and Lev and Masha are going to need to find something to hold on to, because it's going to try to throw them off. They can't let go, no matter what happens, or everyone on this ship is dead. Got it?"

Tae was already muttering into the com.

"It's alright, sweet angel," she whispered. "It's OK." There was a lump in her throat. "Ten. Nine. Eight."

The ship shook harder, like it was trying to pull itself to pieces.

"Seven. Six. Five. Four. Three."

It was dying. It was dying, and still, somehow, she could feel it trying to save her.

"Two. One."

She tightened her fingers on the controls.

"Now."

With one hand, she pulled everything online. The ship screamed in protest, every system sparking and jumping. The acrid smell of burnt wiring scorched her nose, and the floor paneling shook beneath her feet. She sucked in her breath, slid her fingers across the power bar, and, as gently as if she were smoothing a dying friend's brow, pulled it down.

For a moment, nothing happened. Her pulse spiked. She must have done something wrong, or Ysbel hadn't released the button in time, or Lev and Masha had been thrown off the manual bars—

And then, like a child falling asleep, the ship sighed, shuddered, and stilled.

She blew out a long breath, suddenly lightheaded. Beside her, Tae did the same, dropping his head against the panel in relief. Then he turned, and they grinned at each other. She hit the com.

"Well you idiots, you managed to hold on. Not bad."

"I honestly thought we were all going to die," said Lev, his voice still shaky.

"Probably should have. But then, you don't get a pilot like me every day," she said, still grinning.

Then she glanced down, and sobered.

You didn't get a ship like this every day either.

She ran her hand along the controls softly, lying quiet and dead under her fingers.

"Well, Jez," said Tae. His voice was slightly shaky as well. "I think that's the second time you've saved us in the last twenty-four standard hours."

"Yeah? You're not even counting all the times before that," she said. She hoped her voice sounded cocky, rather than hollow.

A few moments later, Ysbel, Lev, and Tanya came into the cockpit. She took a deep breath, bracing herself, and looked over at them, trying for a jaunty grin.

From the look on Lev's face, it wasn't a success.

"I'm sorry, Jez," he said softly, and it was too much, and she had to bite down hard on her teeth to keep herself from breaking down.

"What's the damage?" Tae asked.

"Well, thanks to our crazy lunatic pilot, we're still alive," said Ysbel. "But other than that, it's not good. The emergency oxygen generator wasn't online for long enough to make any difference, and the meltdown killed most of the power cells, I think. We're going to start losing power soon."

"Where's Masha?" asked Lev, frowning. Jez glanced around, and shrugged.

It was just as well, really. She wasn't entirely certain she could face Masha right now.

"Maybe the bastard decided to take her chances in deep space," she said.

"Maybe 'the bastard' stopped by to find out what caused the meltdown," said Masha sharply, stepping into the cockpit.

Jez frowned.

There was a small device in Masha's hand.

Tae stood slowly, staring at it. "Tracking?" he asked.

Masha nodded. "It's a tracking device. We didn't find it, because it was placed behind the main reactor. That's why none of our searches picked it up, and also why the reactor was overheating."

"But—it would only have triggered an overheating if there were heavy signals—" he trailed off.

Jez felt suddenly sick.

"Exactly," said Masha grimly. She tossed the device to Tae, and he grabbed it without a word. He turned it over, ejected the chip, and slipped it into his com, pulling up the holoscreen as he did so.

His face went grave.

"Masha," he said quietly.

She nodded. "I know."

"What?" snapped Jez. Tae turned to look at her, and she was shocked at the grim expression on his face.

"They've been tracking us this whole time, and they've honed in on our position. That's what indirectly caused the meltdown—the core was damaged, and then with the beacon drawing power and focusing it, it was too much. And now—" he paused, glancing down at his com. "I've shut it off, but they already know our coordinates. Their ship is about twelve hours away. And from the looks of it, they've fired off a pair of heavy missiles that will reach us about an hour before they do. Looks like we won't have time to run out of oxygen after all."

She stared at him, a numbness catching her chest. Tanya had gone slightly pale, and Ysbel put an arm around her.

"It's not just that, though," said Tae quietly. "Lev, you might want to come over here."

Lev frowned and crossed over to Tae, scanning the information on the screen quickly. His eyebrows rose, and he gave a soft whistle.

"Well," he said. "Masha, I assume you've seen this?"

Masha nodded.

"Seen what?" asked Ysbel sharply. "I'm not sure if you realize this, but there are people in this room who aren't currently looking over Tae's shoulder."

"I'm sorry," said Lev, looking up. He took the device from where Tae had laid it on the control panel. "This is a government tracker, and it's got the full authorization code on it. If it had been stolen, the code would be out of date, but this one is current. So there's no way this is coming from Lena only."

Jez swallowed hard, trying to keep her voice steady. "Hey, genius. I thought you said you were sure this was Lena. And I'm pretty damn sure that whoever it was that jumped you back in the zestava was smuggler crew."

"Maybe," said Lev, his forehead creased in a frown. "I don't know. We may have to assume that the government is working with Lena."

Jez scoffed. "Lena? Work with the government?"

"If you recall, I worked in the government for quite some time," Masha murmured. "I had access to some very classified information.

Let me tell you, if they'd wanted Lena badly enough, they could have had her. But they prefer not to use those methods on a smuggler crew, no matter how effective that crew may be. They'd only utilize them in a matter of system security."

Jez tried to grin, but she didn't really feel like grinning. "So what, Lena's going to assassinate the Secretary General or something?"

Lev shook his head. "No, Jez. I have a feeling they wanted her because of something else." He hesitated. "Someone else."

The cold in her chest tightened. "But—"

"I assume, someone they knew Lena could locate, where they may not be able to. We never found who betrayed us in the prison. But from what I know of Lena, it wouldn't surprise me if she knew someone on the inside. Someone who could have recognized you. And, if you'll forgive me, you weren't exactly inconspicuous."

"But—" There was something like panic spreading through her. If Lena had been after her, that would have been bad enough. But the government?

Bad things happened to people the government was after. She knew that damn well.

Lev held up a hand. "I don't think it's just you, Jez," he said. "They'd have records of who Masha recruited for this team. We disappeared, for all intents and purposes killed off. But if they somehow found out one of us survived? It wouldn't have been a stretch to assume we all had, and furthermore, that we were all together somehow."

"Is this about the heist, then?" she asked, her voice barely a whisper.

"I—don't know," said Lev. His tone was level, but she could hear the worry in his voice.

"That's the thing," said Tae, squinting at the screen. He expanded his screen, tapped it, and expanded it again. Then his eyes widened slightly.

"Those tags they had on the rest of us," he said quietly. "They're here, too. And there's a note under the tags."

"What does it say?" asked Ysbel.

"It says—" he paused. "They want us dead. All of us. There's our names, and a date, and a death reward. C-level credits."

There was a moment of silence as everyone in the cockpit turned to stare at him.

Something sick and numb was spreading through Jez's whole body. She couldn't push from her mind the image of her old apartment, everything inside torn to shreds, the red stain spreading from the neighbour woman's throat.

"Why, though?" asked Lev quietly. "Why kill us? What would the government want with the five of us? Yes, Masha, what you did on the heist would have certainly inconvenienced them, but—C-level credits to kill us? Even with the jailbreak, that seems excessive."

"And the dates," said Masha grimly. "If this had been about the heist, the dates should have matched up with something in the heist —when we planned it, when we pulled it off, when we disappeared. No. I believe this is something else entirely."

There were a few moments of silence.

Finally, Ysbel raised her head. "Alright then. So, if I understand correctly, we have eleven hours before Lena's missiles blow us into space dust. And we currently have no weapons, no shields, and no power. Is that more or less correct?"

Lev nodded.

Jez closed her eyes for a moment and took a deep breath.

They were probably all going to die. They were almost certainly all going to die.

She probably shouldn't be feeling, for the first time since her beautiful, perfect ship had gone silent, completely alive. But there was something about the adrenalin pounding through her that made it impossible not to grin.

"Alright then," she said. "She's come a long way to find us. Least we can do is to get a welcoming party together for her."

18

Impact minus 11 hours, Lev

There were a few moments of stunned silence.

In all honesty, Lev was feeling slightly stunned himself.

The headache didn't help.

"Well, come on, genius, let's go," said Jez, pulling herself out of the pilot's chair with some effort. "Guess we got some shields to fix."

He stared at her.

She was grinning. She was actually grinning.

She bumped his shoulder on the way by, then sauntered off down the hallway.

Ysbel sighed and shook her head. "I will never understand that girl. But she's right. Tanya and I will go see what we can do with the weapons, I suppose."

"Probably better go with her, Lev," said Tae, his voice still strained. "Masha, can you help me in the reactor bay? I need to check the damage."

Lev turned and started after Jez. He caught up with her a few moments later.

"You're actually enjoying this," he said. He could hear the disbelief tinging his own voice. "You're actually happy that Lena's hunting us down."

She stopped in front of the ship's compartment, and turned to face him. She wasn't even trying to hide the grin on her face.

"Well, genius, we might not be able to get away, but I bet we can make Lena wish she'd never found us. I'm good at that."

He shook his head as she stepped inside.

It was good to see the old Jez back. But he wished, somehow, that it didn't always seem to involve someone about to get blown up.

"Alright, Jez. I assume you know the basics of the shields—"

"Nope," she said casually. "I mostly was worried about making the ship go really, really fast. And the hyperdrive. Which is basically the same thing, I guess."

He rolled his eyes. "Alright. I'm going to pull up the specs, and—" he stopped, glancing around quickly. "Did you feel that?"

Jez frowned as well and hit the com. "Hey. Tech-head. Gravity's flickering in here."

A moment later, Tae's voice came over the earpiece. "Yeah. The meltdown messed up a bunch of the systems. I'm still trying to figure out the damage, but it wouldn't surprise me if the gravity is unreliable. I'll do what I can, but I can't promise anything."

"Thanks, Tae." Lev tapped off his com and turned back to Jez. "We might be working in zero-grav in a minute here."

"I heard." She paused, sobering. "Um. Lev. Are you—how are you feeling?"

He gave a slight smile. The headache was still there, but manageable now. "I'm doing OK. I—thank you. For bringing me in."

She tried to smile back, but there was something haunted in her expression. "I—was worried about you. I thought maybe we'd been too late. I—"

"It's OK," he said, stepping forward slightly. "I'm OK. Just a headache."

"You—were almost dead. When I brought you in. I thought—I thought—" She swallowed hard, and without thinking, he reached out and put a hand on her arm.

"Jez. It's alright. I'm fine. Thanks to you and Tae."

She nodded, a slightly stricken look on her face. "OK. But—tell me if you start feeling—I mean, I don't want—I—don't do that again, OK? I don't know if I can—if I—"

"Jez." He took her other arm and turned her to face him. "Jez. Listen to me. I'm fine, and it's going to be fine, and I'm harder to kill than you might think."

She was looking directly into his eyes, and he couldn't seem to look away, and that faint memory of him lying on a cot with her head on his chest and his arms around her felt suddenly more real. He'd taken a step closer to her somehow, and in the cramped space of the engine room, they were almost touching.

He swallowed, but he couldn't take his eyes off her, and she didn't seem to want to take her eyes off him either.

"How do the shields look?" came Tae's voice through the earpiece, and they both jumped. He released her hastily, and tapped his com.

"Give us a sec."

When he looked up, Jez had already turned away and was crouched in front of the paneling, removing the bolts. He took a deep, slightly shaky breath and joined her, pulling up a list of specs on his com.

She removed the paneling and set it aside, and they both peered inside.

"Well," she said after a moment. "Like I said, I never paid much attention to how the shields worked. But pretty sure they're not supposed to look like that."

He reached past her and lifted out a blackened, warped cylinder. "Yes. You'd be correct," he murmured.

This wasn't good, because he was pretty certain he remembered every single blackened piece that Tae and Jez had managed to salvage from the supplies room, and he was pretty sure this wasn't one of them.

"Well, good thing we have wire-brushes and a mallet," she said, reaching in and pulling out another blackened component.

Something shifted in the compartment again. Lev had a momentary feeling of weightlessness, and when it ended, he landed on the floor off-balance and had to throw out one hand to catch himself.

"Damn grav controls," Jez mumbled.

"You have another wire-brush?" he asked. "I'll get started on this one."

She handed him one, and he started gingerly scrubbing at the carbon buildup on the warped piece of metal.

The feeling of weightlessness returned, and he grabbed for his tools before they could drift away, and this time when the gravity returned he fell a good ten centimetres. Jez landed on the floor next to him on her wrists, and swore under her breath. She hit the com.

"Tae! Stop fiddling with the grav field."

"It wasn't me," came Tae's slightly-irritated voice. "I told you, the melt-down affected all the systems, OK? You want me to work on that, or do you want me to finish going through to see what else might kill us in the next ten minutes?"

Jez rolled her eyes. The gravity flickered again, and she grabbed for the part she'd been working on as it drifted a millimetre or so into the air and then fell again. And then the gravity cut completely.

"Yes, Jez." Tae's resigned voice came over the earpiece a moment later. "It's out everywhere. I'm looking into it. Hold tight."

Jez grinned at Lev. "You ever tried to work in zero-grav before?"

He sighed. "No, Jez. I have not. And so far, it doesn't seem overly productive."

"Well, guess it depends on what you consider productive,"she drawled. She pulled back her arm carefully and tossed the wire-brush at him. The movement sent her drifting backwards, and the brush hit him on the shoulder, leaving him turning slow circles towards the far wall.

"Jez—" he began. She snickered.

"Come on, genius, let's get to work."

"It would have been easier if you hadn't just—"

"It's good for you. Teaches you how to work in difficult conditions."

"I'm fairly certain this entire last sixteen-some hours has been an exercise in working in difficult conditions," he said through his teeth

Jez had maneuvered herself over to the panel, and was holding on to the engine room wall with one hand while she rummaged around inside the compartment with the other.

"See, whoever built this little beauty was thinking," she said chattily as she worked. "See the hand-holds? Guess they probably had to do a little zero-grav work themselves at some point."

Lev shook his head and began scrubbing at the cylinder with the wire-brush again. "I know we've had this conversation. 'Whoever it was' was Sasa Illiovich."

She shrugged. "I'm supposed to remember that?"

"Jez. Even you had to have heard of Sasa. They were the most brilliant inventor the system has ever seen." He paused a moment. "Although now that I've met Tae, I may have to revise that opinion."

"Were they a smuggler?" Jez asked. She now had a small collection of burned, carbon-scored parts floating in a halo around her.

"No, Jez, I just told you—"

"Were they a pilot?"

He sighed. "No."

"Well then." She shrugged. "Like I said. Probably not going to remember their name." She paused a moment, and her voice softened slightly. "Although, if they were the one who built my sweet baby—" She swallowed hard, and turned back to her work.

He watched her in bemused silence.

He wasn't entirely certain he'd ever figure Jez out. For someone who, on the surface, seemed so entirely uncomplicated, he was never exactly sure what she'd do next. Although, a part of him whispered, he could probably make a fairly good guess by thinking of the most outrageous reaction he could imagine to any given situation, and then multiplying it by a factor of ten.

They worked in companionable silence for a while. It was strange, floating between the walls and the floor and the ceiling as he worked. It was hard not to think of the floor as down, and when his feet were pointing towards the ceiling, he kept making unconscious efforts to right himself. Every so often, when he got too engrossed in his work, Jez would throw something at him, sending him spinning slowly off in a new direction.

He shook his head, not certain whether to be irritated or amused.

She'd somehow managed to take the shielding system apart, and was now struggling to work the mallet, as every blow pushed her backwards.

He watched her for a moment in faint amusement. She'd hooked a foot around one of the hand-hold bars to brace herself, but with one broken arm that was the best she could do, and every strike sent her drifting off the wall. At last, shaking his head, he grabbed the nearest wall and pushed off towards her. She looked up as he grabbed a bar next to her, and he let the wire brush and the cylinder drift off.

"What," she snapped. He smiled slightly.

"Jez. Let me do that."

She glared at him. "Pretty sure I have more experience fixing ships than you do, genius."

"I'm quite certain I could figure out how to work a mallet."

"This is my ship. She's been through enough already."

He sighed. "Fine." He paused. "I supposed I could brace you so you can use both hands, if you'd like."

She watched him for a moment, and finally gave a short nod.

He hooked an arm through one of the hand-holds, and his foot through another. She was still watching him. He took a deep breath.

"I'm going to have to—" he gestured at her. She raised an eyebrow, and he blew out his breath. "I—sorry. Do you—mind?"

She shook her head, still watching him, and he put his free arm around her waist, pulling her against him so her body was braced against his chest.

She glanced over her shoulder at him, then turned hurriedly back to her work.

For some reason, he was having a hard time breathing normally. The feel of her angular, wiry body against his felt—almost too natural. Almost like she fit there. Like she was meant to be there.

"Does this help?" he asked. His voice was strangely unsteady.

"Yeah." She didn't look up, but he could feel the tension through the muscles in her back.

"Are you sure? I don't have to—"

"It's better," she said. She'd pushed the part up against the wall to hold it steady, and seemed to be focusing abnormally hard on directing the mallet.

Her voice sounded slightly breathless as well, but it could just be his imagination.

He shifted his grip on her slightly, and she settled back, leaning into him to steady herself.

Damn.

He couldn't seem to catch his breath, and he felt shaky, and weightless in a way that had nothing to do with the grav system.

She smelled faintly of ship grease, and the sharp scent of burnt ozone, and the sweet, musky smell of the ship's interior. It was a nice smell, somehow—the smell of flying, and space, and freedom.

He'd never realized, until he met Jez, what flying was. What freedom was.

She swung the mallet again hard, and turned over her shoulder to grin at him. "Got it," she said. "Hand me that cylinder you were working on."

She stopped speaking suddenly, her eyes widening slightly. Their faces were only centimetres apart, and he found himself staring at her lips, still bruised and cracked from her run-in with the prison guard days before. He blinked and took a deep breath, releasing her for a moment to grab the part she'd asked for. When he turned back, she was still watching him. He handed her the part, and then, his heart hammering, put his arm around her again, pulling her in close.

Because they were working, and if he didn't hold her tightly enough, she couldn't repair the shields. That was the only reason they were doing this, and it would be prudent for him to remember that.

But somehow his brain wasn't functioning as clearly as it usually did, and he felt a little like he had on the outside of the ship with his oxygen running low—an odd sense of euphoria mixed with disorientation, and the feeling that he couldn't seem to breathe just right …

She hadn't turned back to her work yet. She was still watching him, and she shifted slightly, settling herself more firmly against his chest, and there was an expression on her face of slight wonder, like she'd just run her hands over the controls of a new ship. And her lips were parted, ever so slightly. Why was he noticing her lips? And why couldn't he seem to make his heart settle down? And why the hell was he leaning into her, shifting his grip on her body so she was turned to him instead of the wall, and …

"Sorry, still working on the grav controls," said Tae through the earpiece, and they both jumped.

"It's going to take me a while though."

Lev sighed shakily and shot a wry glance at Jez, then tapped his com against the wall.

"Thanks, Tae," he said, trying to keep the irritation out of his voice.

"Best get working then, I guess," said Jez. She'd turned away again, and her voice was unsteady, and he could feel, though her back, her breath coming a little more quickly than it had been.

She could probably feel his heart pounding as well.

He sighed. "You're right. We have plenty to do."

She half turned, and grinned at him. "Looks like I'm the one doing all the work here."

He rolled his eyes and didn't bother to answer.

To be honest, at this point he wasn't certain he'd trust himself to do anything anyways. He wasn't entirely sure how his brain had completely short-circuited and his body had become suddenly shaky and unreliable at the feel of Jez's body against his, and the sight of her staring at him, lips slightly parted, eyes wide, but whatever it was didn't seem like it would go away any time soon.

He didn't know how long they stayed like that, Jez working her way methodically through the warped parts, he holding her steady. But as far as his now-completely fuzzy brain was concerned, they could stay like this forever. In fact, even getting the oxygen online seemed slightly less important than him being able to hold on to Jez, and not having to let her go.

Jez herself was strangely quiet. She didn't make any smart remarks, which was a change in itself, and she seemed to have leaned her head back against his shoulder as she worked, and he could feel her breath hitch slightly, every time a blow of the mallet pushed her back against him.

He shook his head at himself. This was actually ridiculous. They were all going to die in about a few hours' time. He should be able to focus, at the very least.

Another mallet blow, and her body shifted against his, and his heart jumped, his throat going suddenly dry. He closed his eyes and tried to breathe normally.

"I think I've just about got it," she said at last, and he took another deep breath and managed a smile.

"Good. Let's—"

There was a jolt, and for a moment he was clinging to both Jez and the handholds, ducking his head as tools and parts fell around him, and then the gravity shut off again and he was once again weightless.

Jez grinned slightly. "Haven't been in a sketchy grav-field for a while. Almost forgot what it was like."

"You—did this often?"

She smirked, turning slightly in his grasp. "You should have seen the ships Lena had me flying. She gave me the worst crap she had, and I still pulled off jobs no one else could." She paused a moment. "I—I'm sorry. I forgot."

"No need," he said, smiling slightly. Yes, she'd gotten him thrown in jail, indirectly, when she was about sixteen and before he'd ever met her, but the longer he knew her, the more he figured he'd been lucky to get off that easily.

And, if he were being honest with himself, she could probably get him thrown in jail again tomorrow and he'd still smile and tell her there was no need for an apology. He couldn't seem to help himself.

"Yeah. Well, I'm sorry anyways." She paused again, perking up. "But you should have seen that job. It was amazing."

He shook his head, smiling despite himself. "I imagine any job you flew would have been amazing, judging from my personal experience."

"Any job I still fly is amazing," she said, still grinning.

"It is." He paused a moment, then, with a force of will, said, "We should probably get to work putting this back together."

"Yeah." She gave him a small smile, and after a moment he forced his arm to release her.

It was harder than he'd thought, and the feeling of his body without hers pressed up against it was emptier than he'd expected it to be.

She pushed lightly off the wall and grabbed a handful of parts, and he let go of the handholds and prepared to do the same. And then there was a jolt, and he grabbed for Jez, pushing himself forward, and they landed on the floor in a heap, Jez on top of him, her elbow digging into his ribcage. He grunted at the impact, and she swore loudly into the com.

"Could have warned us, tech-head."

"I'm sorry. I told you, there's something haywire with the system."

She rolled her eyes, then glanced down at Lev. "You OK?"

"Yes. I'm fine."

She was probably as heavy as he was, and he was going to have bruises.

Still, better than her landing on her broken arm or bruising up her ribs any more.

She rolled off him, and he sat up. They were still slightly tangled together, and again, for one brief moment, their faces were closer than he'd intended.

"You did that on purpose, didn't you?" she asked. "Landed under me so I wouldn't hit the ground."

He shrugged slightly.

She looked at him for a long moment. Then, abruptly, she pushed herself to her feet, wincing and swearing as she steadied herself against the wall.

"You should think about taking care of yourself a little more, genius," she said, turning back to the control panel. The old snark was back in her tone. "Pretty sure I'm not the one who basically almost died a couple hours ago."

He sighed regretfully and ran a hand through his hair.

He wasn't totally sure how she did whatever it was she did to him, and he wasn't sure if it was the best thing that had ever happened to him or a completely unforgivable amount of stupidity.

But he couldn't seem to do anything about it, and to be honest, he probably wouldn't even if he could.

"Going to need your specs in a sec," she said over her shoulder, and he pushed himself to his feet and tapped his com on, pulling up the holoscreen.

It didn't take long to get everything reassembled. For someone who said she'd never bothered to look at the shielding system, Jez seemed to have an almost intuitive knowledge about what should go where, and the wire-brushed and hammered parts fit back into their places better than he'd imagined. He reached in beside her to help with the wiring, and when their hands brushed, more than once, he tried to ignore it.

"Tae," he said at last, tapping his com. "Can you try turning the shields on, just on the backup system?"

"Yeah. Give me a minute to get into the cockpit."

There were a few moments of silence, and he tried not to look at Jez, even though he wanted to, even though the memory of her face close to his, her body pressed up against him, was a little like a drug, and he was feeling distinctly inebriated at the moment.

"Alright. I'm going to start it up."

"Slowly," snapped Jez, slapping her com. "You'll have to dial it up slowly, and make sure the power is dialled down before you do."

Over the com, Tae sighed heavily. "I do actually know a few things about tech, Jez."

"Yeah, well this is my ship, OK?" She knelt and squinted into the access hole, and Lev joined her.

"Turning it on now," said Tae. Lev held his breath as something inside coughed, shuddered, and then, finally, whirred to life.

He turned to Jez, and they grinned at each other.

"Think you got it, tech-head," said Jez into the com.

"I think it's actually working," said Tae, a sort of exhausted wonder in his voice. "I think for once, something is actually working."

"Well, probably shouldn't get used to it," Jez smirked. She pushed herself to her feet, still grinning, and reached out a hand to help Lev up. He took it and stood, and she glanced down at her com.

"Well, genius, looks like we have about eight hours before Lena's missiles get here. I'm going to check on something, be right back."

"I'll clean up in here," he said with a sigh. She gave him a grin and slipped out the door.

Still shaking his head at himself, he gathered up the tools and headed back towards the cockpit.

He could still feel the shape of her against him, and the front of his jacket still carried her faint scent.

19

Impact minus 8 hours, Jez

Jez hummed to herself as she made her way down the corridor.

Her ship was still dead. Lena was coming to kill them all, and it was at least partly her fault.

But she couldn't seem to help it.

She almost had to glance at her feet on the ground to make sure the grav-control was still working.

There was no reason whatsoever for her to feel like she was floating. Absolutely none at all, and there was really, really no reason for the completely stupid grin on her face.

Still …

She could still feel his arm around her waist, the warmth of him against her back.

The moment when she'd turned in his arms, and their faces were almost touching, and his grip on her had tightened, just a little, and he'd leaned in towards her, his dark, thoughtful eyes intense and not, in that moment, thoughtful at all.

And it was stupid that the memory made her breath catch and her heart pound.

He was Lev. He was a soft-boy, and a scholar, and not even a little bit her type, and she should know, because she'd been with plenty of people who were her type. Whatever that was.

Never lasted for more than a few months, because somehow a few months seemed to be the outside limit on how long she could handle things being the same without going completely crazy, but it had always been fun while it did last. She was certainly no innocent, and Lev was certainly not the first person whose body warmth she'd enjoyed.

But this … was different, somehow. Because it wasn't just that. It wasn't just the fact that her heart couldn't seem to stop pounding when she was around him, and it wasn't just the heady breathlessness of being too close to him. There was something about Lev that was —comfortable, somehow. Like the feel of ship's controls under her fingers and open space around her. Something that felt like home, even though she'd never really had a home for as long as she could remember.

And that was the part she was afraid of. Because if she was being honest, she was completely terrified.

No. Lev was definitely a bad idea, and she was definitely going to tell him that.

Soon.

Probably.

She was humming again, and she could still feel the warmth of him against her shoulders, the way her body had somehow fit with his, like ship's parts slipping into place.

Yep. This was definitely a very, very bad idea.

She shook her head to clear it, and glanced around. She'd reached the hatch that led down to the storage room, and she pulled it open gingerly, wincing at the pressure on her ribs.

The thought of going down there, of seeing the scorched bones of her perfect, beautiful ship, like some burned corpse, made her feel almost sick to her stomach.

But—she was pretty sure, when she'd been down there last time, that she'd seen something. It had been nagging at her ever since, even in the unnervingly-pleasant circle of Lev's arms and his chest. And she was pretty sure that as she'd finished putting the shields together, she'd figured out what it was.

She took a deep breath, and started down the ladder, holding on gingerly with her broken arm.

Thank goodness that the prison doctor, or whoever the hell it was who'd patched her up, had used bone-set instead of a cast, because she'd be basically useless otherwise.

She stopped half-way down and peered along the blackened corridor, then pulled one hand free from the ladder and switched on the light in her com.

There. She'd been certain she'd seen it. That slight indentation in the ceiling, near the wall. And she was pretty sure she knew where it had come from.

She grinned, and pulled herself back up the ladder.

When she reached the door to the reactor deck, she paused.

Either this was a fantastic idea, or it was a really, really stupid idea. Which were basically the same thing, really.

She shoved open the door to the massive, echo-y reactor bay, the steel walkways lining open space that took up all the three levels of the ship.

It only took her a moment to locate what she was looking for. There, in front of the power core, inside a heavy blast-proof casing almost as tall as she was, tucked into an enclave in the wall.

The hyperspeed drive.

She circled the walkway until she reached the access panel.

Unlike tech-head, she didn't go starry-eyed over tech. But this—this was different.

This was a reason she might have to remember that inventor's name, whoever they were. Illiovich, maybe?

Because this was beautiful. Or, at least, it had been, before she'd torn it to shreds trying to keep them all alive.

She took another deep breath, and carefully unlatched the heavy panel and pulled it open.

Tae had looked this over, she was pretty sure. But if she hadn't seen the dent in the ceiling of the storage room, that happened to be the floor of the tiny enclave, she would probably have missed it too. There, just below the bottom fin, there was a small chunk of metal lodged deep into a self-made divot in the metal flooring. And … yes, you could see it if you were looking. The strain along the entire hyperdrive shaft, the slight twisting in the metal.

The pressure on it would be immense.

But …

She grinned and pulled the handheld heat-torch out of her tool kit.

But she was pretty sure she could get it running again. Just take a sec.

She ignited the heat-torch, and waited until the tip of it glowed white-hot. Then, gingerly, she reached into the narrow space beneath the fin and touched it to the lower end of the chunk of metal. The metal hissed and sputtered at the heat, sending up a thick stream of black, acrid smoke as it began to soften and warp.

She heard the soft 'click,' and threw herself backwards as the twisted shaft sprang free, throwing the half-melted chunk of shrapnel across the room. The drive spun madly, hissing with speed, and there was a creaking sound as components groaned under the strain.

Damn. She hadn't realized it was so tightly wound.

A bolt broke free with a loud 'crack,' and she flung herself instinctively to one side as it whistled past her cheek.

This was not going to end well.

She glanced around quickly, then snatched for a wrench.

Not enough to stop it. But she didn't really need to stop it, she just needed to slow it down, so it could release the pressure without breaking itself to pieces …

Another bolt hissed by overhead, leaving a deep dent in the wall behind her head.

Damn. Damn, damn, damn. She didn't need to be giving her ship any more dents, for heaven's sake.

"Jez? Where are you? I thought you were on your way back." It was Tae, and he sounded slightly worried.

"One sec," she managed, then dived to the ground again as a thin sheet of metal embedded itself in one of the walls.

Get it under control. Get it slowed down, and get it under control. What did she have …

She looked down.

Cord. There were a couple lengths of cord in the tool kit.

Shred her hands to the bone if she tried to hold onto it, but if she could just get some weight behind it …

She looped it back and forth between two of the railing spokes a few times, then holding her breath, she edged the end of the cord towards the wildly-spinning drive shaft.

There.

A scrap of spinning metal caught the end of the cord, yanking it from her hands. She watched breathlessly as it wound between the metal spokes fast enough to smoke.

For a moment, nothing seemed to happen. The drive was shaking harder now, and she was certain it would tear itself to pieces.

Something else flew past her, slamming into the door frame and tearing out a chunk of the beautiful old wood, and she winced.

Plan B, then. Whatever the hell plan B was.

But …

Was it her imagination?

No. It had slowed, a little. She was pretty sure.

But now there was a thin curl of smoke from the spinning shaft.

Damn. Time to slow it down more.

She grabbed another piece of cord, wound it through the railing, and fed it carefully into the drive.

It was definitely slowing now, but the smoke from where the first cord wrapped around the shaft was thickening and blackening.

She glanced around again, then grabbed a crowbar. She pulled out a utility knife and hacked a long strip from the bottom of her tunic and wound it tightly around the tool as padding.

Probably a bad idea, but then again, most of her most brilliant ideas were, at their core, bad ideas.

She nudged the bar gently towards the spinning motor.

There was a 'thunk' as it caught, and for a moment the drive slowed enough that she could see the individual components, straining against the bar. Jez sprang to her feet and sprinted for the door, and just as she reached it, the drive picked up one last burst of speed and flung the crowbar, whirling end-over-end, into the air. She dived for the entrance as it hit the wall of the bay with enough force to dent the metal, ricocheted, bounced off the ceiling, and embedded itself in the paneling of the door frame.

She breathed a sigh of relief, and turned back to the drive.

It was still spinning, but much more slowly now, almost sedately.

The cords were wound tightly around the shaft, and they were blackened, but, thank heavens, not yet on fire.

She grinned.

Well, that had worked. Hadn't been completely sure it would.

Lev would have had an absolute fit if he'd been here.

She waited a few moments as the drive slowed more.

There was a faint popping sound from the floor and walls, and she frowned. Maybe just a reaction to the shrapnel of bolts and hyperdrive components that had been flung at them over the last hectic couple minutes?

No, didn't sound like that. It sounded more like—a power issue, maybe. She couldn't tell.

She glanced back over at the drive. Compared to what it had been doing before, it looked like it was almost standing still. But if she were to try to put her hands in there now, she probably wouldn't have any hands left by the time she pulled them out again. Give it another couple minutes. No hurry now that it didn't look like anything was going to start on fire.

The popping came again.

The anti-grav, maybe?

"Hey, Tae," she said, tapping her com. "You got the gravity fixed?"

"No. It wasn't a grav issue, it was a power issue. The meltdown messed up the core. Where are you?"

"I'm just in the reactor bay. Wanted to check something out. I'll be back in a sec."

She picked up the crowbar, now twisted almost in half, and poked carefully at the drive. It slowed noticeably.

That was good.

She watched the spinning shaft for a moment.

It had been under a lot of pressure, but she'd checked that it was unhooked from the rest of the ship before she'd tried this. Shouldn't even have turned anything on, just a pressure release. So what was the popping?

Power issue, Tae had said.

She wrapped her hands in the sleeves of her jacket and touched the warped piece of metal that had been a crowbar gently to the drive shaft again. It clunked, almost jerking the bar out of her hands, slowed, and, finally, stopped.

She breathed in a long sigh of relief and, hands still protected by her jacket sleeve, reached in gingerly.

It spun freely now, when she gave it a cautious tap. Lost a few minor components, but looked like nothing structural damaged.

She cut the blackened cords off the axel with a utility knife and pulled them gently free. She'd have to come back here sometime and put it back together right, but the sight of it, still functional when everything else on her ship seemed to have been torn to pieces, felt like a weight lifting off her shoulders.

She gave a slightly shaky smile.

Maybe she was wrong. Maybe they could get used to things going right every so often.

The popping came again, louder, and she glanced around uneasily. She stood, and peeked out into the corridor. The warm, old-fashioned lights set into the walls were flickering.

She frowned, her unease growing slightly stronger.

Then again, maybe not.

20

Impact minus 11 hours, Ysbel

Ysbel made her way to the weapons tower, Tanya close behind her. Neither of them spoke, but Ysbel could see the concern on her wife's face.

Still, at least this was a threat they could fight. And, at least if they were going to die, she'd prefer missiles to slowly suffocating.

When they reached the tower, Ysbel pulled out her familiar tools and set to work disassembling the guns. Tanya sat beside her, their knees touching, and the familiar rhythm of working together made Ysbel's heart ache unexpectedly.

"It's been a long time, hasn't it?" asked Tanya. Ysbel nodded, because for some reason she couldn't seem to speak.

They worked in silence, and even with the five lost years between them they moved with the rhythm of each other's work, she handing Tanya a tool before Tanya needed to ask, Tanya placing a part in her lap before she knew what she needed. Her hand brushed Tanya's once, and Tanya leaned in to kiss her, and she had to blink back tears.

"How's it coming?"

She started as Tae's voice crackled through her earpiece. She glanced down at the com. It had been almost three hours, but working together with Tanya had lulled her into a sort of trance.

She looked at the components in her hands, and then over at Tanya.

"My love?"

Tanya frowned. "I have everything together that I can, but I'm missing the S-clamps. It looks like they were burned through when the ship went down."

Ysbel tapped her com. "Tae. Do we have S-clamps? I have the guns mostly together, but I won't feel comfortable until we get the S-clamps replaced. All of the ones here are burnt out. I'll need thirty or so. Do we have them?"

There was a short pause. "I don't know. I'll go back to the main deck and sort through, see if I can find anything. We may have to see if we can find a work-around."

Ysbel looked at Tanya, shaking her head. "I'm not sure how—"

Tanya held up a hand. "Ysi? Did you hear that?"

Ysbel paused, frowning. "Hear—"

Then she did hear it, a faint popping sound.

"What—"

It came again, slightly louder. She exchanged looks with Tanya, and tapped her com. "Tae. While you're up by the cockpit, maybe check the ship's com. I'm hearing something back here that I don't think I should be hearing."

"What is it?" came Tae's voice instantly.

"It's a popping noise. It's coming from under the floor, I think."

"Give me a minute. I'm almost there," said Tae, voice strained.

The popping sound came again, louder this time.

"It sounds like something sparking," said Tanya, her face cut with unease. "Ysi, I think we should—"

"Get out!" Tae's voice snapped over the com. "The reactor meltdown cut the power matrix. The blast doors are shutting down. Get out, or you're going to be locked in."

Tanya and Ysbel looked at each other.

"The children," said Ysbel.

Tanya was down the ladder first, and sprinting towards the back of the ship where the cabins were, with Ysbel close on her heels. She came to an abrupt halt, and Ysbel barely managed to stop before running into her.

A steel lockdown door had clanged shut at the end of the corridor, barring their passage.

"Tae! Can you open it? The children are in the cabins," Ysbel shouted.

"I'm sorry. I can't get it back online," said Tae, his voice strained. "I'm trying now."

"I'm going to blow it up," said Ysbel grimly. "Stand back."

"Ysbel. Don't. Those blast doors are completely non-reactive. Your explosion won't do anything but use up oxygen," said Tae.

"I'm not leaving my children there alone," said Ysbel grimly. "If the blast doors have shut, the life support systems back there will shut off too. I won't leave them like that."

"Hey Ysbel. What, you worried I'm going to be a bad influence?"

She stared at her com for a moment. "Jez?" she said.

"Yep. Saw the doors shutting down and I figured someone had to grab the kids. They're not old enough to swear properly yet."

For a moment, Ysbel felt lightheaded with relief.

"You beautiful pilot," she said.

"Careful, pretty sure you're married," Jez shot back, and Ysbel could hear her grin through the com. "Better get going. I'm guessing everything's going to be shut down pretty quick here."

Ysbel nodded, still staring at the com.

"Ysi. Come on. We can't get to them. We'll have to trust Jez to get them out," said Tanya grimly. Around them, the popping, sparking sound of the power shutting down was growing louder.

She shook her head, grabbed Tanya's hand, and they sprinted for the main deck.

21

Impact minus 7.5 hours, Jez

Jez slapped her com off and glanced around the darkening corridors, then took off running towards the cabins, ignoring the pain knifing through her ribcage.

The doors out were already shut. She'd heard them slam in front of her. Still, there'd be time to worry about that once she'd gotten the kids.

The lights dimmed as she pulled herself up the ladder-hatch, and by the time she reached the cabins, the hallways were all the way dark.

Of course. If the blast doors were shut, the emergency systems would be shunted to the front of the ship.

No light, no fresh oxygen. But then, they wouldn't have to worry about that, because there'd be no heat, either, so they'd freeze to death long before they had time to run out of air.

She hit the light on her com, and in its narrow beam, she found the door to the children's room. She pushed it open gently, and by the light of her com, she could see Olya huddled up against the wall. She was holding Misko, who had shoved his head into her shoulder.

Olya's face was very pale.

"Mamochka?" she whispered.

Jez tried to grin. "Nope. It's your favourite aunty."

"Aunty Jez!"

The relief in the girl's voice made her feel slightly uncomfortable.

"Aunty Masha's my favourite aunty," came Misko's muffled, slightly sullen voice.

"Well, no accounting for taste," said Jez. She came over and sat down on the bed beside Olya. "Hey, kid. You OK?"

"I'm fine, Aunty Jez," said Olya. Her voice was trembling a little. "We heard the noises, and we woke up, and Mama and Mamochka were gone. But I knew you wouldn't leave us here."

For some reason, something choked in Jez's throat.

"Yeah," she said. "No way I'd do that. Who'd I be able to teach to gamble if you weren't around?"

"Are we going to go find Mama and Mamochka?" asked Misko, lifting his head off his sister's shoulder. He looked like he'd been crying.

"Yep. We'll go find them. It … just might take a little while," she said, trying to keep her voice carefree. "You stay here. I'm going to go into the hallway and talk with Uncle Tae for a minute."

"Are you going to come back?" asked Olya. "Promise?"

"Promise," she said with a grin, holding the light up so the girl could see her face. "I'll be right back. Just need to check on something."

"OK," said Olya. She was watching Jez steadily with her pale face and her big eyes, and Jez swore quietly as she slipped through the doors.

"Hey. Tech-head. I've got the kids here. What is it looking like?"

There was a moment's pause. "Not looking great, Jez," came

Tae's voice after a moment. "Lev is going through all the specs he can find, but it's not going to be easy to get you out of there. And— it's going to start to get cold in there pretty soon."

"Yeah? Well, I used to live in Prasvishoni, so guess it'll feel just like home," she said, in what she hoped was a jaunty voice.

"We'll get you out as fast as we can. But you may have to hold tight for a bit," said Tae quietly.

"Yeah," she said. "Will do. Just … tell genius-boy to hurry it up, OK?"

"I will," said Tae. "We're working as fast as we can."

She turned slowly and pulled the door open to the kids' room again.

"Aunty Jez? Are we going now?" asked Olya immediately.

"Nope. Not quite yet, kid." She came over and sat down beside the kids again. She pushed herself back farther on the bed and leaned her back against the wall.

The cold was already seeping in through the small cabin. Out in deep space like this, if the power core wasn't running the heater, it wouldn't take long to get cold.

"Olya, can you grab the blankets? Put them around you and your brother, and I'll tell you a story, OK?"

Olya was still pale-faced, but she nodded and hopped off the bed. She gathered up the blankets from Misko's bed, and pulled up the ball of blankets at the foot of her own bed. Jez tucked them in around the children.

"How are my babies?" asked Ysbel quietly through the com.

They're fine. I'm teaching them swear words, she tapped back.

"Jez. I need to know. How are they?"

"Hey kids," said Jez. "Your mama wants to say hi." She hit the com. "Hey Ysbel. I got Olya and Misko here."

"Olya. Misko. How are you?" Ysbel's voice sounded almost unnaturally calm, but Jez heard the tremor in it.

"Hi Mama," said Olya, swallowing hard. "We're doing good. Aunty Jez is going to tell us a story. But—" She paused, and swallowed again. "But Mama, I want to go see you and Mamochka. Can we?"

She was blinking hard, as if trying to push back tears.

"Sweetheart," said Ysbel, her voice choked as well. "Mamochka and I are working to open up the doors. We'll see you in just a few minutes, OK? Listen to your Aunty Jez."

"You want me to listen to my Aunty Jez?" asked Olya, clearly skeptical. "Because last time Aunty Jez came over, Mamochka said —"

"This time, yes, my heart," said Tanya. "This one time, I do want you to listen to your Aunty."

"We're going to remember you said that, aren't we, Olya?" broke in Jez, trying to grin. Her voice was shaking a little with cold, and she couldn't seem to stop it.

"I'm cold," said Misko. Jez looked over at him. He had started to shiver a little as well.

"Hey, Misko," she said quietly. "Why don't you come over here and sit on Aunty's lap? That'll keep you a little warmer. You too, Olya."

"I don't want you. I want Aunty Masha," Misko grumbled, but he came over and settled himself in her lap. Olya joined him, and Jez pulled the blankets up around them.

Misko was a small, warm bundle against her, and Olya snuggled into her side. She put her arm around the kid and pulled her close, hoping her own body heat would somehow keep them a little warmer.

"You want to hear about the time that Aunty Jez got through three sets of police checkpoints with a ship full of counterfeit credit chips?"

They did. She told the story, and maybe she might have added in a couple parts to make it a little more interesting, but at least it seemed to keep the kids' attention. She glanced inconspicuously at her com as she talked.

They'd been down here for ten standard minutes so far, and already she had to concentrate to keep her teeth from chattering as she talked.

As long as the kids were bundled up, they'd last a little longer, but at this rate, it wouldn't be long.

She pulled off her jacket and added it to the pile of blankets. Goosebumps rose on her arms, but when Olya looked at her curiously, she shrugged and grinned.

"Talking makes me too hot. Thought maybe you kids could use the coat, since I'm doing all the talking."

"OK," said Olya.

She looked like she believed every word Jez was saying.

Jez had to swallow hard against the sick feeling in her throat.

They trusted her. What had Olya said? She knew Jez wouldn't leave them.

People didn't depend on Jez. No one depended on Jez. Hell, before this whole thing had happened, she'd been about to blow this damn company anyways.

You stupid, irresponsible girl. She could still hear the disappointment in her father's voice. There always seemed to be disappointment there. *I wish for once in my life I could depend on you.*

She couldn't help it. She was pretty sure she hadn't ever been able to help it. She just couldn't seem to remember all the things she was supposed to do, the little, important things that she'd forgotten, or screwed up, or blown off, again.

You stupid innocent. It was Lena's voice this time. *I can't count on you to do anything. You can fly. Is that all? Is there anything else in that head of yours? Because I'm beginning to think there isn't. You aren't capable of being dependable.*

Well, she hadn't been wrong. After all, when she'd taken her leave of Lena for the last time, it was with Lena's ship and half the cargo she'd stolen as part of her last job.

I knew you wouldn't leave us, Olya had said.

She glanced down at the children again.

Lena was coming for her, after all this time. Well, according to Tae, she was coming for all of them. Some big rewards for all of them dead. But she knew Lena, and Lena wouldn't have agreed to work with the government unless she was desperate. So there was something else, too, something that had frightened even the smuggler boss.

In the end, Tae was right. Jez had spent her whole life running—running away from the messes she'd made, running away from her screwups, running away from relationships that had gone sour.

I'm not certain if you're even capable of fixing your problems, he'd said.

But looked like her problems had decided to come to her. And this time, there was nowhere to run.

She glanced down at the children again. Olya had started to shiver as well, and Jez pulled her a little closer.

I knew you wouldn't leave us.

Well, not leaving them may not have been enough.

"Hey! Jez, you there?"

She broke off the story and hit her com. "Yeah. I'm here. What's happening?" Her voice was shaking with cold.

"Listen to me. I think we can get you out. I'm just going to have to talk you through a procedure, OK?"

She stared at her com for a moment.

That did not sound anything close to OK.

Still—

Olya was watching her, wide-eyed, her teeth clenched determinedly to avoid letting them chatter.

"Yeah. Sounds good."

"Alright. I'll need you to get to the blast doors at the far end of the hallway. Can you get there?"

"Yep. Give me a sec."

She reached down and hoisted Misko off her lap. "Come on, kiddo. Time to walk."

"I'm cold, Aunty Jez."

"I know. I'm getting you somewhere warm as fast as I can. Come on, up you go. You too, Olya. Bring the blankets with. I don't know how long this is going to take."

The two children slid off the bed and stood shivering on the floor, the blankets and Jez's coat wrapped around them.

Her com cast a narrow beam of light as they walked to the blast doors, and Misko slipped his hand into hers. Olya walked ahead, clearly trying to pretend she wasn't scared, and Jez felt a slight pang. How many times had she pretended not to be scared, as a kid?

"We're here," she said over the com. "What do you need me to do?"

Tae sighed deeply. "Alright. I want you to open the panel to your right."

"Got it," she said.

"Now, I need you to listen carefully, OK? There are ten sets of wires in there. They're various colours, but I want you to grab the blue one."

She shined her light into the mass of wires and components, trying to push down the creeping tension rising in her chest.

This was the kind of thing she'd never been good at. Because you had to pay attention and focus, and neither of those were what she'd call strengths of hers.

"Alright, tech-head, there's about five different blue wires. Which one?"

"No. There's a turquoise, and a navy, and then there's a—a true blue."

She glared at the com. "What?"

He sighed again. "Look. Like, this colour." The holoscreen flickered, and Tae's face appeared, worried and slightly exasperated, then he pointed it at a small bundle of wires under the control panel.

She squinted at the screen. "Sorry, looks green in this light."

Tae's face appeared again on screen. He was pressing his finger and thumb of one hand into his temples, as if staving off a headache.

He looked tired. But then again, she was starting to wonder if she'd recognize him if he didn't look tired, since that basically seemed to be his entire mode of existence.

"Can you turn the screen around and show me?"

She obliged, and for a moment he was silent.

"That one," he said at last. "Up in the top corner."

"This one?" she touched a wire.

"No! Not that one. The other one. On the other side."

She rolled her eyes and grabbed the other wire, jerking it out of its casing.

"What are you doing? You're not supposed to pull it out! Anyways, you got the wrong one again. It's the one just below that. You'll have to put that one back in."

"Make up your damn mind," she muttered, shoving the wire back into its hole. It was harder than it looked, since she could only use one hand, as her other wrist was holding the com light steady. At last she managed it, and flipped the screen around.

"Got it."

"Good. At least we're not actually worse off than when you started," said Tae, through his teeth. She grinned at him through chattering teeth.

"Lighten up, tech-head. Told you this wasn't my thing."

"Well, it's going to have to be your thing for at least the next ten minutes," he ground out. She shrugged.

"I'm smart. I'll figure it out."

He muttered something that was probably uncomplimentary.

"OK, so I got your stupid wire. Which, by the way, is not blue."

"It is blue!"

She peered at it closer. "Nope. I'd say more of a purplish."

"Is this important?" Ysbel's voice sounded impatient, and there was a not-very-veiled threat in it.

"Fine. It doesn't matter. You're going to need to take that wire—"

"The purple one?" she broke in.

"Fine. The bloody purple one. Follow it to the other end, and it should be connected into a computer chip. Do you see it?"

She ran her finger along the wire, and touched a small chip.

"Got it." She peered closer. "Is it supposed to have ice crystals on it?"

Tae swore. "No. No it's not. Can you warm it up somehow?"

She bent down and blew on it. The ice crystals in the centre softened, but didn't melt.

"Just—"

"Don't worry. I got it." She pulled the heat-torch out of her back pocket, where she'd stashed it, and fired it up. Tae's expression went frantic.

"No! Jez, you can't just—"

She ignored him, bringing the white-hot tip close enough to the mass of wires that she could smell the chemical scent of softening plastic.

"Jez!"

"I know what I'm doing," she murmured. "Not an idiot, you know."

"No, I absolutely do not know that! What in the system—"

"Got it," she said smugly, shutting off the torch. "No more ice."

"If you'd gotten that torch even a tiny bit closer and melted a wire sheath—" His voice was strained. She grinned at him.

"Well, I didn't. So no need to worry."

He shook his head disbelievingly. "Remind me never to ask you to work on tech with me."

"Not going to get any argument from me on that one."

He sighed again. "OK. Now that you found the chip, you're going to need to disconnect the blue—" she opened her mouth, and he sighed. "The purple wire. But you need to pay attention to where it's connected, because once you get that off, I'm going to need you to connect it through a wire in your com. I think if you do that, I should be able to program in a temporary override which should, technically, open the door for long enough for you to get out."

"Yep." She jerked the wire free.

She was pretty sure she remembered where it had gone, anyways.

"Jez—" said Tae in a strangled tone.

"What?"

"Never mind." His teeth seemed to be permanently clenched by now.

She smirked at him for a moment.

"Aunty Jez, I'm cold," said Misko. She glanced down. He was shivering, and there were tears starting in his eyes. She crouched down.

"Hey buddy. It's OK. Uncle Tae and I will get you out, OK?"

He nodded mutely, and she stood up.

"Alright, Tae, what do I do now?" She found she didn't feel like grinning anymore.

"Open the back of your com. I'm going to explain it to you first, because I won't be able to talk to you while you're doing it. You'll want to pull out the red wire from your com chip, and then slip the chip out. Pull out the chip from the door control, stick it into the slot in your com, and connect the red wire where the bl—purple wire was before. OK?"

"Yeah," she said.

She actually had no idea what he was talking about, but she was pretty sure that he could explain it fourteen more times and she'd still have no idea what he was talking about.

Anyways, it didn't matter. She was just going to have to figure it out.

"Got it. I'm going to shut my com off, then."

"Alright," he said. His face was creased with worry. "When you get it connected it will show up on my com. Once I get the override programmed in, you'll only have a few seconds to get through the door."

"Got it," she said again. She took a deep breath and tapped off the com.

Damn.

She pulled the com off her wrist and flipped open the back. It was almost impossible to see the colour of the wires, since the only light came from the front of the com, but by shining it at the wall she was able to get enough of a reflected glow to sort of make them out.

"What are you doing, Aunty?" asked Olya. Her teeth were chattering now, even though her attempts to hide it.

"Just putting something together for Uncle Tae to work on," she said, trying to make her voice sound careless.

They weren't going to last a whole lot longer in here. The temperature was dropping noticeably now, and their breath puffed out in white clouds. She reached into the back of the com and tried to grab what she was pretty sure was the red wire, but her fingers were stiff and clumsy with cold, and it took her three tries. She finally managed, though, and wiggled the com chip out, slipping it into her pocket. Then she reached with cold-numbed fingers into the control panel for the chip. She got it out, but somehow she pulled another of the wires loose in the process.

Damn. Damn, damn, damn.

She had no idea where it went. She hadn't even been paying attention.

She closed her eyes for a moment, squeezing them tightly.

It was fine. She'd figure it out. She always figured it out.

"Aunty?"

She looked down. Olya was standing next to her on tiptoes, peering into the panel.

"It goes there, Aunty," she said, pointing to a tiny hole. Jez raised an eyebrow.

"How do you know?"

She gave Jez a look that somehow managed to be slightly superior, even through the obvious fear on her face.

"I was listening to Uncle Tae talk to you. And I'm good at remembering things."

"Well, that makes one of us," Jez muttered.

"What?"

"Nothing." She slipped the wire into the hole, and then, hand shaking slightly with cold, shoved the whole thing into her com. She grabbed the red wire and stared at the chip blankly for a moment.

"It goes there," said Olya, pointing.

She pushed the wire gently into its slot.

For a moment, nothing happened. And then there was a faint whirring, and then a 'bang' as the doors behind them slammed open.

"Go!" Jez shouted, yanking the chip free of her com and scooping up Misko. She sprinted for the door and half-shoved him through to the other side, then turned.

Olya was still standing where she'd left her. Her face was pale.

"Come on, Olya!" she shouted. The girl shook her head mutely, eyes wide and terrified.

The doors were shuddering. They only had seconds.

She sprinted back for Olya, snatched the girl bodily off the ground, and ran for the doors.

They were already closing. They were closing too fast, she and Olya were never going to make it—as she reached the doors, she pulled Olya in front of her and shoved her as hard as she could, through the crack that was barely wide enough to admit her.

Too late for Jez, but then that wasn't really what mattered at this point.

And then, just before the doors slammed shut, something was shoved into the narrow crack.

A steel bar.

What—

And then, slowly, the doors crept open. She stared.

The blast doors were impossible to pull open. The pressure would never let you—

"Get through here, you idiot!" came Ysbel's strained voice. And Jez jumped, and slid through the entrance, and the door slammed shut behind her, twisting the bar out of Ysbel's hands and crushing it.

She stood panting and shivering in the corridor.

"Are the kids alright?" she managed, through chattering teeth. And then Tanya had grabbed her in a hug, her grip so tight Jez almost couldn't breathe.

"Thank you," Tanya whispered, her voice choked. "Thank you."

She let go of Jez and grabbed up Olya. Ysbel was already holding Misko, and he was crying into her shoulder.

She smiled to herself for a moment, and then she felt something on her own shoulder. She turned. Lev slid his jacket over her, and his arm lingered around her for just a few moments longer than strictly necessary.

"Jez. You alright?" he whispered.

"Fine," she said through chattering teeth. "Just a little cold."

He studied her. "You look—sad."

She tried to grin. "Nope. I'm fine. Just got used to being off Prasvishoni, I guess."

He watched her for a moment longer. At last he nodded. "Alright." He turned to Ysbel and Tanya. "Let's get Olya and Misko into the mess hall. I imagine they're hungry, and it's warmer in there."

At the mention of food, Misko stopped crying and perked up, and the eight of them made their way down the corridor towards the promise of food and warmth.

Jez waited until everyone had started off before she followed.

I knew you wouldn't leave us.

She'd never been dependable. Never. That was basically the opposite of who she was.

But—the thing was, you couldn't run forever.

The moment she snapped at Masha, told her she was leaving, she'd known that, but she hadn't *known* she'd known it until she was sitting in the dark with Misko and Olya.

You couldn't run forever.

She'd run when her family had kicked her out, run from Lena, stolen her ship and took off, run from job to job to job, run from the police and from other crews, from the explosion in her old safehouse, from every damn mistake she'd made in her life.

But it had caught up with her now. Here, on this broken corpse of her ship, with these stupid idiots who drove her crazy, and who she'd die to save, it had caught up with her.

That was the thing. One day, you had to turn around and face the thing you were running from.

And, well—maybe, for once in her life, she'd actually do the right thing.

Because no matter what Tae said, they weren't going to get away before Lena got here. Even if they got the ship running they weren't going to be able to out-run Lena. But if she could get on board Lena's ship by herself, get caught—she was pretty damn sure she could keep Lena distracted. Yeah, Jez would never make it back to the ship, but hell, she'd cheated death so many times in the past few hours, it was probably about time for it to catch up with her.

And maybe she could actually protect her crew, for once, those two kids, instead of running off and getting them farther into trouble.

Sure, Lena was after all of them. After the reward. But she knew

Lena.

And Lena hated her.

And one day, you had to face things. You'd always have to, one day.

22

Impact minus 7 hours, Tae

Tae looked around as they huddled in the mess hall.

The lights were flickering, but at least the heat and grav system seemed to be functioning.

As a list of things they had going for them, it was pretty short. But it was something, he supposed.

Ysbel placed Misko on his chair, and Olya climbed into hers. Her face was still pale.

"I'm sorry, Aunty," she whispered as Jez walked into the room. "I'm sorry I didn't come when you told me to. I—I got scared. I'm sorry."

Jez had a strange look on her face, half affection, half something else he couldn't read. She came over and knelt beside Olya's chair.

"Hey Olya. Listen. You were the only reason we got out of there. Ask Uncle Tae. There's no way I would have remembered where all those wires went on my own."

Tae blew out a breath, half of exasperation, half of amusement.

The fact that Jez had managed to survive this long was something of a miracle, on more counts than one.

"We all get scared sometimes," Jez continued softly. "It's OK. Not a big deal. Aunty's been pretty scared before."

"I thought—I—I thought I was back in jail," Olya whispered. Jez patted her on the knee.

"Nah. No need to worry about that. If someone threw you back in jail, your aunty would break you right back out."

Olya had recovered enough to shoot Jez a skeptical look. "You got beat up pretty bad last time you did that."

"Yeah? Well maybe it was all part of the plan," said Jez with a jaunty grin. "You think he could have beat me up if I didn't let him?"

"Yes," said Olya firmly. Jez grinned.

"Guess you don't know your aunty well enough, then." She stood and started to stretch, then swore colourfully. Tanya shot her a look, but it contained less animosity than it usually did.

"Tae," said Masha at last. "I'm sure you've looked through the systems. What are we working with at this point?"

Tae sighed and gestured helplessly around the small table. "This. We're alive, and there's still a spot on the ship that's warm and has power. That's all I have."

Jez raised an eyebrow and shot the room a slightly smug look. "Well, I have something."

He turned to her, frowning. She grinned at him.

"Guess you haven't checked the hyperdrive lately."

He stared at her. "What?"

"I said—"

"I know what you said! What are you talking about?"

She shrugged, still looking very smug. "Well, I fixed it."

"You—what? I didn't spend much time with it, but I couldn't even get it to—"

"Good thing you have someone on the ship who's good with tech," she said, smirking.

"I—"

"I believe we got the shields online as well," said Lev quietly. Tae noticed that he shot a glance at Jez as he said it, and his face flushed slightly, and Jez steadfastly refused to catch his eye. Tae raised an eyebrow.

Whatever had happened in the engine room, it was pretty obvious that neither of them wanted to talk about it. Which was just fine with him. What with Tanya and Ysbel, he'd walked in on enough kissing in the last few days to last him a lifetime.

"I didn't finish wiring up the guns," said Ysbel, "but I did get all the components in. We won't be able to get into the gun tower, obviously, but I think I may be able to rig something up so we can fire them from here. Or if not, at least put in some mods for some of the front guns. They aren't the guns you used to take down the wall cannons in prison, but they should still be able to do a substantial amount of damage."

"See Ysbel? I knew there was a reason I liked you so much," said Jez, grinning. "Any woman who can blow things up like you can can't help but be hot."

Both Tanya and Ysbel turned to glare at her, and she snickered.

Still—

There was something strange in her expression. Something a little bit wistful, and a little bit sad, and she was trying very hard to make sure no one saw it.

"You said you got the hyperdrive back online?" asked Tae again.

"Yep. There was a piece of shrapnel lodged in the floor that was blocking the shaft from spinning."

He frowned. The pressure on that would have been immense.

"How did you release it?"

She shrugged. "Melted the shrapnel down with a heat-torch."

"What?" He stared at her. "You—you just—"

"Yep." She was smirking.

"You—how are you still alive? That amount of pressure—"

She shrugged. "I'm good at ducking."

"It should have torn itself apart!"

She shrugged again. "Slowed it down with some cord. And a crowbar."

"You—" he stared at her for a moment, speechless.

"You're just jealous you didn't think of it first."

He couldn't formulate a response, so he just stood there, shaking his head in a sort of awe.

"Well then," said Masha briskly, "we may have more going for us than we thought."

"I—suppose I should go back into the cockpit and check, then," Tae murmured.

Jez grinned. "Don't worry, tech-head, I'll come with. Probably could use a hand. You know, someone who's actually good at tech."

"Jez, you're not—" He gave up.

When he reached the cockpit, he crouched down in front of the paneling, and Jez slid into the pilot's seat. There was still a trace of old anguish in her expression as she ran her fingers over the lifeless control panel. Then she turned to him with a sort of forced cheerfulness.

"Well?" she said. "You want to check how much of a genius I am?" She paused. "I mean, we all know I'm brilliant, but still—"

He shook his head with a faint smile, and ducked his head inside the compartment.

He'd spent hours, fiddling with the burnt wiring, replacing the tiny components, until he felt as if he'd rebuilt the entire control panel of the ship from the ground up. His legs were cramped from crouching, and the burns on his hands, even through the bandages, throbbed.

But if this worked …

He squeezed his tired eyes shut for a moment.

"Here," said Lev from behind him, and his com light illuminated the small space. Tae glanced up at him gratefully, then gingerly followed the path of the wiring.

"OK Jez," he said softly. "I'm going to reconnect the wiring to the power core. You'll have to be delicate with it, but now that the tracker's gone we should be able to pull it back online without another meltdown."

Technically.

"Ready when you are," Jez murmured, her voice serious for once. He took a deep breath and connected the wires, then flipped the switch to allow power flow.

"Alright," he said, glancing up.

Jez's eyes were half-closed, as if she was trying to listen to the ship through her fingertips. Gently, gently, she tugged back on the lever that would pull the ship online.

Below him, he could feel the faint hum of a ship powering up. It was jerky and unsteady—only to be expected, since after the meltdown they had maybe a fraction of the power the ship needed to stay alive—but it was there.

She pulled the stick back further, and the humming grew. The ship trembled slightly, and Jez froze. And then, gently, she pulled it that last few centimetres, and it clicked into place.

He didn't dare move for a moment, hardly dared breathe as he waited for the shaking, the ominous racing of an unstable power core on the verge of meltdown.

But there was nothing.

He blew out a long breath, his shoulders slumping in relief. Jez turned to him and grinned, and something glistened in the corners of her eyes.

"She's back," she whispered, almost reverently. She swallowed hard. "I mean, I know she's not going to be able to—we won't be able to—But—" She swallowed again. "Even just for a few minutes," she said almost to herself, voice soft. Her hands were spread on the control panel, as if she wanted to catch every movement, every hum, as if she was trying to memorize them, even weak and sick as they were. Like he'd imagine you'd memorize a loved one's face as they lay dying.

He took a long, steadying breath, blinking back his own tears.

The *Ungovernable* had been a good ship. She'd been more than a good ship, and even though he didn't go completely off his head for ships the way Jez did—losing her hurt more than he'd expected it to.

But maybe, just maybe, she'd save their lives one last time.

"Alright," he said after a moment. "I'm going to try to pull the shields online. Hold tight, and watch the power. If she starts to run away, shut her down."

Jez gave a brief nod, and, carefully, Tae re-connected the shields, wire by wire.

"Try it," he whispered, and Jez eased back on the shielding controls.

The shield section of the control panel lit up, and on the ship's holo screen, a faint blue glow appeared surrounding the dot that was their ship.

Tae couldn't fight a relieved smile.

"Don't have all of them online, and the ones we do have don't have much power. But might be enough to hold us together until

Lena shows up." Jez was grinning again, a weak sort of a grin, but still a grin.

They pulled the weapons online next. Finally, he looked at Jez.

"Ready to try the hyperdrive?" he asked.

Her shoulders were tense, her whole posture tight, but she gave a shallow nod.

He re-connected it, and gingerly, she pulled it online.

For a moment, nothing happened. Then an entire section of the control panel lit up, and the ship's hum steadied slightly.

Jez turned to him, her grin almost as wide as her face. "Told you I was good with tech."

He shook his head, but he was smiling.

"So," said Ysbel from behind them. "Does this mean we might live through this after all?"

"We might," he said softly. "It will take a few hours to get the hyperdrive powered up, but … as long as it powers up before Lena gets here, it's just possible that we might."

It took him and Jez a few more minutes to pull the weapons online. They were able to power them up, but Ysbel had been right —the gunner tower wasn't going to come back online, and even if it did, they had no way to reach the tower and actually use the guns. They'd be limited to what she could do from the cockpit controls. Still, the fact that the weapons system was functional again was an almost dizzying relief.

"Alight, Ysbel," said Lev quietly. "This is your expertise. What do you need from the rest of us?"

"I'll need someone to go out again to work on the external parts while I work from in here," Ysbel said tersely, without looking at Lev.

There was a sudden tension in Lev's posture, and then, as if with an effort, he relaxed slightly.

"I'll go," he said, his voice quiet.

"You'll go out there again over my dead body, genius," Jez said, her grin turning dangerous.

"Jez—" Lev turned to her with some irritation. "I'm not—"

"There's a lot of things you're not," she snapped, "and one of them is going out that damn airlock one more time."

Tae smiled slightly to himself and shook his head.

Who knew Jez was the protective type?

"Jez," Lev tried again in a pained voice. "I'm no more likely to get hurt out there than anyone else."

Tae noticed that, as he spoke, he cast a quick glance at Ysbel, and he frowned slightly.

Ysbel wouldn't. Would she?

But the thing was, she could have. If she'd wanted to.

And despite the fact that everyone on this damn crew was going to leave him once they were able to get back planet-side, the thought hurt.

"Look," said Jez in a strained voice. "I almost watched you die out there once, OK? I'm not doing it again, not right now. Got it?"

"Anyways," said Ysbel grudgingly, "Tae is probably going to need you in here, to get the ship ready for when Lena arrives. So Jez is right."

Lev turned to look at Ysbel. He studied her for a long moment, expression a mixture of caution and curiosity, but finally he nodded. "Very well."

"Which leaves me and Masha," said Jez, her dangerous grin returning. "And since Masha's a useless bastard—"

"Useless bastard or not, I'm going to need two people out there if you're going to do what I need you to do," Ysbel broke in, "so you may as well save your breath, pilot-girl."

Jez smirked at her. "Don't worry, Ysbel. I have plenty of breath to go around."

"Yes, well you'd better start using it to get your suit and helmet on." Ysbel glanced down at her com. "We only have about seven hours left."

"Seven hours left before what?" asked Olya in a small voice, and Tae glanced over at her. She seemed to have recovered somewhat from her ordeal in the lockdown, but her face was still paler than usual.

Jez grinned. "Seven hours until your mama shows you what it looks like when smuggler ships get shot down." She pushed herself painfully out of the pilot's seat. "Anyways, guess Ysbel's right. No point in wasting time. Going to need some weapons to hold her off until—" she broke off abruptly, grin faltering for just a moment, and Tae frowned, watching her. "Until we can get the hell out of here," she finished at last.

He watched her as she left the room, her gait somehow jaunty even with her limp. Masha was watching her too. Then she turned and followed the pilot out of the room, and Tae sighed and turned back to the control panels.

It was still a basic problem of timing. The missiles were going to get here in seven hours, and Lena was going to get here in eight, and the hyperdrive would take at least seven and a half to fully power up, maybe more. With the hyperdrive fixed, it was just possible that they'd be able to get away, and with the shields and weapons repaired it was just possible they'd survive long enough to make a jump, even without the thrusters online. But if they did, it would be a very, very close thing.

23

Impact minus 6.5 hours, Jez

Jez glanced over her shoulder at Masha as they pulled on their suits.

Thankfully, the blast doors between the airlock and the cockpit hadn't shut down in the power outage, but the only suits they had were the ones hung in the airlock itself. Which meant Jez was pulling on a suit that was noticeably too small, while Masha's suit hung on her slightly, making her look like a kid trying on her parents' clothing.

The comparison worked until you actually looked at her. And then you realized that there was no situation in which Masha would not look competent, pleasant, and damn scary.

Jez took a deep breath. The others would be in here soon, and she only had a minute, but somehow the words were hard to say anyways.

"Hey. Masha," she said finally. Masha raised an eyebrow and turned to look at her.

"Yes, Jez?"

Jez blew out a long breath. "Um. Listen. You—know how to work the hyperdrive, right?"

"Yes, I believe I do," said Masha, still studying her. "I haven't flown with it, but I believe I understand it well enough."

"Good." Jez paused. "I—OK, look, if something—if I—anyways, I thought it might be good if we had someone who could fly the ship out. Someone else, I mean."

Masha gave a slow nod, but her eyes were sharp. "I see."

"So listen. If you're going to make a hyperdrive jump without thrusters, it's going to be a bit complicated. Ship isn't going to survive it, but I guess we knew that already. And it's going to take some time to power up, especially with the power core damaged like it is. So what you're going to need to do is, take everything offline for a minute—leave the oxygen and the air pressure on, but even cut the gravity. Pull the weapons and the shields offline. And then, once everything's offline, you'll have to jam it in hard. You'll be able to feel it. It should jump, and you should get all the way through, not like last time when we were skimming on the edge of a jump. Hyperdrive will burn out after a couple minutes, so get Lev to plot you a course as close to a planet as you can make it. Figure once you get out of the jump, you probably won't have any sort of power left, because when the hyperdrive burns out, it will probably take out whatever's left of the power core. The hyperdrive will divert all the energy, so it shouldn't melt down, but it's not going to be functional. Get everyone in helmets before you go, and get the emergency oxygen tank as full as you can. You might still have enough backup power to run the life supports, but I don't know. But as long as you can get to shallow space, reach a busy shipping lane, you should be fine. You'll still have communications, I'm pretty sure, and someone should be willing to tow you, or at least pull you off the ship." She paused, and swallowed back the lump rising in her throat. "It—

probably won't even be worth towing her in at that point," she finished softly. "Don't think there'll be much left of her after a cold hyper jump."

Masha was still watching her. "Why are you telling me this?" she asked at last. Jez shrugged irritably.

"Told you, you bastard. Because as much of a damn plaguer as you are, Lev certainly isn't going to be flying this ship."

"And nor are you?" the woman asked quietly. Jez shrugged again.

"Never know what might happen. Figured it was better to have a backup plan."

She turned away to finish pulling on the too-tight suit, but she could feel Masha's eyes on her.

Tanya and Lev arrived with the oxygen tanks a few moments later, and Tae followed them into the room.

"I checked the tanks this time," he said. "There's no leaks in these ones, at least none I could find." His face was creased in concern. Lev said nothing, but he was watching her, and there was sharp worry on his face. She tried to grin at him.

A space walk sure as hell wasn't going to kill her.

He managed a small smile in return, and for some reason she remembered the feeling of his arms around her, the warmth of his body against hers, and a small, pleasant shiver ran through her body.

Which was completely stupid, because first, falling for someone like Lev was probably the stupidest thing she'd ever contemplated doing, and she'd contemplated doing a lot of stupid things in her time. And second—

Well, second, she was going back to face Lena. And after Lena was finished with her, she was pretty sure that anything else would be irrelevant.

She shrugged into her oxygen tank. Lev stood behind her, lifting it, and once she'd strapped it on, his hands rested on her shoulders for a brief moment, almost brief enough to have been an accident. She took a deep breath and cast a quick glance over her shoulder. His eyes were filled with concern, but he managed a small smile.

"Good luck," he said through his com. She nodded.

She wasn't nervous about the space walk. She'd done this about a million times.

But she was suddenly sure that leaving this damn soft-boy behind was going to be almost as hard as leaving this ship.

She and Masha stepped into the airlock, and Tae sealed the doors. She grabbed for the ladder as the gravity cut.

"You ready?" asked Tae through the com. She glanced at Masha, who was holding on below her.

"Got it, tech-head. You can open up."

"Alright. I haven't had time to work on the coms, so once you get out, you may or may not have communication. Three tugs on the line means you need to come in. But hopefully it was just a malfunction in Lev's helmet."

"Yep. We're good." She hit her com off, and a moment later there was a soft puff of pressure releasing, and the outer doors slid open.

She held onto the ladder until the pressure had equalized, and then she clipped her mag boots to the ladder rungs and began to climb.

Once out on the hull of the ship, she stood and stretched, glancing around. It had been a while since she'd done a walk, and even now, even with her ship lying cold and dead, there was something achingly beautiful about the vast black expanse surrounding them. Far off to one side she could see the faint green glow of a distant nebula, a swirling of colours and patterns too far off to make out, the fierce glow of distant stars and suns pricking tiny holes in the cold, endless black.

She sighed and turned. They'd have to go around to the underside of the cockpit, Ysbel had said, and moving with mag boots on took longer than you'd think.

"Jez." Masha's voice came through her earpiece, on the single channel.

She stiffened. "What?"

"You aren't planning on being there when we make the jump, are you?"

For a minute Jez didn't answer, just focused on moving her heavy mag boots across the ship's surface.

"Look," she said at last. "Don't know if Tae told you this, but it's going to be a timing thing. Missiles hit us in six hours or so. Hyper-drive takes about seven more hours to fully power up, maybe a bit more. Lena gets here right around the same time if we're lucky, and a little too soon if we're not. But I'm pretty sure I can keep her busy for a while, if I have to. OK?"

There was a moment of silence. At last Masha said, "While I appreciate the sentiment, Jez, you realize that she's not just after you."

"Yeah. I know that. But here's the thing—" she managed a jaunty tone, "I don't think you have any idea how much Lena hates me. Figure if push comes to shove, she'd trade the rest of you for me."

"I see," said Masha at last. They were silent for a few moments, and Jez focused on her boots.

Because she really didn't want to focus on what she'd just said. And she really, really didn't want to focus on what it would be like, trapped on Lena's ship, watching her angel ship disappear for the last time.

"Don't tell the others," she said finally. "They probably won't agree. Figure you won't care, though. I mean, it's not like I wasn't going to leave anyways, and besides, you pretty much hate my guts."

There were another few moments of silence before Masha spoke.

"Jez," she said at last, a strange note to her voice. "My first goal has always been to keep as many of this crew alive as possible. And there have certainly been times when I believed your actions were working against that goal. I will admit to having been frustrated, more than once. But—I've never hated you."

"Yeah? Not even when I got completely smashed right before we hit Vitali? Or when I staked all your credits on a game of fools tokens?"

"No, Jez. Not even then."

Jez shot a glance over her shoulder, but she couldn't make out Masha's expression inside her helmet.

She gave a small shiver.

Probably wasn't telling the truth. But—somehow, it had been a lot easier when she knew that Masha loathed her, and she loathed Masha back.

"Anyways," she said finally, "like I said. I wasn't planning on sticking around, so this is probably for the best. Besides, I guess Tae was right. You can't just run away forever. I'm going to have to face her sometime. May as well be now."

There was another silence.

"You know this may not be necessary," said Masha. "If Lena doesn't get here until after the hyperdrive is powered up—"

"Yeah. But seems like not a lot of things have been going according to plan lately."

They'd reached the cockpit now. She could see the others through the window, their faces focused and cut with strain. She managed a faint smile.

No. She'd been right. Getting these idiots back somewhere safe—that'd be worth it. Even if the thought of going back to Lena made her sick to her stomach.

"Well, Jez," said Masha finally. "I suppose I underestimated you. It's happened before."

"Look," said Jez, turning slightly. "I don't care. Doesn't matter. Just—get them out safe, OK? And don't let Ysbel kill Lev?"

There was a slight smile in Masha's voice. "I'll do my best."

"Yeah." She paused. "Thanks."

"Do you copy?" Ysbel's voice crackled over the main line, and Jez jumped.

"Loud and clear," said Masha, tapping the side of her helmet for the general line.

"Alright then. You'll need to do some hard work, so Jez, if you can't do something because of your ribs or your arm, let me know and I will try to think of a solution."

Jez tapped her helmet. "Ah, come on, Ysbel, you know me. I can do basically anything."

"I see." Ysbel made no attempt to hide the skepticism in her tone. "Then let's see if you can get the guns to release. I don't even want to think about how badly they're jammed up."

"On it," said Jez, grinning.

Ysbel had been right—the two massive front-cannons that poked out just under the cockpit were badly jammed. The strain on the blackened metal was visible even before Jez got close.

"We're here, Ysbel," said Masha into her com.

"Good. Can you show me what it looks like?"

Masha pulled up her suit's holoscreen, and swung it around so Ysbel could see the position of the guns. Over the com, Jez heard Ysbel suck in a quick breath.

"That's not good. But I think I can still make it work. Alright, here's what I need you to do."

Jez wasn't entirely certain how long they wrestled with the first gun, but it must have been almost an hour. She and Masha had brought cables and tackle lines, and she clipped the mag-winch to the hull of her beautiful ship, gritting her teeth the whole time, and finally, finally, with a grinding, twisting sound of tortured metal, the gun began to break free.

"Get back!" Ysbel shouted, and Jez and Masha retreated as quickly as they could with their mag boots sticking to the hull as the gun wrenched itself loose and swung free.

For a moment they stood there, breathing heavily.

"Good," said Ysbel. "Now I need you to do the same with the other."

The other gun was less badly jammed than the first, and even though the sound of the mag-winch scraping against the *Ungovernable*'s perfect hull made her wince, it didn't take nearly as long before they heard the tell-tale creaking and groaning.

"Get back," Ysbel grunted again, and Jez and Masha retreated.

And then Jez noticed the small loop of cord caught on a protuberance on the edge of the gun, and her breath caught. She started forward, hitting her com to shout to Masha, as the gun wrenched free.

Like she was watching in slow motion, she saw Masha jerked forward, saw the impact as the woman was slammed into the side of the gun and knocked sideways. The already-strained line tightened, frayed, and snapped. And Masha was flung outwards, towards deep space.

In Jez's earpiece, Ysbel swore and shouted something, but Jez didn't have attention to spare. She glanced around quickly.

Masha was already too far for her to reach with her line intact.

OK, well, that just made things interesting. She snatched the heat-knife out of its sheath on her suit.

"Jez." Lev's voice was panicked, "What are you doing? You can't —"

She grinned at him through the cockpit window. "Lesson one, genius-boy. I can do basically anything."

"Jez—" It was Tae this time.

She hit off her com.

There. Floating lazily beside the now-free gun, a wide, flat sheet of metal torn off the gun port. Something she'd never be able to lift in gravity, because it probably weighed double what she did, but that was the nice thing about zero Gs.

She remembered, for a moment, the engine room, and Lev.

One of the nice things, anyways.

Masha was drifting out further. Her body was limp. The impact must have knocked her out momentarily.

Served her right to be the one passing out for once. Jez was usually the one doing that, and to be perfectly honest, she was getting a little tired of it.

She grabbed the metal, hitting her suit controls to dial up the strength of the mag boots and letting them hold her in place as she pulled the twisted chunk of metal around in front of her.

The others were signalling frantically from inside the cockpit. She gave them a jaunty wave, took a deep breath, and with the heat knife, cut her line. Then she bent her knees, glanced up at the direction Masha was floating, and cut the power to her mag boots as she kicked off with both legs.

She glanced up and couldn't hold back her grin.

Perfect trajectory.

Then again, this sort of thing was kind of her specialty.

She wasn't going fast—her kick-off, which would have normally sent her shooting off in her chosen direction, had put her on a staid course with the added mass of the metal. Still, probably better this way. Yes, there were vanishingly-few times that going fast was not the best option, but this, she supposed, was probably one of them. As long as she was going faster than Masha …

She glanced ahead again.

Yes. She'd reach her in a moment …

There. She was just close enough to touch the woman's space suit.

As Jez grabbed her, Masha stirred.

Good. Because it would have been really irritating if she'd done all this and Masha turned out to be already dead.

She managed to shift the metal to one arm, and with her free arm she wrapped the end of her line around Masha's waist, strapping the woman as tightly to her as possible, with a slightly disgusted expression.

There were certainly people in the system she wouldn't mind being in close quarters with, but Masha was not one of them.

Then she moved so as much of her body as possible was in contact with the chunk of metal. She glanced behind her at the *Ungovernable*, receding into the distance, and for a split second, watching the dark of space that surrounded them, the gorgeous, velvety perfect blackness, she realized that if she didn't make it—well, she could think of a hell of a lot worse ways to die.

Still, that soft-boy idiot Lev was back there, and Olya.

I knew you wouldn't leave us.

Her stomach was tight with adrenalin. She maneuvered the bottoms of her boots against the chunk of metal, glanced back one more time to calculate her trajectory, and shoved as hard as she could.

The metal accelerated its course towards the perfect, endless black, and Jez, with Masha strapped to her, was pushed at a slow, almost leisurely pace back towards the *Ungovernable*.

She managed a shallow breath of relief.

She'd calculated it right. They were going to make it. All she had to do now was—

And then another piece of space-junk from the freed cannons, traveling so slowly it was ridiculous, bumped her shoulder.

It wasn't much, just enough to knock her into a slow spin. But—the ship was approaching fast, and where they were going to hit now on the hull, there were no handholds.

She gritted her teeth and tried to maneuver herself downward.

She had to hit feet first. She had to let her mag boots anchor them, because if she couldn't, they'd bounce off and now she had nothing to change her momentum.

She could probably save herself if she cut Masha free and shoved her off to one side, which was honestly somewhat tempting, but considering that the whole point of this damn exercise had been to save Masha's life, it seemed somewhat counterproductive.

She was getting closer, too close, and she wasn't going to hit with her feet at all, she was going to hit with her shoulder, and there was nothing she could do.

For a moment, cold, irrational panic washed over her.

She was going to die. She was going to have to make a decision, and either she or Masha was going to die.

She hit the ship, the impact enough to jolt her broken ribs. She swore, trying to twist in the air, scrabbling for something, anything to grab on to, but there was nothing, and her fingers brushed helplessly over the rivets on the smooth paneling that she loved so much. And then she was straining to reach them, and then they were out of reach as she drifted helplessly out towards deep space.

She closed her eyes for a moment and grabbed for her heat knife, and even as she did so she wasn't certain about who she'd push back towards the ship. And then something jerked her around, and she opened her eyes with a start.

Masha was standing on the hull of the ship, her mag boots hooked down to the metal. She untwisted the line, where Jez had tied them together, and pulled Jez in.

Almost in shock, Jez activated the mags on her boots and stood there breathing heavily.

She looked up and met Masha's gaze. The woman had blood running from her forehead and into her eyes from the impact with the gun, but for a moment the two of them locked eyes. And then Masha gave her a slight smile, and somehow, Jez found herself smiling back.

Masha tapped the side of her helmet with a finger, shaking her head, and Jez tapped her com on.

Lev was swearing in a long, steady stream, and she was secretly somewhat impressed at his vocabulary. She'd never known he had it in him. Tae was also swearing, and Ysbel was saying something that was probably very uncomplimentary, although her accent had thickened, like it always seemed to when she was upset, and besides, with Tae and Lev's admittedly inspiring diatribes, it was hard to hear.

"Hey," she said, smirking. "Didn't know you could swear like that, genius."

There was a moment of silence.

"Jez?" said Lev in a strangled tone.

"Yep."

"Where are you? Are you alright? Are you—"

"Relax. I'm here. Masha and me. We're good."

There was another moment of silence. Then Lev let loose another string of expletives.

"What the actual hell were you thinking?" he sputtered at last. "What in the name of everything holy or unholy were you—"

She shrugged, even though she knew he couldn't see. "I know what I'm doing."

"No, I don't actually think you do. Because no one in their right mind—"

"Who said I was in my right mind?" She was grinning broadly.

"Jez. Do you have Masha with you?" asked Tae, his voice just as strained as Lev's.

"Yep. Right here. She got hit, I think the impact killed her com."

"Alright." Tae took a long breath, clearly trying to remain calm. "Alright. Neither of you have anchor lines anymore, so I need you to make your way back to the airlock, OK?"

"Ysbel? You want us to do anything else first? Because I'm going to be honest with you, at the rate we're going through space suits, I'm not totally sure how many more times we're going to make it out here."

"You stupid, ridiculous, idiotic, crazy lunatic—"

"Take that as a no, I guess?"

There was the sound of Ysbel drawing in a long breath. "No. You did what I needed you to do. You hopeless—"

"Yeah, yeah, I got that part. Alright Tae, we're heading back. Meet you on the other side." She hit her com off and turned her grin to Masha. Masha raised an eyebrow. Jez jerked her head in the direction of the airlock, and they made their slow way back.

When they were inside, and the airlock re-pressurized, Jez unclipped her helmet and pulled it loose, taking a long breath of the ship's air.

Always tasted better, somehow, than the canned air in the suit tanks.

Masha did the same, and a moment later the inside doors slid open. Lev grabbed Jez, holding her at arm's-length to inspect her, then pulled her into a tight embrace that still managed to be gentle enough not to hurt.

For a moment she was too surprised to react, and somehow the feeling of him holding her, even through the bulk of her space suit, sent a tingling sensation through her body, and the side of her face was pressed up against his, and his warm skin against hers was surprisingly pleasant. She closed her eyes for just a moment, breathing in the familiar smell of him.

Since when had this soft-boy become so familiar? And since when had she thought that being held like this by him would be a good thing? It wasn't a good thing. In fact, it was a very stupid thing, and she was probably going to protest in just a minute.

As soon as she stopped feeling lightheaded.

Because to be honest, her head was feeling a little fuzzy at the moment, and she thought perhaps she'd enjoy it for a few minutes before she'd do something about it. And somehow, without her really thinking about it, her arms had gone around him as well, and he was whispering in her ear in a choked voice something about "You crazy, wonderful, ridiculous idiot." She'd never actually had someone call her an idiot in that tone of voice before, like it was something you'd say to a lover. And considering that she was completely unhurt, it made no sense at all that she was leaning against him like she wouldn't be able to stand on her own if he let go of her.

The sound of Ysbel clearing her throat jerked her back into full awareness.

"I said," said Ysbel, her tone a mix of irritation and amusement, getting back to her feet from where she'd crouched beside Masha, "while I am also very happy Masha and our lunatic pilot are alive, if we want them both to stay alive, I would suggest that we get back to the cockpit and make sure our weapons are functional, and then perhaps make a plan for what we're going to do when Lena's missiles get here in—" she glanced at her com. "Four and a half hours. Tanya and I will hardly be able to get it done as it is, and my understanding is, Tae, that you will need Jez and Lev if you're planning on getting everything online and functional."

Lev cleared his throat and stepped back slightly, and somehow she managed to stay on her feet. She turned a glare on Ysbel, who looked like she was fighting down a laugh, then to where Tae was finishing applying a bandage to Masha's forehead, and studiously avoiding looking at her and Lev.

"Alright, tech-head," she snapped. "If we're going to fix my damn ship, let's get going."

He glanced up, shaking his head slightly. "Jez, what in the system were you thinking back there?"

She shrugged. "I know how to work in space. Wasn't a problem."

"Except for the part where you almost died," he muttered. He glanced over his handiwork. "You alright, Masha?"

"Yes, Tae. Thank you," she said. She got to her feet, somewhat unsteadily, and caught herself against a wall for a moment before she straightened. "And I will second Ysbel's suggestion—while I'm very grateful that I'm alive, I don't think that will last long unless we get back to work."

Lev sighed. "She's right. Let's go. I don't even want to think about what trouble Misko's gotten into while we've been gone."

As they made their way out of the airlock and back towards the cockpit, Masha fell back so she was walking beside Jez.

"Jez," she said quietly, and Jez was surprised to see that her eyes were hard. Still, wasn't like she'd expected Masha to be particularly grateful—she hadn't done it for Masha. She'd done it so there'd be someone on the ship who could get them all out after she left.

And, if she would admit it, much as she hated the woman, she probably would have felt guilty watching her drift out into space without even trying to save her.

"What?"

Masha turned to look at her, her face grave. "You should have left me. My life wasn't worth the risk you took, and if we'd both died, everyone else would have as well."

Jez's stomach tightened with a familiar anger. "Yeah? Well, maybe I should have, you bastard. But an idiot tech-head told me something once, when he and the rest of them came back for me when maybe they shouldn't have—he said people don't do things like that to people. So shut up, OK?"

Masha studied her for a long time, head cocked slightly to one side. At last she gave a small smile. "I see." She paused. "I—suppose I should thank you. Although I disagree with what you did."

Jez gave her a smirk. "Well, guess that's better than no gratitude at all, you plaguer."

"I guess it is," said Masha, her tone ever-so-faintly amused.

24

Impact minus .5 hours, Tae

Tae clipped a connector in carefully. "Jez, power it up," he said, and a moment later there was a familiar hum. He let out a breath of relief and wriggled out backwards. The others watched him as he brushed himself off and stood, their faces a familiar blend of concern and the blind trust that he'd know what he was doing well enough to get them out of this.

"It's ready," he said. "At least, as ready as I can make it."

Tanya's face broke into a relieved smile, and Jez grinned widely.

"Knew you could do it, tech-head," she said.

He shook his head. He'd actually had no idea he'd be able to do it. But on the same token, he'd had no idea that Jez could cut her lifeline, push off out into deep space, and somehow make it back, so he supposed they were all pushing the limits of the impossible at this point.

"How much time before we can make our jump?" asked Masha, her face taut.

He glanced at his com. "The shields are up now, but it's going to be a solid hour plus before we can do a jump."

"So now we wait," said Lev. Tae nodded.

"That's all we can do." He tried to feel relieved rather than worried.

Still, he'd never have believed a few hours ago that they'd be this close to getting away. Not when they were sitting crippled and helpless in deep space, with their oxygen running low and their power dead and no shields as two missiles blasted towards them.

"Well," said Ysbel at last, "I should get the children ready for the jump."

"Put them in helmets in case the oxygen goes," Jez called over her shoulder.

"I'll go calculate our coordinates," said Masha. "Lev? Would you come please?"

Lev looked up and nodded. His face was unaccountably grim. He turned and shot a last worried look at Jez, then stepped out of the cockpit.

Tae shook his head slightly.

Apparently, being stuck on a dying ship was something of a relationship builder. In the airlock, in Lev's arms, Jez had looked completely drunk, and Lev had looked like someone had hit him over the head. Who would have thought?

He smiled to himself and glanced over at Jez.

Her eyes were closed, and she ran her fingers over the control panel like she was trying to memorize the feel of it.

He knew as well as she did how the ship would come out of this jump. Maybe with the thrusters, they would have lost the components designed by Sasa Illiovich. It would have been tragic, but they could probably have put something back into her and got her running again, as a sort of pale, weak shadow of her former self.

This, though—this jump would leave her a broken hull. There

wouldn't be anything worth salvaging.

"Tae," she said, after a moment, without opening her eyes.

"Yeah?"

"I—I'm sorry. For screwing everything up with Masha."

It seemed so long ago he could hardly remember it.

"Jez—"

"You were right, you know," she said quietly. "I always have run away. I guess I just got into the habit of it. But—I guess running away works better if you don't care about what you're leaving. Guess I hadn't really thought through what I'd be leaving this time."

He stared at her for a moment. Finally, he shook his head. "Jez, listen. It's fine. I'm sure—"

She opened her eyes and looked at him, and her grin had a tinge of weariness to it, and something that was almost regret.

"Nah. Don't worry about it. I'm sure everything will work itself out once we get away. I just—I wanted to tell you that. Because here's the thing—you're a good person. And I don't want to screw everything up, which I tend to do, and have you not know that."

He looked at her oddly. "I—"

She grinned. "Anyways. I'm going to grab something to eat. See you soon." She pushed her way to her feet and made her jaunty way out of the cockpit, and he stood looking after her, frowning.

There was something about the tone of her voice, the look in her face, that made him uneasy.

He shook his head and tapped his com.

Fifteen more minutes.

It took him about three minutes to clean up the wires and the extra components from the floor of the cockpit, and another two minutes to organize the tools neatly back in their places.

Waiting was always the worst part.

Ysbel appeared a few minutes later. Tanya and the children were with her. Misko looked slightly ridiculous in the oversized helmet, but it should keep him alive, at any rate.

Lev and Masha came in next. Lev glanced at the empty pilot's seat, but he didn't say anything, just sat down in the copilot's seat and began typing coordinates into the com.

Five more minutes.

Jez sauntered back in and dropped into the pilot's seat. She didn't look at him or anyone else, and for a moment he could have sworn he saw traces of tears on her face.

"Alright, Ysbel," said Masha quietly. "We'd best get the shields prepped."

Ysbel nodded and moved over to the side of the cockpit. Tanya joined her.

"I'm pulling the shields online, Ysbel," Jez said, still without looking at them. Ysbel nodded, and Jez pulled down the shielding lever.

"We're going to have impact in five minutes." Lev was watching the ship's com screen.

Ysbel had Misko, and was bracing herself against the wall. Tae pulled off his portable harness and tossed it to her. She shot him a grateful look and strapped the protesting Misko into it.

"Four minutes."

Olya slipped her hand into Lev's. Without looking up from the screen, he stood and lifted her into the copilot's seat, strapping her into the harness. He knelt beside the chair, bracing himself.

"One minute."

Tae took a deep breath, trying to steady his nerves.

"Four. Three. Two. One."

There was a moment's silence. And then the ship bucked and

rolled, tools and loose parts were flung across the cockpit. Tae put up his hands to shield his head, and Misko screamed, a thin, terrified sound.

Another explosion rocked the ship, and from behind him on the main deck came sounds of smashing and breaking.

And then, finally, the rocking and jolting subsided. Cautiously, he lifted his head from his arms and glanced at the ship's holoscreen, which was somehow still active.

"It looks like—" he let out a long breath of relief. "It looks like the shields held," he said, almost not recognizing his voice. "It looks like they actually held!"

They looked at each other, their expressions slack with relief.

Then he froze, staring at the screen.

No.

It was impossible.

He stared for a moment more, almost unable to breathe. He felt as if someone had hit him in the stomach and knocked the wind from him, that moment where his body seemed to have forgotten how to pull in air.

Lena's ships. Close enough for a visual. Maybe twenty minutes away.

"We miscalculated," he said, his voice sounding strange. "Looks like they were traveling faster than we thought."

And then there was a jolt, something almost like a puff of air, and the ship rocked, ever so faintly.

He locked eyes with Lev for the briefest second.

And then, without warning, the lights flickered and died, and the soft hum of the ship that had become so familiar over the past few hours he hardly noticed it anymore, disappeared.

"What—" Lev began in the darkness.

"Why are the lights out, Uncle Lev?" asked Olya, her voice small.

"Tae?" asked Masha, her brisk voice showing a sudden hint of concern.

He didn't answer for a moment.

Twenty minutes out. That was about the right range.

He'd recognized that feeling, recognized the wild spike of lines on his com screen.

He'd seen them before. He'd seen them plenty of times before. Because he'd been the one who had made them.

"Jez," he said quietly.

"Yeah." The tone in her voice told him she'd figured out the same thing he had. "That EMP tech the government stole from you."

He nodded, even though in the dark no one could see him.

There was a moment of silence.

"Well, tech-head," said Jez at last, and there was a tone in her voice he couldn't read. "Guess that's the disadvantage of being so good. Least it didn't take out the life support backup."

"Lena will shoot us out of the sky, then," said Ysbel softly.

"Nah," said Jez. "I know her. Probably sent those missiles so we'd power up, get the shields going, so she could knock us offline. She won't kill us until she talks to us first. Always looking for an angle, Lena."

Tae stared down at the blank screen.

Not that they needed a screen. Lena was close enough for visuals now.

And there was nothing he could do.

25

Post-impact, Jez

It was pitch dark, but Jez knew this ship like she knew the shape of her own body, and she could get around it as instinctively as you twisted sideways to get through a narrow doorway. She slipped out the cockpit door as Lev's com light illuminated the space.

The cabins were cut off, but she headed back for the small storage closet behind the cockpit, where she stored her spare clothes and whatever else she might need on short notice.

Lena would be here in twenty minutes.

I knew you wouldn't leave us.

Funny how a kid could make you rethink your whole life.

It wasn't like she'd thought about it. It wasn't like she'd sat down and thought to herself, as soon as I start getting soft-eyed over that ridiculous scholar-boy, as soon as these idiots start feeling like friends instead of coworkers, that's when I'm out. It had been Masha, and her damn rules, and her ideas that everything had to happen just so, and her inability to take risks.

But Tae had been right. It had been almost a reflex—she got into a fight with Masha, and she didn't know who would win the fight, and she didn't want to find out if Lev and Tae and Ysbel would take her side, or Masha's. And she couldn't deal with everything that would come with trying to make things work even after everything she and Masha had said.

So she'd decided to run again, like she always did. And she hadn't even thought about what that would do to the others, because she was never around for that part. She'd go in and start a fire and get back out again before she had time to get burned.

But there was something about this damn crew that had pulled her back in, right into the middle of the flames.

Still, probably came a time in everyone's life where they just couldn't run anymore.

Lena.

It had been a long, long time, but that name still had the power to scare her, just a little.

Lena, who had once, almost, been the mother and father she'd lost. The crew that she'd once naively believed would replace her family, after her family threw her out as a skinny, frightened fourteen-year-old, with nowhere to go and no-one to turn to.

And for five years, she'd chafed under Lena the same way she chafed under her father, but at least under Lena she'd been allowed to fly.

And she had flown. She'd flown things no one else in that damn crew could fly, even as a fourteen-year-old.

She opened the tiny ship's closet and pulled down a couple of pieces of old clothing. Behind them hung her pilot's jacket, and she pulled that out as well and reached into the pocket.

Her fingers brushed something inside of it, something small and round and hard, and she smiled to herself.

A piece of the cargo she'd lifted off Lena, when she'd stolen her ship and run. The thought brought a smile to her face, even now.

Hell. Lena would be ecstatic to see her. Probably be the best day of her damn life. Because Jez was pretty sure after she stole Lena's ship, and then after the others had almost blown up Antoni when he'd come after her on Prasvishoni, killing Jez had probably become Lena's fondest dream.

Jez grinned to herself slightly. She wasn't exactly looking forward to this, but still, she had to admit, it was nice to be appreciated.

She rolled the change of clothes into a bundle and shoved them into her tattered bag, and shrugged on the pilot's jacket. She flipped on her com light quickly and looked around.

Anything else she needed? Probably not.

Anyways, she had no idea what Lena would have planned for her, and it may not involve her living long enough to need a change of clothes and some toiletries.

But the thing was, whatever it was, whatever Lena had planned, Jez was almost certain she'd be able to make it last long enough to give the others a chance. Masha was at least a little bit right. Jez had never been good at not attracting attention. And good thing, because she was about to attract a hell of a lot of attention in just a few minutes from now.

She looked around one last time and sighed. Her hands shook slightly, and her heart was beating a little faster than it probably should be.

Guess after everything, she was more afraid than she'd thought she would be.

Still—she gave a slight shrug. If you weren't afraid of something you were about to do, you probably weren't living hard enough.

She'd use an escape pod. Even if the EMP tech had disabled everything, there were manual controls on those. She should be able to eject, and then manually steer the thing in the direction of Lena's ship. And once she got close enough, she could use the harpoon to pull herself in.

Shouldn't be a problem.

And the best part was, there was no one else on this ship who could pull that off. Once she was gone, there was no danger that any of the others would come after her.

It was an odd feeling, really, to think that they probably would have. They almost certainly would have.

There was a lot about her idiot crewmates that she didn't understand. And there was a hell of a lot about the strangely-lightheaded, giddy feeling she got every time she damn well brushed fingers with Lev that she didn't want to understand. But somehow, she did understand that. They'd never leave her behind, not if they could help it. Which was exactly why she was going to make sure they wouldn't be able to help it.

Least she could do, she figured.

She hoisted her small bag and stepped back out of the confined space and back into the main hallway of the ship, and almost bumped into someone.

She tensed.

"Jez." It was Masha, and she let out a breath of relief, shoulders dropping.

"Hey Masha. Just on my way off ship. Remember what I told you, OK?"

"Of course," said Masha, in her usual calm tone. She flipped the light on her com, illuminating her face in shadowy light. "Good luck."

She managed a grin. "Thanks. Same to you."

She made to step past the woman, but Masha put out her hand.

"Jez. A moment. I think you forgot something."

Jez half-turned, and Masha's hand came up, and she only had time to realize the woman was holding something small and white, and to catch a whiff of the strange, sweet smell of it, before the world went completely black.

Lev caught the unconscious Jez as she fell and lowered her gently to the floor, then flipped on his own com light, illuminating the small corridor.

"Well," said Tae at last. "That was almost frighteningly effective."

"I did tell you," said Masha. "I am somewhat proficient in sleeping gasses."

Lev looked down at Jez, her eyes closed, her face somehow almost peaceful, and shook his head. "She was going to the escape pods?" he asked.

"I suspect so," said Masha. "Although I didn't wait to find out."

"How long until she wakes up?"

Masha glanced down. "From the amount I gave her, I'd say maybe twenty minutes."

Lev sighed again. Something inside him hurt, just a little, to see Jez like this. Still, there's been no other way, because talking Jez out of something once she'd decided it was a good idea was, he'd learned, singularly ineffective.

"Alright," he said, straightening. "I guess we have twenty minutes to come up with a plan, before she wakes up and decides to go anyways." He paused, and glanced at Masha. "I—thank you. For telling us."

Masha smiled her pleasant smile, but there was a trace of warmth behind it that he wasn't sure had been there when he'd first met the woman. "You were right, Lev. Jez has gotten the rest of us out of enough sticky situations in the past. I believe it's our turn to do the same for her."

Tae glanced at his com. "We'll have to work fast. Lena will be in com distance in ten minutes, and close enough to initiate boarding maneuvers in fifteen."

Lev nodded and gestured at the floor, and the rest of them took their seats. The bluish glow from the com lights threw strange shadows on their faces, and on the unconscious Jez lying behind them.

"Alright," he said, pulling up his com holoscreen. "What do we have on our friend Lena?"

26

Post-impact, Ysbel

The dark bulk of Lena's long-haul ship blocked out any view of the sky from the cockpit windows. Ysbel glanced over at Lev, who'd taken his customary seat in the copilot's chair.

"You ready for this?" she asked quietly. He glanced over at her and gave her a quick, strained grin.

"Ysbel. I may have mentioned this before, but I don't love getting shot at."

"Well, let's hope they don't shoot at us, then," she said.

The ship shuddered as Lena's airlock hooked on. If it had been running, the *Ungovernable* would have held them steady. But besides the soft whir of the life support backup systems, their ship was as dead and lifeless as a piece of space-rock.

"Prepare to be boarded," came a woman's voice over the com. It was hard and cold, the voice of someone accustomed to being obeyed. "I warn you, do not try to fight. If you do, I promise you, I'll blast your ship to space dust."

"Are you ready?" asked Ysbel. Lev sighed and nodded, pushing himself to his feet. He came to stand in front of her, and put his wrists behind his back. She looped them together and pulled them tight, and he winced slightly as the cord cut into the skin of his wrists.

"I'm sorry," she said automatically.

He shook his head. "Don't be." He paused a moment."Ysbel," he said in a low voice. "I know there's nothing I can do to take back what I did to you, and to Tanya, and to Olya and Misko. You have every right in the system to kill me after this is all over. But I—I'm sorry. I can't tell you how sorry I am, and how many times I've regretted it, and how many nights I've stayed awake thinking about it, and I—" he paused for a moment, his voice choking, and she frowned. She couldn't remember ever hearing Lev choke up.

"I'm sorry. That's all. I'm sorry for what I did to you, to all of you. To little Olya. I just wanted you to know that, before—in case—" he broke off abruptly, head dropping to his chest.

His shoulders shook slightly.

Was he crying? Lev?

He took a deep breath and wiped his cheek against the shoulder of his jacket. "I'm—sorry."

She stared at him, speechless for a moment, something uncomfortable twisting inside her.

How was it possible to hate someone this much, and at the same time care about them so much that watching them cry hurt?

She opened her mouth to say—something. She wasn't sure what.

And then there was the sound of heavy boots along the corridor, and she pulled out her heat pistol and shoved him forward. He went down on his knees, and she placed the pistol against the back of his head.

And then the cockpit door burst open, and five armed figures burst through.

For a moment they stared at Ysbel and Lev, weapons raised.

"Drop your weapons! Hands up! Now!" the leader of the smugglers screamed, shoving through the others. Ysbel threw her heat pistol to the ground with disgust and raised her hands.

"That's fine. As long as you don't take your weapons off this scum."

Two smugglers jumped forward and grabbed her, wrenching her arms behind her back and securing them with mag-cuffs. They patted her down quickly, removing another heat-pistol from her boot holster, then turned her around and shoved her face-first against the wall. Out of the corner of her eye, she could see them doing something similar to Lev.

"Where are the others!" the leader shouted. "Tell me now! Where are they? I'll shoot you both!"

"There's no point," said Ysbel, her voice heavy. "They're gone."

"Turn her around," the leader growled, and two smugglers took Ysbel by the shoulders and shoved her to her knees in front of the woman. The hard knot of a gun barrel ground into the back of her skull, but she didn't look down.

The woman stood in front of her. She was medium height, with pale skin and pale hair.

Not Lena, then.

But, judging from the look in her eyes and the arrogant tone in her voice, someone with some sort of position in the crew.

"Tell me," she growled, glaring down at Ysbel.

"That man over there," said Ysbel, jerking her chin towards Lev. "He killed them."

The woman frowned. "He doesn't look like he could kill a space jelly."

Ysbel gave her a bitter smile. "As you can see, our ship was damaged in the hyperjump. The oxygen converter went down, and we only had enough oxygen for forty-eight hours, give or take. At least, with eight of us on board, that was all we had. We've been trying for the last day and a half to fix it, to no avail. And then an hour ago I came back from where I'd been working on the shields. And I found this man. Alone. It was a good thing I'd been gone. He vented sleeping gas into the cockpit where the others were working, and then he loaded them into the escape pods and ejected them. My—" She paused, swallowing hard. "My family was on those pods." She stopped again, dropping her head. She had watched her family go to their deaths twice already, and the memory of it still sent panic racing through her veins and tears welling in her eyes.

"I wanted to kill him," she said, when she'd recovered her speech. "But I knew you were on your way. And so I thought perhaps I could use him as a bargaining chip instead."

The woman was watching her coldly. At last she gestured with her head, and two of the smugglers dragged Lev in front of her.

"Is this true?" she asked. Lev tried to raise his head, but the guard behind him forced it down again with the barrel of her pistol.

"Yes," he muttered. "There was no way we were all going to survive, not with the oxygen as low as it was. With only two of us, there was a chance we'd last at least until you got here."

"So you killed the others," she said, faint amusement in her tone. "Well, boy, you may have miscalculated. My boss wanted them. There was one of them in particular she wanted badly."

"Jez?" he asked, looking up finally. There was a weary expression on his face. "She's long gone. She was killed by a piece of shrapnel about twelve hours back, when she was trying to get the power back online after a core meltdown. We let her body go into space."

"Ah," said the woman, her smile growing just a little. "And that's why you didn't mind killing the others. We heard from our informant that you and she may have had an—understanding."

Lev didn't answer.

The woman turned back to Ysbel. "So we're here just in time to save you from suffocating. If that's the case, you won't object to being brought on board our ship, then." She gestured to the smugglers holding Ysbel and Lev.

"Get up," said the man behind Ysbel, shoving her forward. She almost lost her balance, but managed to stumble to her feet. Someone planted the nose of the heat pistol hard into her ribs.

She could, of course, grab it. With how close the man was standing, she could twist out of his way and grab the heat pistol in her cuffed hands, and then she could pull back the heat sink and set off an explosion that would kill every person in this room.

But instead, she bowed her head and walked forward, with Lev shoved along behind, out of the cockpit and down the silent hallways of the dead ship to the airlock, and on to Lena's ship.

27

Lena's ship, Lev

Lev stumbled forwards, trying to keep his balance on the smooth flooring of the smuggler's ship. After the blackness of the last twenty minutes, lit only by the dim glow of their com lights, the brilliant, cold lights of Lena's ship half-blinded him. The smuggler shoved him ahead of her, the barrel of the gun a hard, dull pain in the back of his head.

"Keep moving," she grunted, and at her sharp push he almost lost his balance again.

He caught only jumbled impressions of the ship they were passing through—harsh lines, stark panels, bare hallways. And then the woman grabbed his shoulder and shoved him up against the wall, his face pressed hard against the cold metal.

Beside him, another smuggler stepped forward, and with a soft *hiss*, the doors in front of him slid open. Lev's captor jerked him around and pushed him hard, and he stumbled through the doorway, lost his balance, and fell hard without his hands to catch him. He winced as his face slammed into the deck, and then some-one grabbed his shoulder and hauled him into a kneeling position.

She shoved the gun back into position, and he dropped his head at the pressure on what was shaping up to be an impressive bruise at the base of his skull.

From the corner of his eyes he could see Ysbel kneeling beside him, although he was pretty sure she hadn't landed on her face on the deck first.

In front of him, the sharp sound of boots clicking off the hard floor approached. He looked up for half a second before his head was shoved back down.

A woman was walking briskly towards them. She was strong-looking, with straight black hair and sharp features and eyes that were as cold as deep space.

And even from that brief glance, he knew exactly who she was.

The footsteps stopped in front of him, and he stared down at shiny black boots.

"Where's Jez," the voice snapped, and there was a cold menace in it that sent a shiver down his back.

"Sorry, Lena. These were all we found. This one—" someone kicked him, and he almost lost his balance again. He gritted his teeth and drew in a long breath. "Apparently he knocked the others out and sent them out on the escape pods so he could conserve oxygen. He said Jez was killed earlier, when they were trying to deal with a meltdown."

There was a long pause. Then something cold and hard pressed into the hollow under his chin. The pressure on the back of his skull eased, and the woman in the black boots tipped his chin back with the muzzle of a heat-pistol.

Lena.

She wasn't tall—Jez would be a head and a half taller than she was easily—but there was something about the way she stood that demanded respect. He recognized her from pictures he'd seen, but none of them fully conveyed the hardness in her eyes, the sense of menace in her posture. There was a tension about her now, like a hungry dog that had sensed its prey.

"Where is she?" the woman asked, her voice soft with threat.

He allowed some of the strain of the last few hours to show in his face. "Jez? She's dead. I put her body out the airlock myself."

Lena's expression didn't change as she pulled the pistol out from under his chin and swung it sharply against the side of his head. His vision burst with stars, and he fell awkwardly, teeth gritted against the sharp, shocking pain. She let him lie there for a moment, then gestured, and the smuggler behind him hauled him upright again.

Something warm and wet trickled down the side of his head, and he had to blink to steady his vision.

"I asked you a question," she said calmly.

"I—"

She hit him again, and again he went down, his ears ringing with the blow. Again, the smuggler hauled him back upright.

"Where is Jez Solokov?"

"No point in that," came Ysbel's voice from behind him, heavy with disdain. "She's dead."

Lena straightened and turned towards Ysbel. Through the blood trickling into one eye, he could see the thoughtful expression on her face.

"Tell me what happened," she demanded. Ysbel narrowed her eyes.

"Jez died about twelve hours ago. The rest of them—" she took a deep breath. "The rest of them, this man killed, to conserve oxygen. He knocked them out with sleeping gas and put them in the escape pods. You can kill him if you want. I don't mind."

Lena glanced over his head at the smugglers who'd brought them. "Did you check this?"

The woman behind him nodded. "Two escape pods were launched, but I have people checking the ship now. They're scanning for heat signatures. If there's anyone alive on that ship, we'll find them."

Lena nodded, and crouched in front of Lev again.

"You must be Lev," she said. "I've read your files. You're a cold-hearted bastard, aren't you? If someone was going to kill the rest of the crew, it would be you."

He tried to fight back a faint annoyance. It would be nice if people didn't automatically believe that he'd spent his life patiently waiting for the opportunity to kill all his crewmates.

"But you didn't think this one through. You have no idea how badly I wanted Jez. If you were as smart as your files say, you'd have saved the body to show me."

He clenched his teeth and didn't say anything, and a slight amusement appeared on Lena's face.

"I'm sure Jez would have been a very enthusiastic lover, until she got bored of you. Was that it? My prison contact guessed the two of you were sleeping together. So you kill an entire crew, including two children, but you can't bring yourself to hold onto your lover's dead body to use as leverage? That was very stupid, Lev." She pressed the pistol harder into the hollow under his chin and he strained his head back and shifted to ease the pressure.

She smiled. "Or is it something else? She's still alive, and so are the others, and the two of you are trying to save them? You might want to re-think that. I've known Jez for longer than you have. If there's one thing you can depend on about her, it's that she'll run. Not someone worth dying over."

He didn't answer, but there was something cold and angry stirring in his chest.

Lena, he'd discovered, was not someone whose company or conversation he enjoyed.

Lena leaned forward. "If there's someone hiding on the ship, I'll find them. I can make you hurt in ways you can't imagine, and if I find anyone hiding, I'll do it. And I'll do the same to them. The government wants you. They want you bad. And I have a reward coming for proving I killed you. So if there's someone alive and you want to keep them that way, better start talking now."

"There's no point in appealing to that man's higher sentiments," said Ysbel from behind him, disgust thick in her voice. "He doesn't have any. When this dirty bastard looks at the system, all he sees is what he can get out of it."

Lena glanced towards her, then back at Lev. She gave a small smile, then removed her gun carefully from under Lev's throat. He almost relaxed. Then she swung, and again he fell awkwardly to the deck, his head singing with lighting pain. Lena crouched beside him, and through the blazing stars in his vision could see the expression on her face, a hard fury that she was no longer even trying to disguise.

"I wanted Jez," she hissed. "And if I don't get her, you and your friend will pay for it."

She stood, examining him for a moment, then kicked him hard in the stomach. He doubled over, gasping for breath, and Lena turned away.

"Take them somewhere you can watch them until you're done searching the ship," she said over her shoulder.

Lev was hauled to his feet and shoved, half-staggering with the pain pulsing in his head, out the door.

'Somewhere you can watch them' turned out to be a narrow room somewhere behind the main deck, with a couple uncomfortable chairs and a bare, stark metal table, welded into the deck. One of the smugglers pushed him into a seat and cuffed his ankles to the chair legs, and another did the same for Ysbel. Then the smuggler took her place in the doorway, heat pistol loose in her hands and posture that of someone who knew how to use it.

Lev blinked against the throbbing pain and shifted slightly in his seat. The woman raised her pistol a fraction, although he wasn't entirely sure what she thought he was going to do—bite her to death, maybe, since that seemed to be the only part of him that was unrestrained.

It didn't matter, though. He'd managed to shift so his wrist com was touching the back of his chair. He jiggled his leg, channeling Jez, and hoped it would be enough to disguise the faint tap of his com against the back of the chair.

Tae. Did you get enough of a visual through my com? I was doing the best I could, but it wasn't much.

"Got it," Tae's voice whispered in his earpiece. "But I don't think I'm going to show Jez that footage. Are you alright?"

I've decided I prefer not getting hit in the head with the butt of a heat pistol, he tapped back. *But barring a concussion, I'm fine. I've been going through my specs. I think this is a PKT class, probably a redwing model. Five, six years old.*

"That helps," said Tae. His voice was slightly distracted. "I'm going to pull Jez on and see what other info she needs." He paused. "She's probably going to swear at you. She swore at me. And Tanya. And Masha. And I think basically the system in general."

Lev sighed. *I think I can handle Jez swearing. Put her on.*

Jez did, in fact, swear at him. Fluently and at length. When she finally seemed to run out of either breath or creative ways to curse him, he tapped, *I got Tae some specs. He'll send them on to you. Is that enough?*

"You scum-sucking plaguing bastard," she said through her teeth. "I can't believe Masha told you. And I can't believe you let her use sleeping gas on me, you plaguing—"

Jez.

"Fine. Yes, that's enough. I'm not a plaguing egghead like you and Tae. Don't need nearly as many specs as you all seem to." She paused the familiar jaunty edge returning to her voice. "Lena's losing her touch, by the way," she said. "Guess losing her best pilot put her down in the ranks a bit. This ship is kinda crap, to be honest. Even with the fancy government mods."

Is that all you need? He tapped out patiently. *Because if it's not, I can try to—*

"It's enough, genius," she said, and he could hear the grin in her voice. "Trust me. I've been waiting for this for a long damn time."

28

Lena's ship, Jez

Jez tapped her com off and glanced off to her side. Masha was crouched to the side of the small walkway beside her, her face set and slightly grim, but still, somehow, pleasant.

Of all the damn people in the damn system to work with. She'd much rather do the job alone.

Of course—she put out a hand to steady herself against the wall. Of course, when Masha had plaguing drugged her with plaguing sleeping gas, she'd basically put that option out of commission. Because it was surprisingly hard to stay steady on your feet when you were just waking up from being plaguing well knocked out by your plaguing crewmates.

It wasn't necessarily being knocked out by her crewmates that surprised her—quite frankly, she'd always figured if she was crewmates with someone for long enough, they'd probably eventually want to knock her out.

It was the fact they'd knocked her out to save her damn life.

And that Masha had been the one who sold her out.

It was annoying as hell, but—well, but at the same time, if she stopped to think about it, about Lev and Ysbel tied up on Lena's ship and Tae and Tanya and the kids hiding back in the engine room, and Masha—who, by the way, she still basically hated—crouched beside her, she was pretty sure she was going to maybe start crying or something.

Which, again, was completely stupid.

"Ready?" she whispered. Masha gave a short nod. Jez stood, swayed slightly, cursed under her breath, and grabbed the wall for support.

"Do you need a hand?" Masha asked, with a slightly ironic smile. Jez narrowed her eyes.

"Go to hell, Masha," she whispered. Then she took a deep breath and stepped forward onto Lena's ship.

A heady mixture of anticipation and fear tingled through her body as she stepped into the main body of the ship.

Lena.

It had been years.

She closed her eyes for a moment and pictured the diagram Tae had sent through to her com, and then slipped off down a corridor to her right. Masha's footsteps followed close behind.

This corridor should lead down to the lower deck, and from there, she should be able to access the hatch that would take her into the engine room. This ship was a soulless thing, all metal and hard lines, nothing like her beautiful *Ungovernable,* but it was a ship, and she knew her way around a ship.

They weren't going to steal it, although stealing a second one of Lena's ships would have been frankly amazing. But she wasn't going to leave her *Ungovernable*, she would have died rather than do that, and—well, and the others must have known that when they were making plans.

Nope, they were going to do the second best thing. They were going to damn well cannibalize it. Lena'd given her the best smuggling ship in the system last time Jez had left her. Well, 'given' might be a stretch. And now she was going to fix the *Ungovernable.*

Maybe she'd learn to appreciate Lena one of these days after all.

They'd only made it about ten metres when she heard footsteps from the junction behind her. She looked ahead to where the corridor branched, then glanced back at Masha.

"Rafal?" came a woman's voice from the opposite corridor. "That you?"

They flattened themselves against the walls of the corridor, Jez hardly daring to breathe.

"Rafal?" the woman's voice called again, and the footsteps hesitated at the branch in the corridor. Jez glanced around quickly.

The corridor was narrow, and brightly lit with stark white bar-lights set into the ceiling. Nowhere to hide.

Then from the other branch of the corridor, an irritated voice called, "Rafal is on the other plaguing ship, hunting for warm bodies."

The footsteps, which had hesitated for a moment, restarted, and the smuggler woman said in clipped tones, "Andrik? I thought you'd have finished in the engine room a long time ago."

"Not as easy as it looks," the man's voice grumbled. "Natalia is still down there, trying to make up for how hard we've been running her for the last sixty hours. She wasn't built for this kind of strain."

Natalia. Jez gave a fond smile. The woman probably still wanted to skin her alive, honestly.

The footsteps moved off, and Jez let out a quick breath of relief.

And then the second set of footsteps turned purposefully at the fork in the corridor. Jez locked eyes with Masha for a moment, and they ran.

Jez had no idea where she was going, except that it was away from the sound of following footsteps. She turned a corner, blinking as her vision blurred slightly.

Damn Masha and her sleeping gas.

The footsteps turned as well. She swore.

There. Ahead. A maintenance closet.

She reached it, jerked the door open, and swayed slightly as Masha slipped past her. Masha grabbed her by the elbow, pulled her in, and swung the door shut behind them just as the smuggler rounded the corner.

Through the crack in the door, Jez could see the man coming down the corridor. He was short and wiry, with dark hair and medium-brown skin, and she didn't recognize him, which meant he must be new to Lena's crew in the past four years.

He frowned slightly, looking up and down the corridor. Then he shrugged, and started walking again.

The door to the maintenance closet was open a crack, and Jez bit the inside of her cheek as he came close.

He paused in front of the door, and she felt for her heat pistol, but he just shoved it all the way closed and continued past.

Jez let out a breath and turned on her com-light.

"Well," she said, her voice only a little shaky. "Guess we didn't do too bad." She pushed at the maintenance cupboard door.

It didn't budge.

She swore, and pushed it harder.

Nothing.

"Seriously?" she whispered.

Masha's disapproving sigh came from close behind her. "Are we locked in?" she asked.

"Not locked. Just no handle from the inside," she said.

"Let me," said Masha, stepping past her. Jez stepped grudgingly out of the way, and the woman pulled something sharp out of the pocket of her coat. She twisted it a couple of times, and there was a faint 'ting' as something small and metal hit the floor on the outside of the cupboard. She gave the door a slight push, and it swung open.

She didn't even glance back at Jez for her reaction, which was actually slightly irritating, because Jez had had no intention of showing that she was impressed. She slipped out of the door, and Jez followed.

They walked quickly, and it was only a minute or two before they reached their destination—the hatch to the engine room.

And three smugglers, standing over it, deep in conversation.

Jez narrowed her eyes and stepped quickly back around the corner. Lena'd let things slip since she'd been on the crew. Pretty sure the damn woman would have threatened to slice her throat three different ways if she'd been lazing around the plaguing engine room chatting.

She could shoot them, which would be satisfying in its own way, but would also probably mean they'd be caught and killed. So probably not the best plan.

She turned and gave Masha a wink, and, before Masha's face had time to register alarm, she straightened her coat, pulled her toque down over her hair, and strode out into the room.

"What the hell are you dirty plaguers doing! Does Lena know you're bloody well using up all her oxygen chatting? Because I'm just about to—" She was shouting as loudly as any of Lena's crew-managers, but probably the other crew-managers wouldn't have been grinning like complete idiots.

The three smugglers scattered down the hallway like their boots had been scorched with a heat-torch. She threw a jaunty grin over her shoulder at Masha, who was glaring at her, bent to pull open the hatch, and almost toppled over.

She muttered something about plaguing idiots with their plaguing sleeping gas as Masha stepped around her and lifted the hatch. She shot Jez a look as she started her climb down, and Jez could swear there was a hint of smugness in her eyes.

When her head had stopped spinning, Jez touched her hand to her pistol, took a deep breath, and started after Masha.

The engine room at the bottom of the ladder was small and cramped, with a roof low enough that she had to hunch over uncomfortably to avoid banging her head on the ceiling. But there, in front of her—what they'd come for. Two beautiful thrusters, newer than the ship if she was any judge, practically glowing in the faint reflected light from the open hatch.

Be a little less beautiful once she'd pulled out their insides, but still —

She took an almost-unconscious step towards them.

Then a woman with shoulder-length grey hair and wiry muscles stepped around the side of the thruster. The momentary flicker of shock in her eyes disappeared almost instantly, to be replaced with a dangerous satisfaction. "Jez," she said, her tone a mix of smugness and loathing. "Should have known you'd come sneaking around here, let someone else take the fall for you."

Jez grinned, every muscle in her body singing with adrenalin.

"Good to see you too, Natalia. Don't often meet someone so plaguing stupid that they run the wires wrong on a brand new ship, so I always figured you were something special."

The woman's eyes narrowed. "Jez Solokov," she almost purred. "Look at you, all grown up now. But you haven't gotten any smarter, have you?"

"Well, at least I haven't gotten uglier." Jez managed a smirk, then she threw herself to one side as the woman's right hook grazed her face. Pain jolted through her ribcage and another wave of dizziness hit her. She staggered, grabbing for the thrusters behind her for support. She threw up a hand in a probably-futile attempt to guard her broken jaw.

And then there was an unpleasant crunch, and Nataila dropped, eyes rolling back into her head.

Behind her, Masha dropped the crowbar she'd been holding, a slight smile on her face.

Jez raised her eyebrows, impressed despite herself. Then she blinked back her dizziness and knelt gingerly, pulling a length of cord from her pocket to truss the unfortunate Natalia.

"Hey Tae," she whispered into her com. "We're in. And guess what? Lena brought us some very nice replacement parts."

29

The Ungovernable, Tae

It was almost concerning how quiet the children were as they crouched behind the *Ungovernable's* ravaged thrusters. But Tae understood that kind of quiet. Olya was looking at him wide-eyed, and Tanya held Misko's hand lightly in hers, her finger to her lips.

From outside, the sound of boots crossed and re-crossed the engine room.

He'd gambled that the residual heat from the overheated thruster engines would block their heat signature, but that would only last for so long. They'd have to move eventually, because eventually someone would figure out the same thing he had.

Alright, Jez, he tapped carefully into his com. *I checked the thrusters. I'm going to send a list of parts through to your com. Do you know what make Lena's thrusters are?*

"They're Belokamsk," she whispered, in a voice that was almost reverent, and he rolled his eyes.

Alright. The parts won't be compatible on their own, but we should be able to rig them in. It looks like Sasa designed this thing to be pretty easy to work with.

"Watch what you're calling a thing," she whispered. "That's my angel you're talking about there."

He tapped his com again, sending off the list of parts.

"Got it," she whispered a moment later. "Hey Masha. You know how to use a wrench?"

Masha murmured something in the background, but Tae was fairly certain that Masha knew how to use a wrench. Tae was fairly certain that if you were stranded on a desert planet and the only way off was to tame and ride a wild harocat, it would just so happen that Masha had had some small amount of experience doing that exact thing at some point.

Outside, another group of boots tramped through the engine room.

"Have you checked in here?" asked a man's voice.

"Yes," a woman answered. "But everything is residually warm from where they pulled online to bring on the shields." She paused a moment. "Looks like they had a core meltdown at some point. I'm actually surprised this thing is still functional."

"Did you get behind the blast doors?" the man asked.

"Yeah. I checked, and they got the core reactor stabilized, so I was able to plug it into our ship's power core. Once she had full power, blast doors opened right up. Chilly back there, though. If there was anyone in there, they'd be an icicle by now."

The man sighed. "Well then, I suppose we go through room by room. Anywhere there's residual heat, there's the possibility they're hiding and their signatures won't show up."

Tae bit his lip and glanced down at the kids. They were completely still, hardly breathing, and Tanya's posture was a tense crouch.

He caught Tanya's eye. She nodded, and the four of them slipped around the opposite side of the thruster towards the engine room door. Tanya, Misko in her arms, reached the exit first. She peered outside and beckoned him forward. He gently pushed Olya after her mother, and with his heat pistol drawn, he crept out after them.

The hallway was deserted, for the moment at least, and he hesitated, gesturing the others after him into a small storage closet.

They needed to get the kids to safety—if there was any such thing on this plaguing ship at the moment. But he also needed, desperately, to get to the power core and get Jez a list of parts he needed.

"Tanya," he whispered at last. "I have to get the information for Jez. You take the kids and try to find somewhere safe."

Tanya gave him a look. "No. You stay here with the children. You tell me what you need to see and I'll show you on my com screen."

"I—suppose that would work. But if one of us is going to—"

She gave him a faint smile. "Tae. You are very, very talented at tech. But, and please don't be offended, you are not very good at sneaking around."

He sighed.

She wasn't wrong—over the last twenty minutes, he'd learned she was very much better at this than he was.

But—he glanced down at Olya and little Misko.

He'd never be able to live with himself if they lost their mamochka.

"I'm not asking you for permission," she said, slight amusement in her voice. "I'm only asking you to tell me what parts of the core you need to see over your screen."

"I—"

This time she did smile. "As I said. I'm not asking for permission."

He sighed. "Alright. Listen, then." He pulled up his holoscreen and flipped to a 3D model of the power core. "These are the places I'll need to see to start off. Once I know basically what's going on, I'll probably need to see more."

She studied the screen for a moment, then nodded. "Very good. I'll be back shortly, then."

She knelt. "Olya, Misko, my hearts, behave yourselves. And listen to Uncle Tae. Mamochka will be back soon." She stood, gave him a slight smile, and slipped off towards the reactor bay.

When she was gone, he leaned his head back against the wall and swore under his breath.

Ysbel would kill him. Lev would probably kill him too. Possibly Jez would also kill him, just for the fun of it. He'd just let Tanya go into what was probably a suicide mission, and he hadn't even tried to stop her.

She was right, of course. She didn't need his permission. But somehow Ysbel's visceral fear for her wife must have rubbed off on him. And he'd never be able to look the children in the face again if anything happened to her.

He strained his ears, listening to the voices, waiting for them to raise in alarm. She'd wait until they moved, of course, and who knew how long that would be. The hallway in front of the reactor deck was narrow, and there was nowhere to hide.

A faint tapping in his earpiece caught his attention.

I'm in. Turn on your screen.

He stared dumbly at his com for a moment, then flipped up the screen. Tanya's face appeared in it for a moment, then the view switched to the power core.

Behind the core, he could make out the forms of the three—no, four—smugglers in the hallway outside.

"How did you—" he began. Then he gritted his teeth. No time for that at the moment.

He studied the power core through the holoscreen, frowning. "There's an access port at the bottom of the outer shell, probably right about where your feet are," he whispered. "I need to see inside it."

She pulled it open, and he ran his eyes quickly over the connections. A few connectors melted, like he'd suspected, but not as bad as it could have been. The wires were a melted mass of metal and plastic, but that he'd assumed.

"Alright," he whispered. "I'd like to see the port on the other side, but it looks like—"

The screen shut off for a moment.

"Tanya, no!" he hissed. "It's not worth getting caught over."

The screen popped up again, showing a clear view of the open port.

She must be standing right behind the smugglers.

His stomach was a tight knot as he looked over the components, carefully noting each damaged piece. At last he whispered, "Got it."

Her screen flipped around, and he sucked in his breath in alarm. She was standing so close behind one of the smugglers that if either of them had leaned back, they'd touch. Tanya gave a quick nod, and then the screen cut out.

He squeezed his eyes closed for a moment and let loose a long string of curses under his breath.

"Uncle Tae?" Olya whispered. He glanced down at her, his chest constricting even further.

This was her mother. She's almost certainly seen the screen, and she was smart enough that she'd have figured out—

"You're worried about Mamochka, aren't you? Don't worry, Uncle Tae. She'll be fine." She didn't look even slightly concerned, a superior smile on her face. "She's very good at being quiet."

He knelt. "I'm sure you're right, Olya." He was speaking past a knot of combined panic and terror in his throat. "I'm sure she'll be fine."

She raised a superior eyebrow at him. "Well, you don't look very sure."

"Tae."

He jumped and bit back a curse. Tanya stood beside him.

He hadn't even heard her come in.

"If you have what you need, let's get somewhere a little safer. I heard them talking while I was in there. They're going to go over this sector for a second time very soon now. And it seems Lena's not overlooking anything. She instructed them to leave someone in each of the rooms with heat signatures, to ensure that no one can access a room that's already been checked."

He just stared at her for a moment, his entire body weak with relief, but there was no time for relief at the moment. They still needed to find a way to hide the children.

He paused a moment.

Behind the blast doors had been frozen for hours. Which meant everything in that sector would be freezing cold, including the first-aid kits.

He looked up at Tanya. "The cabins," he mouthed. "If we cover them with the reflective blankets, the cold should disguise our heat signatures, at least temporarily."

She glanced at the children, and there was momentary indecision on her face.

Of course. Her children had almost died behind the blast doors.

Then she nodded, her face set.

They crept down the hallway on silent feet. Tae's throat was dry, and his pulse pounded in his ears.

There were footsteps in the corridor in front of them, and Tanya slipped into a small cross-hallway. Tae pushed the children after her.

Ahead, the blast doors hung half-open. The power from Lena's generators must have been enough to get the doors to open, but not to lock. If the power went out again, even momentarily, they'd slam shut, trapping them in the icy, airless cold.

Still—it spoke to the desperation of their situation that this was by far the best option they had.

They chose Ysbel and Tanya's room. There was room in there for the four of them, if they packed in tightly. Once the children were settled beneath the double-cot, he rummaged around quickly in a hallway storage compartment and pulled out a kit. He yanked out as many of the heat reflective blankets as he could grab, then slipped back into the room and passed them down to Tanya.

"It'll be cold," he whispered. "Make sure the kids are bundled up."

She nodded, her face grim in the reflected light of his com.

"Hey, Tae," came Jez's voice into his earpiece. "Got your parts."

He looked around quickly. Tanya and the children were huddled back into one corner under the cot, out of sight, the heat blankets pulled over them. "Tanya," he whispered. "I'm going to meet Jez to get the parts. We'll deal with putting them in once I get back."

"Very well," Tanya whispered from behind the blankets. "Go, quickly. We'll be waiting."

He nodded and turned back out the tunnel. His teeth were clenched so hard his jaw ached.

But Jez had the parts. Thanks to Lena, the *Ungovernable* had power again.

And maybe, for the first time in a long time—they had a chance.

30

Lena's ship, Lev

"We got the parts, genius. Time to go." Jez's voice hissed through Lev's earpiece.

He glanced quickly at Ysbel. She didn't look at him, but he could read her face. She'd heard it too.

He shifted his arms slightly and held his breath.

This was much more Jez's specialty than his own. Still …

He tapped his com against the chair, once, twice—there. There was a slight hum, and the cuffs loosened on his wrists.

Tae's key had worked.

He glanced at Ysbel from the corner of his eye. She tapped her own com against the chair, and he saw her muscles tense—

And then something hard and cold was jammed into the bruise across his temple, and he bit back a gasp of pain.

"Looks like those cuffs are a little loose," said the smuggler, the amusement in her voice cut with menace.

Slowly, he turned.

A guard stood at Ysbel's side as well, heat gun pointed in a no-nonsense way at her head.

Someone pushed his hands together and bound them tightly with cord, then slid the useless cuffs off and dropped them on the floor.

"Up," the guard growled. Someone un-cuffed Lev's feet from the chair legs. "Good thing Lena called for you, I guess."

He cast a quick glance at Ysbel, but she was bound as tightly as he was.

"Up!" the smuggler barked, jamming the gun harder against his temple. He tried to stand, but he ended up losing his balance and toppling awkwardly to the floor. His bruised cheekbone connected hard with the textured metal of the floor, and he winced. The smuggler laughed and grabbed him by the bound arms, dragging him painfully to his feet. He sucked in a quick gasp at the pain in his head and only just caught his balance as the smuggler let go of him. Beside him, Ysbel stood with much more grace, and much less incident. Although, in fairness, even cuffed, she was intimidating enough that it was unlikely even Lena's crew would purposely antagonize her.

"Come on," the smuggler guard said again. "Lena wants to talk to you."

When he stumbled to a halt on the main deck, Lena sat in a chair at the back of the deck, waiting for them, a handful of her crew around her. This time, though, there was a faint smile on her face, and at the sight of it, unease stirred in his stomach.

She'd been furious when she'd spoken to them before. But now she seemed to have resumed her good humour, and somehow that frightened him much more.

"Sit," she said, gesturing, and the smugglers shoved him and Ysbel into hard-backed chairs against the wall close to the port-side door. For a few moments she watched them calculatingly, then she stood and crossed over to them.

"Lev. Ysbel," she said at last. "The government gave me a file on all of you." She shook her head. "You're talented, sure. But even still—the government is willing to pay a hell of a lot to make you disappear. So tell me." She leaned forward. "What do they want with you?"

Lev frowned slightly. His palms were sweating, but he tried to keep his tone neutral. "Honestly, Lena, I'm not certain."

Lena smiled, but for a moment he saw behind her expression a flash of her former fury. "I thought you were smart, Lev. So I suggest you think about it very damn hard." She stood. "Before they recruited me, the government sent people to kill me and my whole crew. They only stopped when I told them I could find Jez. And they were asking questions about a cargo-grab she did shortly before she ran off. So I want to know what's going on."

She took a step closer, her eyes narrowing slightly. "Why is the government after you? I'm a crew boss. And I didn't become one by letting people get away with lying to me."

He didn't answer, just watched her. Something cold was spreading through his stomach.

He expected her to hit him across the head again with her pistol, and he braced for the blow. But instead she stepped back with a faint smile. "You don't want to talk? You're more stupid than I gave you credit for. Almost as stupid as Jez." She paused. "Funny, isn't it—Jez, who lived through more crazy jobs than any other crew member I've had, stole my best ship and got away with it, stayed one step ahead of me for four years. Broke out of a prison ship, pulled a heist on Vitali Dobrev, broke into and out of a prison—and in the end she was killed in a core meltdown." She shook her head in mock disappointment. "Honestly, I'm disappointed."

He didn't have to fake the tightness in his jaw. "Lena," he said, trying to keep his tone level, “I’m sorry. I’ll admit it, I wish Jez hadn’t died. But—”

She smiled at him, a tiny sparkle of triumph glittering behind her eyes. “Well,” she said. “I did too. There was a hell of a lot I wanted to say to her. But I guess—” She straightened, glancing up at something behind him, and her smile broadened.

He didn’t want to turn and look. He didn’t have to, really, because he saw everything he needed to know in her face, and something tightened around his chest, compressing his breath.

But he couldn’t help himself. He turned, twisting to peer over his shoulder.

The starboard door to the main deck was open, and armed smugglers shoved three figures through it.

Tae.

Masha.

And Jez.

31

Lena's ship, Jez

The sight of Lena was instantly, sickeningly familiar. Like the sight of a place where you'd crashed your first skybike, when the phantom ache of your broken leg hit you once again, the remembered sick feeling as you realized what you'd done. What had happened to you.

Somehow, though, Jez still managed to keep the grin on her face.

The main deck on Lena's ship was the same semicircular shape as the main deck of the *Ungovernable*, but the similarities ended there. The floor and walls were cold metal, the artificial lights so white they were almost blue. Half a dozen smugglers leaned against the far wall behind the smuggler boss, weapons at the ready.

She glanced around quickly, heart hammering.

There, in the corner. Ysbel and Lev, bound to their chairs, guarded by three armed smugglers, but—alive. The unexpected rush of relief that flooded through her at seeing Lev alive was strong enough to almost make her legs wobble. Then she noticed the dried blood on the side of his face and his sick expression, and her heart rate jumped.

How dare these bastards hit him? And how dare he not even

plaguing mention it? She glowered at him, but he didn't glower back, which scared her more than anything.

Ysbel didn't seem to be hurt. Her face was grim, and her eyes were desperately searching for someone other than Jez or Tae.

They weren't there, yet. At least, not as far as Jez knew.

Then again, she had no real idea.

She took another deep breath.

Damn Lena to hell.

"Hey Lena," she drawled, hoping her voice didn't sound as scared as she felt.

Because she was afraid. Not afraid of dying. Not even afraid of the pain, although she was afraid of those things too.

She was afraid of Lena, with a fear that was gut-deep and completely irrational, like a kid afraid of their dad even years after they were big enough that he couldn't hit them anymore.

Lena looked her, and for a moment her face twisted with hate. She took a step forward and raised her hand, and Jez flinched despite herself.

Lena laughed, a hard, humourless sound.

"Jez," she said. The familiar cold amusement in her voice was almost jarring. "Look at you." She ran her eyes deliberately up and down Jez's body, then she smiled. "Beat to hell, half-dead, trapped in deep space. Your crew do this to you? I wouldn't blame them. Never were as good as you thought you were, were you? Except at getting people to hate you, always were good at that."

"Yeah? Well, must be embarrassing, you bastard, four years to track down someone who's no good." She hoped her voice wasn't shaking. "But I guess can't blame you, seeing as I had basically the best ship in the system. Nicest thing you ever did for me, really." Beneath the fear, the sweet rush of adrenaline was pumping through her veins.

Lena's smile dropped, and there was that familiar hint of fury behind her expression.

Despite everything, Jez felt a warm rush of satisfaction. Nice to know that she still had it, even after four years.

"Jez Solokov," the woman hissed. Lena had to look up to look her in the eye, but somehow that didn't make her any less intimidating, and for half a second, Jez felt the familiar urge to drop her gaze.

Of course, she'd never listened to that urge. Might have led to her being beat up less often, now that she thought about it. Then again, it wouldn't have made Lena nearly so upset, so probably worth it after all.

She smiled lazily, even though her heart was going to beat itself out of her chest. "You ever manage to take out the wall-spikes I put through the thrusters on your ships when I left? Or did you have to shell out for new thrusters? Always wondered about that."

"You scum-eater," Lena spat. "You can fly, sure. But you're not worth spit. You were all talk, never had the backbone to face up to things. You were always going to run, I knew that from the moment I set eyes on you."

"Yeah? Well—"

"Shut up!" This time, Lena did backhand her. Pain like lighting jolted through Jez's broken jaw, and she swore through her teeth, blinking back tears. Lena watched her coldly.

"You're nothing, Jez. I read what the government gave me on you. Jumped from crew to crew, job to job, because no one wanted you enough to keep you around. Just like your family didn't want to keep you around. Too much of a damn liability."

Somehow, Jez was still grinning, even though the words cut into her chest like razor-blades.

"Nah. I left because I wanted to. Just like I left your damn crew." Her hands were clenched into fists under the mag-cuffs, and she had to mumble the words through the knife-sharp pain radiating across her face.

"You left because you're a damn coward," Lena snapped. "Too afraid to own up to your own mistakes. When the government hired me to come after you, I figured I had to work fast, because you wouldn't be able to stick around this crew any longer than you stuck around anywhere else."

Jez couldn't hide the sick acknowledgement in her face. Lena smiled, her expression cruel.

"What were you going to run from this time? Got tired of your lover? Got into an argument with someone and didn't know how to back down?"

"Shut up," Jez muttered. She could feel tears pricking at her eyes.

Because the stupid thing was, Lena was right. Lena'd always been right. So had her parents.

Unreliable. Stupid. Couldn't deal with her own problems, so she ran from them, and got caught, and then ran from them again, because she was too stupid to learn.

But that hadn't really been the reason.

She ran because she knew that one day, she'd screw things up. If she stuck around for long enough, no matter how much they said they liked her, no matter how much they told her she was part of them, she was going to screw up, and someone was going to get hurt. They'd start to depend on her, and she was undependable.

And the thing was, she cared about this stupid, crazy crew. She cared about Ysbel, Tae, Lev, Tanya, Olya, Misko—even Masha, if she'd admit it. Jez might hate her, and the feeling might be mutual, but even so, Jez couldn't bear the thought of the look on the woman's face when Jez inevitably screwed things up for good.

That was the real reason she'd decided to leave.

Sometimes, if you cared about someone, leaving was always going to be your best option.

She'd been too late, of course. She'd already screwed up, run away one too many times, brought Lena after them, wrecked everything, that's why Lev was tied up in that chair, and Tae was cuffed somewhere behind her.

Her stomach twisted with nausea.

Lena was right. No matter how much she wanted not to, no matter how hard she tried, she was always going to hurt people, even if she didn't mean to, because she just didn't understand how not to. And then she'd leave them to deal with the consequences while she ran.

No wonder Masha'd wanted her out.

Lena's face was cold triumph. "Doesn't matter, does it? I got you, finally. You screwed everything up, like always." She shrugged slightly. "We'll find the other woman and the children soon, I have my crew in there searching. They can't hide forever. And the best part is, it was always going to end like this. My little damn innocent." She gave Jez that familiar, mocking smile, and something knotted in Jez's throat, just like it had when she was a terrified fourteen-year-old. Lena leaned in slightly. "As soon as I guessed your lover-boy was lying to me, I knew. Because that's the stupidest damn thing about you—you'll always run before you face your own problems, sure. But I knew the moment you thought I might hurt them? You'd be back here like a tick on a swamp-rat. That's the only thing I could ever depend on about you."

Jez stared at her for a moment, jarred out of her fear. "What?"

Lena shook her head pityingly. "You remember the first job I sent you on? Flew there with Alexi? He was getting shot at, and Bratka told you to leave it, but you went back in there, got your ship shot to hell to get him out. Put you in junkers after that, because I couldn't trust you. But I never could beat it out of you."

Jez just stared. She felt, for a moment, like someone had hit her over the head, and she hadn't got over the dizziness of it.

Was it possible? That Lena had never thought Jez would leave the crew to get captured? That she'd known she wouldn't, she never would? That she'd always come back for them, if they were in trouble?

"I—I thought you said I was unreliable," she said at last, her voice strangely hoarse.

Lena shook her head. "You damn worthless innocent," she said in disgust. "Look at this. Don't know what you paid this crew to cover for you, but you couldn't even follow through on getting out."

Jez blinked, hardly hearing the words. Something was choking in her throat, and the tears welling behind her eyes were pushing at the corners of her eyelids, trickling slowly down her cheeks.

Lena thought—no, Lena knew—she'd never leave her crew to get hurt.

She felt like she'd been hit with a shock-stick.

"I might have worried, if it had been anyone else." Lena was still talking, her voice somehow distant. "But I know you, Jez. I know you better than you know yourself."

Jez swallowed hard. She couldn't seem to get her mouth to form the words.

"I always would have come back for them," she murmured, almost to herself.

The thing was—the thing was, it was true. Lena was right. No matter what she'd told herself, she never would have left them in danger. Not the children, not Lev, not any of them.

Unreliable.

Unreliable, because she wasn't ever going to leave her crew to get hurt.

Tears were dripping down her cheeks now, and her nose was running, forcing her to sniff awkwardly.

She hardly noticed.

She hardly cared.

She felt like someone had ripped away the floor she'd been standing on, and instead of falling, she was floating.

She glanced reflexively over at Masha. Masha was studying her, her eyes sharp, her expression unreadable as always.

But—

But when Jez caught her eye, she raised one eyebrow and gave the faintest of nods.

Jez almost swayed on her feet, dizzy in a way that had nothing at all to do with Masha's sleeping gas.

"So, you innocent, you're going to damn well tell me why the government is willing to pay this much for you." Lena was still talking. "Because if you don't, you're going to be damn well spitting out your teeth in about three minutes."

"I wasn't. I really wasn't," she whispered. "Going to leave them, I mean." She turned back to Masha. "Going to leave you. Any of you. Not like this. Not to get hurt."

"I know," said Masha, quietly. "That was never once the thing I worried about."

For a moment, Jez was completely speechless.

Lena was still talking, she was pretty sure, but then she'd had years of practice ignoring Lena.

Someone grabbed her by the shoulders and shook her, and she

glanced up.

Antoni.

He was scowling into her face, and shouting something.

She gave him a dreamy smile.

It hadn't been what Masha had been worried about, either.

She'd always, deep down, been sure it was. She'd always, deep down, been sure that when Masha talked about keeping her in the ship, about not letting her go down planet-side, it had been because Masha had known how much of a coward, how much of a runner Jez was. That the woman had thought she'd get them all into trouble and take off and leave them, because that was who she was.

But—

But maybe, just maybe—it wasn't.

Antoni was still shouting at her. Again, something she was pretty good at ignoring.

Then he slapped her hard across the face, and the jolt of pain through her freshly-broken jaw jerked her back into full consciousness.

She'd always had a harder time ignoring his fists.

"I said, you damn idiot—" he snarled, his face twisted with rage.

"Jez," came a voice from overhead, almost a whisper, really, and Jez glanced up reflexively. Then she blinked and stared.

Tanya?

The woman had somehow managed to balance herself on the wide support beams across the ceiling. She was smiling, that slight, wistful smile with the hint of steel behind it.

She winked, and held up a small tube.

A EMP blocker?

She pointed it down and clicked it, and the cuffs on Jez's wrist popped loose. Tanya tossed something lightly, and Jez put up a newly-freed hand instinctively to grab it as Antoni blinked in shock.

A grin spread across her face as she recognized the familiar shape in her hand, even though she could hardly see through the tears in her eyes.

She twisted the gas bomb, hauled back her arm, and threw it as hard as she could.

It hit the back wall and exploded in a hissing cloud, and the smugglers nearest it dropped nervelessly to the ground.

"Hold your breath, kids," she called to the others. Her grin felt wider than her face, and she still, somehow, felt like she was floating.

Because she'd been right. She had to face up to her past.

The thing she hadn't anticipated, though, was that she wouldn't have to do it alone.

Antoni still hadn't recovered himself. She gave him her best grin, the one he absolutely hated. Then she brought her forehead down hard on the bridge of his nose. He staggered back, and she stepped in and dropped him with a sucker punch to the gut.

"Guess I got a little better at that since four years ago," she whispered as he lay doubled over on the ground, gasping for breath. She turned to Lena.

"Jez—" the woman began, her face pale with fury. "I—" The cloud of gas was creeping towards them, and it wouldn't be long before it reached where Lev and Ysbel were strapped to their chairs.

"Know what else I've always wanted to do, Lena?" Jez said in a musing tone. She took a deep, satisfied breath, and closed her eyes for half a second, savouring the moment.

"This." She opened her eyes, drew back her fist, and hit Lena right in the middle of her damn face.

She'd never had any idea that almost breaking your knuckles could feel that good.

32

Lena's ship, Ysbel

Ysbel felt faintly sick to her stomach as she watched Jez, head bowed, body tense, facing Lena.

The look on the pilot's face cut her, the scared, vulnerable expression, the way her body tightened like Lena was beating her with a whip, rather than simply with her words.

She'd never seen Jez look like this before. And for the first time, she saw the frightened kid who'd been thrown out by her family, tossed onto the mercy of a smuggler crew, trying just to survive, rather than the cocky, irritating, supremely self-confident pilot she'd thought she knew.

She glanced over at Lev, and the look on his face told him he was having similar thoughts.

She tightened her lips.

"Shhh," came a small voice from behind her, and she glanced quickly over her shoulder.

Olya stood there, crouching against the cold steel wall, a self-satisfied smile on her face. "These smugglers are pretty stupid," she whispered, cutting efficiently through the cords on Ysbel's wrists. She caught the sliced cords as they fell and placed them gently on the ground. "They didn't even see me sneak in."

Ysbel stared. "Where's—"

Olya pointed at the ceiling, and Ysbel glanced up. Then, slowly, she smiled.

Of course.

"Alright, my love," she whispered. "Thank you. Now, get back to your brother, OK? I don't want the smugglers to see you."

"They won't," Olya whispered back. Ysbel glanced to her side. Lev was carefully rubbing feeling back into his wrists. He caught Ysbel's gaze, then glanced up at the ceiling, half-way across the deck, to where Tanya was perched gracefully in the rafters. He raised an eyebrow at her.

"Tanya will be fine," she mouthed.

His expression changed to one of slight confusion, but he shrugged and nodded. His posture, though, as he glanced back up at Tanya, did not look as though he'd taken her advice.

But Ysbel felt like a weight had been taken off her shoulders.

An attack, or a heat-gun blast—something she couldn't control, like the fire in their cabin—hurting Tanya or the children terrified her, with a fear that stopped her heart and thickened the blood in her veins.

But this? She was no more worried about Tanya now than Tanya would be worried about her testing explosives.

They all had things they were good at. And Tanya had always been good.

And, it appeared, Olya was taking in her mamochka's footsteps.

"Did you bring any weapons, my love?" she whispered over her shoulder to her daughter. Olya gave her a long-suffering look.

"Yes, Mama." She dropped a small modded heat-pistol into

Ysbel's hands. "And masks. Mamochka said you'll need one in a minute. I already gave one to Uncle Lev."

Ysbel glanced up at her wife, just in time to see the tiny cylinder fall from her hands into Jez's suddenly-unbound ones.

Jez, she realized, was grinning now, even through tears running down her cheeks. She twisted the gas cylinder and tossed it, with perfect aim, to hit the wall of the deck to Ysbel's left, behind the largest cluster of smugglers. Ysbel jumped to her feet and slapped the mask over her face as Jez, with a beatific smile, dropped the muscular man in front of her and turned towards Lena. Masha had already grabbed the stunned Tae and shoved a heat-pistol into his hand, turning him around and shoving him towards the door.

Ysbel raised her eyebrows. Masha's ability to hide weaponry would never completely cease to surprise her.

Smugglers were falling to the ground behind them as the gas caught them, and others were running for their lives. One of them seemed to remember the prisoners, and turned towards them. His face was frantic, but he was holding his gun on them in a businesslike way. "Come with me," he shouted. "I'm not damn well losing this —"

She could kill him. But—she glanced at Olya, who was watching in wide-eyed admiration, and cracked off a shot at his feet. The blast shimmered in the air, and then he was staring at a ragged hole in the deck, dripping molten metal into the level below them.

He met Ysbel's eyes. She lifted her weapon slightly.

He turned, and ran for his life.

"Go, Olya!" she hissed. "I will meet you back at the ship. Keep Misko safe, OK? We'll be there in a moment."

Olya nodded and disappeared, and Ysbel glanced around the room quickly. The gas was rapidly filling the room, but Masha had grabbed Jez by the sleeve and was pulling her towards the door. Tae was already in the hallway, and from the crackling sound of heat-blasts and the muffled shouts, there were things outside the room that would require her attention in a moment.

Masha seemed to come to the same conclusion, because she gave a final jerk on Jez's sleeve and hissed something to the half-dazed pilot. Jez blinked. Masha handed her a pistol, and the two women sprinted for the door. Ysbel grabbed her own pistol and turned.

Lev.

She hadn't seen him.

She glanced back over her shoulder.

He was sitting where she'd left him, head lolling back. The mask over his face—she went suddenly cold.

It was a child-sized mask. And there was a split seam on one side.

He must have noticed, and talked Olya into trading with him.

Knowing he'd be knocked out the moment the gas hit him, but she'd be safe.

And there it was—the contradiction that had almost killed her over the past two days.

This man, who'd been willing to risk his own life to save her family from a fate worse than death, and who had been the one to send them there in the first place. The boy who little Olya had wrapped around her finger, who would do anything for her, including giving her the last working mask—and who'd been the reason she'd grown up in hell. The man who had asked her about Tanya when she hadn't realized talking about Tanya was the one thing, the only thing, she needed to keep her sane, listened to her memories and her horrors—and who had been the author of those horrors himself.

She'd blown up a whole shuttle site to avenge her family, to kill the people who'd taken them from her. She'd been willing to bring down an entire government building and kill this whole team of idiots for the chance to get revenge on a couple more of them. And this time, she wouldn't need to do anything. All she'd have to do was leave.

And—

And after all that, she'd still wake at nights to nightmares of a burning cottage. The hardness behind Tanya's expression would still be there when she wasn't thinking of it, the unnatural quiet of their children, who she'd never seen grow up, hadn't been there when they'd lost their first tooth or learned to speak without a lisp. All of those things were gone forever.

And—Lev would be gone too. Their easy camaraderie, his dry sense of humour, the quiet, thoughtful look in his eyes. They way Olya stared up at him, half challenging, half adoring, and the doting look on his face whenever he caught sight of her.

His absence, too, would ache. Ache more than she'd ever let herself admit.

She shook her head slightly at herself. Then she bent, hoisted the unconscious Lev onto her shoulders, shifted her grip on her heat-pistol, and headed out into the hallway.

33

Lena's ship, Jez

Jez still felt a little like her feet weren't touching the floor as she followed Masha at a sprint out the door. But when she broke through into the corridor, with heat-blasts searing the walls on either side and Tae locked into a fist-fight with two smugglers she recognized by name, the world settled once more into it's delightful, familiar, comfortable form. She jumped forward, yanked Tae out of the way of a fist, and grabbed the fist's owner by the collar.

"Miss me?" she smirked. Then she kneed him in the groin, and as he folded in on himself, felled him with a pistol-butt to the temple. A fist caught her in the side of the head and she staggered backward, vaguely grateful the blow had missed any broken bones. She caught herself against the corridor wall and braced for the next blow, but Tae, scowling, stepped past her and dropped the man with one well-placed punch to the throat. Then he grabbed her by the arm and hauled her upright.

"Come on, Jez!"

For a moment, she almost hesitated. He rolled his eyes, and they ducked instinctively as a heat-blast blistered the air over their heads.

"If you want to fix your ship, we don't have time for this," he said through his teeth.

Her ship.

Something warm and effervescent bubbled up in her chest.

For the first time since that horrible, awful, hopeless moment when she'd pulled the *Ungovernable* out of hyperdrive—there was a chance they could fix her ship.

She swallowed back tears, vision soft with a rosy glow.

"Come on!" He grabbed her by the arm, and she followed him at a gasping run down the sterile corridors of Lena's ship.

"The others—" she started.

"They're fine," he said over his shoulder. "Ysbel's there, and Tanya, and they've got Lev, and I get the feeling that Masha knows her way around a fight."

"Masha knows her damn way around basically everything," Jez muttered, but for the first time in a long time, she didn't actually hate the woman nearly as much as she probably still should.

When they reached the airlock that led to the *Ungovernable*, a handful of smugglers were already pushing their way down the corridor back towards Lena's ship. When they saw Tae and Jez—specifically, when they saw their modded heat guns—they froze. Jez grinned.

They grabbed for their own weapons, but she'd already lunged for them, and the four of them went down in a heap on the floor. Above her, Tae sighed with exasperation as he brought his weapon up. She grabbed his ankle and yanked hard, and he went down as a laser blast burned a long line in the wall behind where his head had just been.

"That's my ship you're wrecking, you bastards," she growled, turning back to the smugglers. A fist hit her in the ribs, and for a moment her vision turned to white stars at the pain. Then Tae was hauling her to her feet again.

"Consort's bloody blue balls, Jez," he said through his teeth. "You've got four damn—"

"Broken ribs, I remember," she gasped. She kicked out, hitting a smuggler in the stomach, then caught herself against the wall as black spots danced across her vision. Tae grabbed a woman who'd staggered to her feet, turned her around, and shoved her face-first into the corner of the doorframe. She dropped, momentarily stunned, and Jez pushed herself off the wall and followed Tae at a painful sprint down the corridor.

"You know how to fix the thrusters?" he panted. She nodded.

"Alright. You do that, I'll deal with the power core. They probably have it pretty well powered up by now anyways, with the size of cable they're using."

They'd reached the corner where they'd been caught by Lena's people, and Tae yanked open the small first-aid cupboard. She reached in, almost holding her breath.

It had to be there. If the guards who'd grabbed them had noticed Tae slamming the door shut as they rounded the corner—

There it was.

She breathed out in relief and pulled out two sacks. She shoved the smaller one at Tae, hoisted the larger one over her shoulder, and ran for the engine room.

When she reached it, she slid inside, and gently, almost reverently, lowered the sack of parts to the floor. She ran her hands over the damaged thrusters, fingers catching gently on the melted bits, the charred, burned, scabbed chunks of metal. It felt a little like examining a heat-blast victim, wondering if there was a hint of life inside the charred flesh.

But this was her angel. This was her sweet, sweet ship, and it knew her. It could hear her.

And she was one hundred percent sure it would listen.

"It's alright, baby," she whispered. "You're going to be alright. You kept us alive out here, and now Tae and me, we're going to put you back together."

She could have sworn she felt the ship, the faint hum that was the heart of it powering up, answer her through her fingers and through her feet and through her whole body.

A frantic smuggler burst through the engine room door, heat gun raised. She stepped forward, raised her wrench, and brought it down hard across the base of his skull. He staggered, and she wrenched the pistol from his grip.

"Keep your damn weapons away from my thrusters," she growled, and shoved him back through the door.

Outside, there were shouts and screams, the hiss and crackle of heat-guns and lasers.

Jez took a long, deep breath, a soft smile on her face.

It was good to be home.

She tightened her grip on her wrench and set to work.

She wasn't entirely sure how much time had passed when a voice in her earpiece jolted her from her reverie.

"Jez." It was Masha, and her voice was tight with strain. "How close are you?"

Jez blinked, and glanced at the jumble of broken pieces scattered on the floor around her. "Almost there. How's Tae doing?"

"He informed me he's just about finished as well."

"Good. We should be able to power up in a minute or so then. What's happening?"

"We all got back here and managed to herd the rest of the smugglers onto their own ship. The gas should have taken care of them for the moment," said Masha. "We don't have long, though. Ysbel went back to unclip the power cable from their ship, and she's going to seal off the airlock on her way back through. She said we have maybe another five, ten standard minutes before they start to wake up."

"I'll be done before then," said Tae. "I have one more part to replace."

"Well," Jez drawled into the com, "I just finished. Guess I'm better at tech after all."

"Jez—"

She brushed off her hands, glancing one last time around the cramped room.

She'd come clean the rest of this mess up later. Right now …

Right now, the *Ungovernable* was calling her, and she damn well planned on answering.

She made her way to the cockpit. Masha was there, and Tanya and Ysbel and the children. Olya looked up as she stepped in and grinned at her, and Jez grinned back.

Then she saw Lev, lying on the floor, and her stomach dropped.

"What the hell happened to him," she gritted out, dropping down beside him.

He was breathing, at least. That meant he was alive. But the limp droop of his body, his slack face and closed eyes, the crusted blood across his temple, made her feel like she was going to throw up. She spun around, glaring at Ysbel.

"I said, what the hell—"

"He's fine," Ysbel said, and there was a wry, slightly amused tone in her voice. "He got caught in the gas. He'll wake up in a minute or two, I imagine."

She glanced back down at him, her heart rate slowing just a bit. Sure enough, his eyes were moving restlessly under his eyelids, and he stirred ever so slightly.

"Jez," said Masha, in her usual calm voice, "I understand your concern. However, if you'd like him to remain alive, I suggest we get the ship running."

"Yeah." Jez didn't take her eyes off Lev for a minute. "Yeah, you're probably right."

Reluctantly, she got to her feet.

"Got it," came Tae's voice over the com.

Jez took a deep breath and slid into the pilot's seat. The familiar shape and feel of it was a little like stepping through the doors into your home. There was something right about it, something vital and comforting.

She closed her eyes and rested her fingers on the controls for just a moment.

"Ready?" she whispered into her com.

"Ready," said Tae.

Gently, she tapped the power, and the ship hummed into life.

For a moment she could hardly move, her chest tight with a desperate, sickening relief. She'd almost forgotten, with everything that had happened, how much the lack of that soft hum beneath her boots, through her fingers, into her bones, had hurt. How it had been killing her, as surely as a knife between her ribs.

And now it was back, and for the first time in a very, very long time, she felt like she was being put back together. She felt alive. She felt like she could actually breathe.

Without opening her eyes, she pulled the thrusters online, gently, carefully. They hummed to life, and another part of her fell into place.

It wasn't fixed yet, not really. This was temporary, and the parts they'd replaced wouldn't work long-term. They still had to re-wire the hyperdrive into the newly-remodelled thrusters if they wanted to run it without tearing everything apart, and there would be plenty of work ahead of them to get her ship in proper running order. But right now, she hardly cared.

"Strap in, kids," she murmured, and then she nudged the controls, and her angel shot forward. Her stomach lurched with the acceleration, the speed shoving her back in her seat, and she closed her eyes in bliss, revelling in the intoxicating whisper of the ship beneath her fingers.

She reached up to wipe away the tears that were running down her cheeks. Stupid to cry like this when everything was right.

Behind her Tae was swearing and Ysbel was picking herself off the floor, but she hardly noticed.

She couldn't stop smiling.

"This is the *Viper*, paging the *Ungovernable*." Jez recognized the voice over the com instantly.

Lena.

Even that wasn't enough to cut through the haze of joy.

"May I?" asked Ysbel, gesturing to the com. Jez nodded, still unable to speak, and Ysbel stepped past her.

"Lena," she said, her outer-rim accent heavier than usual. "You've lost this one. You sent someone after our pilot back on Prasvishoni, and I sent him away with a warning. Apparently, he didn't listen. So you listen to me now." She paused a moment. "You will leave us alone. You will leave Jez alone. You will never come after her again. And if you know what's good for you, you will stay exactly where you are. You can page for help if you'd like, but I'm warning you, do not try to come after us."

There was a momentary pause.

"If you're stupid enough to fly with Jez," said Lena at last, her voice cold with anger, "then I guess you're stupid enough to think that you can just fly off. You have no idea how badly the government wants you. And if you think you can—"

Her voice cut off abruptly in a burst of static.

Jez frowned and turned to look over her shoulder.

Where Lena's ship had been, there was nothing but a slowly-expanding cloud of space-debris.

She stared at the explosion, then up at Ysbel.

Everyone in the cabin, it appeared, was staring at Ysbel.

"I did tell her not to try to come after us," said Ysbel, a faint note of satisfaction in her voice. "I suppose I could have also warned her I'd rigged explosives into her power core. But—" she shrugged. "I didn't like the way she talked to Jez."

"Well," said Masha, after a moment. "I supposed that solves the problem for the time being." She turned to face Jez.

For a moment, their eyes met.

Jez frowned slightly. Masha's expression was as unreadable as ever, but there was something in her eyes that Jez couldn't remember seeing there before. Something like—affection.

"Jez," she said at last. "Why don't you take us somewhere where we can get the *Ungovernable* put back together?"

Jez stared at her for a moment longer.

She was, for a moment, almost as disoriented as she'd been facing Lena.

But somehow, she felt herself smiling. Not the snarky grin she usually reserved for Masha, but an actual smile.

"On it," she said, and turned quickly back to her controls so that no one else would see the tears filling her eyes.

34

Afterwards

Masha glanced around the cockpit.

It was almost unnerving, the relief she felt at the sight of the seven of them, battered, bruised, slightly worse for the wear, but—alive.

And the realization that that was the part that relieved her. Not the fact they could still, possibly, pull off her plan. Not the fact that they were still, for the moment, a team.

The fact that they were alive.

Ysbel had turned to embrace Tanya, almost unconsciously, her arms protectively around the slender woman who, it appeared, was at least as deadly as Ysbel herself, their two children pressed between them. Tae, nursing a bruised shoulder and shooting the occasional glare at Jez, leaned up against the back wall of the cockpit, his dark hair tangled and the almost-permanent dark circles under his eyes accentuating his exhaustion, but there was a softness to his face when he looked around the cockpit. Lev lay back in the copilot's seat, blinking at the aftereffects of Ysbel's gas. He'd woken just in time to catch a glimpse of what was left of the smuggler's ship disappearing behind them, and there had been a grim satisfaction to his expression that told her he'd heard every word the smuggler boss said to Jez.

And Jez.

She was leaning back in her seat, head tipped back, a hint of tears glistening in the corners of her eyes. She hadn't really stopped crying since the ship had come back to life, and every so often, she reached up to wipe moisture from her cheeks. She seemed almost in a trance, stroking her hands unconsciously along the controls as if trying to reassure herself they were real. Since the ship had hummed to life, the only moment she'd allowed her attention to be dragged away from the controls was when Lev had pushed himself up on his elbows and asked, in a groggy voice, what the actual hell was going on.

Masha had thought the lanky pilot might actually kiss him.

She shook her head slightly.

Even Jez.

She'd stood on Lena's main deck, and she'd watched Jez, standing in front of the smuggler boss as the woman used her words to rip Jez to shreds. And for the first time, she'd realized exactly what Jez had been willing to do to give the rest of them a chance to get away.

The thought made her feel almost nauseous, and she pushed the feeling away determinedly.

How long had it been since she'd allowed herself to look at people—this crazy, irritating pilot, the scowling street-kid who seemed to feel he was responsible for every single member of the crew, and simultaneously to believe that he didn't have the power to save anyone or fix anything, the stoic, matter-of fact Ysbel, and Lev, with his dry humour and his brilliant intellect—and see people, instead of tools?

And why, in the name of everything holy, had she allowed herself to do that with this crew? Because they were, in the end, tools. They were the best tools she'd ever been able to gather. But now they were more than that. More than she'd ever wanted them to be.

And there would be no going back. She could never bring things back to the way they had been. Even if she'd wanted to.

And for the first time since she was seven years old, she wasn't entirely certain that she wanted to.

"Jez," said Tae at last, "you think you can take her through the wormhole?"

"Mmm," Jez murmured dreamily.

"Jez," he snapped, and she looked up.

"What?"

"I said—"

Jez rolled her eyes. "Yes, but it was kind of a stupid question. Of course I can take her through the wormhole. You could sit me on a piece of space-rock and I could take it through a wormhole. And now that my sweet angel is running again—" she broke off, running her fingers lovingly across the control panel. Tae sighed heavily.

"Do you need us to leave you two alone?" he said.

"Mmmm," Jez responded, without looking up.

Masha smiled despite herself.

"Masha," said Lev, turning slightly in his chair and looking up at her. "I believe there was a date under your name as well."

She studied him for a moment, and at last she nodded. "You're correct, Lev," she said. Her voice was steady, but then she'd had years of practice keeping her voice steady.

"What happened on that date?" he asked softly.

"That," she said in a matter-of-fact tone, "is something I'd prefer to keep to myself for the moment."

He watched her for a moment, then nodded.

"I believe," she continued, "that you have some theory. Am I correct?"

He nodded again. "Although," he said, with a slightly rueful glance at Tanya, "it was slightly easier to formulate my theory before I was knocked out by Ysbel's gas bomb."

"I did wonder," said Masha. "Why didn't you put your mask on?"

There was a moment's silence, and Lev looked faintly uncomfortable.

"Because there was a damaged mask," said Ysbel at last. There was a strange tone in her voice. "It was a child's mask, but I believe he noticed it, and wanted to ensure the child would be safe."

Masha looked down at the small family group, huddled tightly together as if the thought of physically separating was too painful to contemplate, then back at Lev.

He looked embarrassed. "I—"

"Uncle Lev!" Olya's voice was equal parts outrage and hero worship. "You told me—"

"I'm sorry, Olya," he said, spreading his hands ruefully. "I didn't think you—"

"You lied to me! You told me you didn't think the big mask was going to fit you!"

"I—"

She glared at him. "You could have gotten killed!"

"I—" he glanced up suddenly, and for a moment he and Ysbel locked eyes. "I—am not completely sure why I wasn't," he said quietly, eyes not leaving Ysbel's face.

"Because if you had, I think it would have broken my child's heart," said Ysbel softly. "And, perhaps—" she paused a moment, swallowing hard. "Perhaps mine as well."

Lev stared for a moment, as if unsure of what he'd heard. And then he dropped his eyes, but Masha noticed him blinking harder than completely necessary.

After a moment, he cleared his throat.

"At any rate. Yes, Masha, to answer your question, I believe I'm beginning to have a theory." He paused. "I don't recall if I told you, but the date on my chip was the date that a professor of mine disappeared from the university. She'd been working on a project for the government. After I started working for the government, that was, in part, what motivated me to search for the records that landed me in prison. Still—" he paused slightly. "Still, no matter how far into the classified documents I went, every mention of her project was censored out."

Masha nodded slowly, but there was something cold growing in the pit of her stomach.

It wasn't possible.

Was it?

"And Jez," Lev continued. "She told me what happened on the date on her chip. The apartment she was living in was blown to shreds, the entire building demolished. But she noticed one thing before she ran for her life, and that was the cargo that she'd stolen from Lena a year or so earlier was gone. Is that correct?" He turned to the pilot, who was still smiling dreamily out the cockpit window.

"Jez?"

"Mmm?"

"Jez!"

She looked up.

"I said, is that correct?"

"Is what correct, genius-boy?"

He sighed heavily, and Masha bit back a small smile. "At any rate," he said, giving Jez a glare that was probably entirely ineffective, as she'd already turned back to her controls, "Lena was saying the same thing, that there was some job they'd pulled right before Jez left, and that's why the government tracked Lena's crew down. Then we have Ysbel."

Ysbel looked up.

"You said your date was the date your family left Prasvishoni for the last time. That did confuse me for a while, because you were only a child then. But then I got to thinking—your father and mother were both war heroes, as I recall. So why leave Prasvishoni in the middle of the war?"

Ysbel was nodding slowly. "Yes," she said, her voice quiet, expression nostalgic. "It wasn't the war. I overheard them once or twice, talking after they thought I was asleep. My father had been working on the beginnings of a project for the government. I don't know what it was, but whatever it was frightened him. He didn't think he could quit the project, and he was terrified to continue it. I believe he and my mother thought if they could get away, the government would find someone else to finish it."

Lev nodded slowly. "And Tae. I looked up your date. That was the day you hacked into Vadym's system, wasn't it? And you found something on that system."

Tae nodded, eyes wary. "I don't know what it was, though."

Lev nodded again. "Nor do I." He turned his disconcertingly-sharp gaze back on Masha. "But Masha. I believe you do."

She took a deep breath and managed a small smile at him.

"Yes, Lev. As usual, you are correct. I believe I do as well." She paused a moment, gathering her thoughts.

"As I told you," she said at last, "I've worked with the government for some time. Seventeen years, to be exact. And I know much, much more about the inner workings of the government than you might suspect."

"It might surprise you what I suspect about you, Masha," Lev murmured, and this time she couldn't entirely bite back her smile.

"Be that as it may, Lev, I assume it would not surprise you to know I had access to some very, very classified information." She paused again.

"There was a government program. It was in the works, on and off, for over twenty years. I believe it was originally designed to help in the war effort, but at some point some government official decided it could be useful in more situations than just war." She sighed, trying to fight back the cold in her stomach. "I don't know what it is, or what it's designed to do. But I will tell you this—it is dangerous." She looked slowly around the cabin, meeting each of their eyes. "Whatever it is, I believe Lena was sent after us because each of us have touched this. What Lev's professor and Ysbel's father was working on. What Tae found when he hacked Vadym's system. The cargo that Jez stole off the ship from Prasvishoni, and then stole from Lena when she took the ship. Whatever it is, the government is determined that it not be discovered."

"But why now?" Lev asked quietly. "These dates are from years ago. If this had been important, I assume the government could have easily contrived to kill each one of us in prison. It isn't like they didn't have the opportunity."

Masha sighed. "I don't know. I wish I could tell you that I understand why it has suddenly become relevant now, when it was not before. If it was something we've done that triggered this, there is a strong chance that the government assumes, considering we all have some connection with this project, that we know more than we do."

Jez looked up from her control panel and grinned. "Guess pretty much everyone must think we know more than we do. Considering we basically know crap."

"Speak for yourself," muttered Tae. Jez rolled her eyes at him.

"If that's the case," said Lev at last, "then I suppose it would probably be prudent if we were to figure out what it is we're all supposed to know."

Jez gave him a look of mild horror. "Listen, genius, if you think I'm going to spend hours going through a bunch of documents—"

"That wasn't exactly what I was thinking," Lev murmured. "I was actually thinking of breaking into my old university. I believe there ought to be some files there still. I couldn't get to them as a student, but if we went in as professors—"

Masha raised her eyebrows, impressed despite herself. "That's not actually a bad plan," she said.

"Thank you for the vote of confidence," said Lev dryly.

"Wait." There was a note of completely unconcealed delight in Jez's voice. "You mean, break into a damn university? As professors? We'd sneak in and pretend to be professors and steal crap from the university?"

Lev gave her a wry look. "I thought you said—"

"Nope, changed my mind. This sounds exactly like my kind of plan."

Lev and Masha exchanged looks.

"I suppose that may be our next step," said Masha at last. "And I suppose there is something I should tell you."

Lev glanced up at her, his eyes sharp, and for a moment she wondered if he'd already guessed what she was going to say next.

She'd always planned to tell them at some point, of course, but she hadn't expected it to be like this. Their ship broken, their company swelled by three. Jez only a few days past her declaration that she would leave the company.

Telling them, not because she knew she had them where she wanted them. Because they deserved to know.

"I did, in fact, have a reason to bring you together that went beyond our heist on Vitali. And I suppose it's time I told you what that reason was." She took a deep breath. "The Svodrani system government is corrupt. It's in the pocket of the mafia, as I'm sure many of you know. However, I doubt you realize the full extent of its corruption." Her hands were shaking, and she wondered absently if any of the others had noticed.

"And, between the eight of us, I believe we may be able to change how the government functions going forward."

There was a moment of silence as they looked at her. The realization dawned on Lev's face faster than on any of the others, as she's suspected it would.

"You never wanted Vitali's tech at all," he said softly. "That was just firing an opening salvo. You want to take down the whole damn government."

She smiled at him fondly. He'd always been a smart one, that boy. "Perhaps not the entire government," she said, her tone depreciating. "Only, perhaps, taking down one faction, and the organized crime backing that allows them to stay in power."

Lev raised his eyebrows. He looked up at Masha. "I see," he said at last. "Well." He paused a moment. "I believe I understand why you didn't want to tell us this right off."

"Tell us what right off?" asked Jez, turning reluctantly from the control panel. Lev gave a long-suffering sigh and shook his head.

"Tell us," Ysbel grumbled, "that the reason we really are here is because we are single-handedly supposed to take down the entire Svodrani system government. And the mafia. And who knows what else."

Jez stared at her for a moment, then turned to stare at Masha.

A slow grin was spreading across her face.

"Masha," she drawled at last. "And here I figured you were a cautious bastard. That almost sounds like one of my ideas."

Masha thinned her lips.

The thought was not entirely comforting.

For a few moments, no one spoke. At last, though, Tae said quietly, "I didn't have much to do with the mafia. They ran in higher circles than the street gangs. But I had enough to do with the government." He turned to her, and she was mildly surprised at the grim expression on his face. "Masha," he said, "I'm not going to lie and say you don't scare the hell out of me. But if you plan on taking this government down—that's the one thing I've wanted to do my whole life."

She raised her eyebrows. That, at least, was something she hadn't expected.

Ysbel was smiling. "I agree with Tae. I've had enough dealing with the Svodrani system government." She turned to Masha. "I have my family back. But the system that put them there—" Masha noticed that she glanced over at Lev, and that Lev did not meet her eyes. "If you want to take them down," she said quietly, "I will come with you."

"And I do not intend to leave my wife ever again," said Tanya, from within Ysbel's arms. "So I suppose you get all of us."

"By the way," said Tae, "Tanya, how the hell did you learn to—to—" he broke off, shaking his head. Tanya glanced at Ysbel with a faint smile.

"I thought you'd told them, Ysi."

Ysbel looked faintly smug. "I did. I told them you went to university in Prasvishoni."

Tanya shook her head and turned to the others. "What my wife apparently neglected to tell you was which university I went to. They recruited me to train as an agent for the internal security committee."

Masha turned to stare. Lev whistled slightly.

"No wonder they wanted to transfer you to the Vault when they thought Ysbel had died," Tae murmured. There was a look in his face, a sort of mortal terror, that he usually reserved for Masha. "Ysbel, it would have been nice to know we were sleeping next door to someone who could kill us all in her sleep without breaking a sweat."

Ysbel shrugged. "In fairness, most of us could kill us all in our sleep without breaking a sweat."

There was a long, long pause. At last, Lev leaned back in his chair.

"I suppose that settles it," he said. "First we break into my university. Then, we take down the government."

Masha watched them for a moment.

They were so confident they could do this.

She wasn't.

Because she'd realized, for the first time, that their lives were no longer expendable in her calculation of risks and rewards.

That was dangerous. That was terrifying.

And somehow, she'd have to find a way for them to pull it off anyways.

Masha waited until the others had finally, yawning and stretching, headed back towards their cabins. Lev had seemed somewhat reluctant to leave, but she'd given him a meaningful stare and finally, reluctantly, he'd left as well.

At last, it was only her and Jez.

Jez studiously avoided her gaze.

"Jez," said Masha at last. Jez looked up, face instantly defensive. "What?"

Masha sighed. "Jez. Do you still intend to leave?"

There was a long silence.

"I don't know," said Jez at last, not looking at her. "I guess you want me to."

Masha shook her head. "No, Jez," she said quietly. "I don't."

Jez frowned at her. "Have kind of a strange way of showing it, you bastard."

Masha gave a slight smile. "I'm sorry. I—was wrong."

Jez froze. "What—do you mean?" she asked cautiously.

"I mean," Masha took a deep breath. "I mean, I've come to realize that this crew would not be what it is if you were not part of it. Over and beyond how you fly, which, I must admit, is more than impressive, the others need you." She paused. "I—suppose we all do."

Jez was staring at her, a frown creasing between her eyebrows, as if trying to parse out the sting in the words.

At last she shook her head. "I guess—I don't know, I've gotten pretty used to this crew. Guess maybe I might stay for a little while longer." Her mouth was twitching slightly, and Masha couldn't tell for certain if it was with a grin or with tears.

"I'm glad." For some reason, Masha found her own words choking a little. "Because you were right, in the end. I have been cautious, but I may have lost sight of the thing that makes this crew unique."

"What, you mean besides the fact that Ysbel could basically blow us all up in our sleep?"

"Besides that," Masha murmured, a slight smile on her face.

"Yeah." Jez tried to grin, but there was something glistening in the corners of her eyes. "Well, guess we'll have to stop trying to kill each other then, you dirty scum-sucker."

"I suppose we must," said Masha.

35

Lev sat back on the main deck and watched as the others left back to their bunks or their calculations. Jez, of course, still hadn't left the cockpit. He wasn't sure if she'd ever leave it again. Like always, the thought of her made his heart stutter slightly. He closed his eyes and took a deep breath.

There would be time for that in a moment.

He'd just learned that they were planning to take down both the Sovdrani system government and the mafia. That should certainly absorb more of his attention than the thought of a woman who liked to run her ship through asteroid belts for fun.

But his eyes lingered on the cockpit door, and he couldn't seem to shake the slightly-inebriated buzz the memory of her smile seemed to illicit in his brain.

"Lev."

He turned, startled out of his reverie.

Ysbel had taken a seat across from him.

The old guilt shoved itself back into his throat, mingled with a familiar fear. Because, all things considered, he was still a coward.

He managed, somehow, to keep his voice steady.

"Yes, Ysbel?"

Would she kill him right now? At this point, he wasn't certain whether that could possibly be a worse fate than letting him wait and wonder when the moment would come.

"I didn't puncture your oxygen tank, you know," she said at last. He looked up at her, raising an eyebrow.

She looked—sincere.

"I—didn't think you had," he demurred. She gave a slightly grim smile.

"You aren't a very good liar."

He sighed. "I hoped you hadn't, then."

"I could have," she said quietly. "I might have, at one point. But I didn't."

He studied her face. There were lines there, of concern and pain and worry. He'd put most of them there himself, as an arrogant, self-confident young man, too self-important or self-absorbed to consider the potential consequences of his actions.

"Why?" he asked finally. "Don't tell me I didn't deserve it."

For a few moments, she didn't answer. Finally she said, "Maybe you did deserve it. I don't know. I thought I knew, once. But—I suppose life isn't as clean as all that. I didn't puncture your tank, for the same reason I didn't leave you behind on Lena's ship. Because at the end of the day, whatever happened, whatever you did in the past —I can't change it, and neither can you. But—" she paused again. "But I did not wish to lose another person I care about because of what you did five years ago."

He frowned abruptly as he realized what she'd said.

"Ysbel," he said at last, speaking around the sudden lump in his throat. "I—I deserve whatever it is you wanted to do to me. I spent the last few weeks trying to pretend I didn't, that there was a way out. But I—"

Ysbel held up a hand. "Then listen. You're right. What you did hurt me more than you will ever know, and it hurt people I care for more than I care for my own life. But in prison, and here on the ship—what you did saved them, too. Saved me. It doesn't make what you did to us go away. But—" she shrugged. "As I said. I am tired of losing people I care for to things that happened in the past."

He stared at her, speechless. She gave him a brief smile, and pushed herself to her feet.

"I will see you in the morning, then," she said, and disappeared out the door.

He stared after her for a long time.

There was a sort of emptiness inside him, nestled in beside the guilt and the fear.

He'd considered the whole thing logically, over and over, trying to find an escape for himself, some excuse, and there hadn't been any. And so, like he'd done to the student who'd turned in his mentor, he'd expected her to take her due.

And then she hadn't.

She'd saved his life, back on Lena's ship. And Tae had worked himself ragged for them, even when he thought they were all going to take off and leave him when it was done. And Lev had somehow managed to go completely off his head for the pilot who had put him in prison, and who he'd spent the better part of seven years planning his revenge on.

Maybe, after all, Ysbel was right. Maybe life wasn't quite as simple as he'd assumed, back in university. Maybe life was a hell of a lot more complicated than that.

And maybe—maybe that wasn't such a bad thing after all.

Ysbel walked slowly back to her cabin. When she entered, Tanya was waiting for her.

"The children are already asleep," she whispered, standing and leaning in for a kiss. "I think they were sleeping before they'd finished lying down."

Ysbel smiled slightly, and ran a hand down Tanya's smooth hair. She'd missed the feel of Tanya's hair. It was a stupid thing to miss, after everything that had been taken away from her, but there it was.

"Are you alright, my heart?" Tanya whispered, twining her arms around Ysbel. "You've seemed so sad."

Ysbel smiled, despite the wetness in her eyes. "Yes, my Tanya," she whispered. "I'm alright."

Tanya pulled back to look at her, then reached up to brush the tears from Ysbel's eyes, the gesture at once so familiar and so tender that Ysbel had to swallow hard.

"Tanya," she whispered. "I've missed so much. You, the children."

"I know," said Tanya quietly. "There is so much we've all missed. I thought—at first, I thought maybe going back to our home. I thought maybe that would be the thing that could heal us. But—" she gestured around her at the small, comfortable cabin. "But, my heart, I don't believe we are the same people we were when we left that home. You are part of this crazy crew now, aren't you? And I believe we are becoming part of it as well, whether we want to or not."

Ysbel pulled Tanya close and buried her face in her wife's hair.

It was short now, not long like she'd always remembered.

But still, somehow, beautiful.

"When I left Prasvishoni," Ysbel said at last, "back when I was a child, I thought my life was going to be over. Everything I loved, and everything I cared about, and everything I knew, I left behind. I didn't think I'd ever get over it." She pulled back slightly, looking at Tanya's face, so much like home.

"But what I found there—I found my life there. I found you."

Tanya's eyes were sparkling now too, and she blinked back tears.

"Maybe it's like my mother told me, when I was crying that first night. She came into my room, and she said, Ysi, you can't get back what you lost. But if you are always looking back, you'll miss what's ahead of you."

"I'm glad you didn't spend your life looking back," said Tanya. "I would have missed you very much."

"Yes. I believe I've missed enough already," said Ysbel. She leaned in and kissed her wife, and Tanya kissed her back, a lingering kiss that for a moment brought her back to a small cottage on a small farm on a planet where the sun glowed warm and brilliant over freshly-plowed fields. And then she pulled away, and they weren't back there anymore. They were in a small cabin, on a ship full of lunatics who she couldn't help but love, Olya and Misko sleeping in the adjoining room.

"Come," said Tanya smiling. "I thought you were tired."

"Maybe not all that tired," said Ysbel with a faint grin, letting her hands slip farther down Tanya's waist. Tanya grinned in return, and Ysbel felt herself relax for the first time in a very long time.

Tae was exhausted. He was always exhausted. He wasn't entirely certain that he remembered a time he hadn't been exhausted.

But somehow, when he left, he didn't turn down the corridor that led to his cabin.

"What?" asked Jez, without looking up from her controls, when he tapped at the cockpit door.

"Can I come in?"

She glanced up and shrugged. "Thought you'd be sleeping by now."

He smiled slightly. "I probably should be." He paused. "Listen, Jez. I'm—sorry about what I said about you. Before."

She turned to face him, and the look on her face was serious. "No. I—I'm sorry. You were right. I do run away. I've always run away." She paused a moment. "I didn't mean to hurt you. But I did. I guess maybe that's what I was trying to run away from. But Tae—" she paused. "I—would have come back. Helped you get your friends, whatever. I—wouldn't really have left you to do that on your own."

"Jez." He shook his head. "I—I didn't even think about who Lena was to you. But you were going to go back there. That's not someone who runs away."

She was still looking at him.

"And—" he paused. "And listen. I've been thinking about the thrusters."

For a moment, there was a pang of anguish on her face. "Yeah. I know. They're never going to be what they were."

"No. But—well, I had some ideas. I think—I might just be able to switch them up a little, modify the design."

There was a cautious glimmer of hope in her face now. "Which means?" she said at last.

"Which means—well, I don't know. I'm no Sasa Illiovich. But I might just be able to improve on their design just a little."

The hope in her eyes was growing bright. "Which means?"

"Which means, you probably won't ever have to look for a speed capacitor again."

Her whole face was transfused with joy. "Are you serious?" she whispered. He nodded.

"She won't be what she was. But I'm thinking, between you and me and Lev and Ysbel, we might be able to make her something better."

She blinked a few times, staring at him with an expression of such rapture that he couldn't stop his own smile.

"Anyways," he said at last, pushing himself to his feet, "I'm going to bed. I just wanted to tell you that first."

She didn't say anything. She didn't have to.

He smiled to himself as he made his way down the corridor to his cabin.

Funny. He'd been so sure she'd just leave, that they all would. She'd said she would, after all. Hell, he'd been almost ready to leave himself. But … well, then everything had gone wrong, and when she could have taken a pod and run—should have, probably—she'd stayed. They all had.

And … well, he knew, deep down, they always would have. Somehow, these past few weeks, they'd built something that wasn't going to crumble at the first hint of pressure.

Despite the bone-deep exhaustion, there was a faint smile on his face as he fell onto his bed and closed his eyes and at long, long last, drifted off to sleep.

Jez woke with a start and glanced around the cockpit, panic jolting through her.

Lena.

Then she remembered, and lay back with a sigh of relief.

Lena was gone. She'd faced her, finally.

And turns out, she'd maybe been wrong the whole time.

Maybe, just maybe, there was a chance she wouldn't screw all this up. Or maybe—maybe she would, and somehow it would be alright anyways. Maybe instead of throwing her out, they'd stick around to help her clean up the mess.

It was a strange thought, and a not entirely comfortable one. She'd spent her whole life waiting to be thrown out. Her parents hadn't been able to handle having her around past her fourteenth birthday, and Lena had spent the whole five years Jez had flown for her alternately insulting and threatening her.

And yet—

Masha. She'd never expected Masha to admit she was wrong.

She'd never expected, once she'd said what she'd said, to be able to take the words back. To tell Tae she was sorry, and she hadn't really meant it, and now that she thought about it, she didn't want to leave, she wanted to help him get his street-kid friends somewhere safe and let him get enough sleep for once in his life, she wanted to teach Olya how to fly and how to gamble and wanted to have Ysbel pull out one of her modded guns and threaten whoever was trying to kill her with violent death.

She wanted Lev to—

She paused a moment, the memory of his arms around her, her back pressed up against his chest, sending a sudden tingle through her entire body.

It still scared the hell out of her, to be honest.

But—

"Jez. Are you awake?"

She spun around as Lev ducked through the door. He looked tired, but less tired than he had, and there was something missing from his expression. It took her a moment to figure it out.

The guilt, haunting behind his eyes.

It wasn't gone, not completely. But it wasn't nearly as strong as it had been, once.

She found she was staring at him, and she pulled her eyes away, back to the controls.

He crossed the cockpit floor and stood behind her chair, peering down at the control panel.

"How's she flying for you?" he asked.

She swallowed hard. "I—" her voice didn't seem to be working. "Alright. For what she's been through, she's flying a dream. But Tae came in last night, before he want to bed. He said he thought maybe —he thought he could—" She wasn't entirely sure why her brain wasn't working, but somehow she couldn't seem to make her words come out in a logical pattern.

"I know. I spoke with Tae before I came in here." There was a smile in his voice. "I think we should have your angel running better than she's ever run before."

The *Ungovernable* would be her perfect self again. That was the only reason she was feeling the way she was feeling, the only reason why her brain had suddenly shut down.

"I—" She forced a jaunty tone back into her voice. "Well, she'll be happy about that. Bet she'd kiss me, if she could."

Lev had wandered over to the back of the cockpit, and was peering out the back window at the rich blackness of space spread out behind them. He turned, and her eyes snagged on his and caught fast.

"I'd like to kiss you," he said quietly, and there was something in his voice, something affectionate and amused and at the same time, very, very serious. "If you'd like to, I mean," he added.

No. Nope, nope, nope. This was a terrible, terrible idea. She was something of an expert at bad ideas, and this was probably her worst one yet.

She wasn't entirely certain how she'd gotten to her feet. Her breath was coming much too fast, her body tingling with a mixture of panic and something else that she really, really didn't want to think about.

She was not going to do this. She wasn't a damn idiot, and she most certainly was not going to do this.

Her traitorous legs had already taken the few steps across the cockpit towards him. He turned, and she was suddenly very aware of how close they were.

Thing was, she didn't do relationships. She'd never really done relationships. Wasn't who she was. She didn't mind finding someone for a few weeks here and there, someone who'd be waiting when she came in from a long run, and then when she got tired of them, she'd just not show up, and that was the end of it. But there was something about this soft scholar boy, with those dark, intense eyes that she couldn't seem to look away from, and she was pretty damn sure that it wasn't the kind of thing you could just walk away from after a few weeks.

No, this was definitely something very stupid, and she wasn't stupid.

She was standing right in front of him.

He reached out gently, not taking his eyes from hers, and brushed a stray strand of hair behind her ear. His hand lingered in her hair for a moment, then brushed down along her jawline, and the touch was so achingly tender that she thought maybe her heart would stop beating completely. He tipped her chin up, ever so gently, his eyes asking a question.

No. Absolutely not. She was not doing this.

Her whole body was shaking.

She gave a tremulous nod, and the corners of his mouth turned up slightly, and the tenderness and the intensity in his eyes was making her drunker than she'd ever been in her life. He leaned forward, and he was close enough for her to notice his chest rising and falling far too quickly. And then he kissed her, gently, and her head spun and her heart pounded so that she thought maybe her whole chest might explode and this was the worst idea in the whole system but she didn't want it to stop, ever. She was floating, and his fingers on the tip of her chin and his lips against hers were the only things anchoring her to the ground.

He pulled back finally, his eyes never leaving hers, and she realized she'd completely forgotten how to breathe. She felt a little like someone had just hit her across the back of the head with a spanner.

He looked almost as stunned as she felt.

She tried to open her mouth to say something, but the words didn't seem to want to come.

"Jez—" he began, his voice unsteady. And then Tae's voice crackled through their earpieces, and they both jumped.

"Lev. I'm worried about this connector in the power core. Would you mind coming down here? I need to see the specs."

Her muscles remembered how to move, and she managed a shallow, shaky breath. Lev sighed shakily as well, and ran his fingers through his hair. He gave her a rueful smile.

"I suppose I should go. We've probably had enough core meltdowns for the present."

She managed a nod. He paused a moment, then leaned in kissed her again, lightly, his lips barely brushing hers. Then and he turned and slipped out the door, casting one last look at her over his shoulder as he went.

She dropped down into the pilot's seat, feeling oddly weak.

Nope, nope, nope.

And yet …

She touched her fingers to her bruised lips, where he'd somehow managed to kiss her without it hurting at all.

She found she was humming to herself as she turned back to the controls, the giddy, intoxicating feeling of staring into his eyes, of his lips on hers, suffusing her chest like a heartbeat.

Masha sat in a chair in her cabin, staring blankly at the wall.

The date on her chip.

So somehow they'd found out, after all these years.

She was seven years old, on her way home from school. She'd seen the figures lurking in the alley close to her home, but it hadn't frightened her. Her mama and papa weren't afraid, they told her, and so there was no reason for her to be.

And she hadn't been.

Until it had started.

She could still feel the splintery wood of the table against her small hands, smell the sickening scent of blood and burning, mingled with the scent of her father's laundry soap wafting from the table cloth that covered her.

She couldn't remember the sight, not exactly. Just the sickness, the blurring in her vision, the vomit rising in her throat.

But she remembered enough to know that, even at seven, she'd understood her parents were far, far beyond saving.

She didn't know how long she stood there after it was over, staring at the bodies, the blood spattering the floor and the walls. They hadn't been quick about it. Her father had shoved her under the table when the figures had pounded at the door. "Stay out of sight, Mari," he'd whispered. "It's nothing. But best if they don't see you here."

But he'd been wrong. About the first part, at least.

She swallowed down the sick coating her throat, finally, and turned towards the door. Maybe the police. Maybe they could help.

But she hadn't made it out the door. She couldn't seem to leave them.

And the police had come anyways.

They hadn't seen her there, hiding under the table. But then, they hadn't been looking. They'd glanced around, at the blood and the bodies, like it was a normal sight, their faces slightly bored.

"Captain said clean this up," said the woman who seemed to be in charge. "Don't want to cause a stir in the neighbourhood." She looked around, a slightly disgusted look on her face. "If they'd wanted to take them out, wish they'd chosen a cleaner way to do it."

And then they splashed fuel over the floor, over what was left of her mother and father, aimed a heat-blast at it. The house ignited in a roar of flame.

She slipped out the back door as her home burned, wandered down the street until she found her way to a transport dock. She didn't have enough money, but somehow she was able to convince the captain that her aunt was expecting her, and would pay for her passage.

Her aunt wasn't expecting her, but she did pay for the passage, although she was slightly puzzled.

"Why did your parents send you, Mari?" she'd asked. "They usually call me first."

She shrugged. "I don't know, Aunty. But don't call me Mari. I don't like that name anymore."

"What should I call you, then?" her aunt had asked.

"Masha."

When her aunt had come in, pale-faced and grave, a few days later, and told her there'd been a fire and her parents had been killed, she was very careful to act the part of a bereaved daughter. She mourned until it seemed that mourning was no longer acceptable, and then she went back to her schoolwork.

But she never, never forgot.

And she'd sworn, that first night, lying in her aunt's guest bed and biting the inside of her cheeks to keep the tears from spilling down her face, the horror from choking her—she'd sworn that one day, the mafia and the government who had protected them would pay for what they had done. And they would never do it again, to anyone else.

She blinked out of her reverie.

It had been a long time. She hadn't let herself think of that memory for a very long time. But she could still feel the splintery table leg against her hand, smell her father's laundry soap mingled with the thick, sickly-sweet scent of blood.

She shivered slightly.

This crew. They'd listened to her. They'd agreed to come.

But none of them had seen what she'd seen, as a terrified seven-year-old, and then again, over and over, as she'd worked her diligent, competent way through the government ranks, biding her time.

And none of them—not Lev, not Ysbel, not one of them—had any idea what they were going up against.

There was a cold chill in the pit of her stomach, a chill she hadn't felt in a very long time.

The End

ENJOYED THE BOOK?

I HOPE YOU'VE ENJOYED Time Bomb, the third book in The Ungovernable series. Thank you for reading!

I have a small favour to ask you: Would you please leave a review? It may seem like a silly thing, but reviews are very important to authors like me, as they help other people find my book, which in turn helps me to keep writing. Even a line or two would be unbelievably helpful.

If you haven't read it yet, Zero Day Threat is the first book in the series, and Jailbreak is the second.

In the mean time, if you subscribe to my mailing list, I'd love to send you an exclusive short story prequel featuring Jez Solokov, *Devil's Odds.* I'll also let you know about future launch dates, giveaways, and pre-release specials. And I always love to hear from my readers, so feel free to drop me a note!

If you'd like claim your free short story and subscribe to my newsletter, head over to my website: www.rmolson.com

Also, feel free to connect with me on Facebook: https://www.facebook.com/rmolsonauthor

or Instagram: https://www.instagram.com/rolson_author/

Printed in Great Britain
by Amazon

49037195R00194